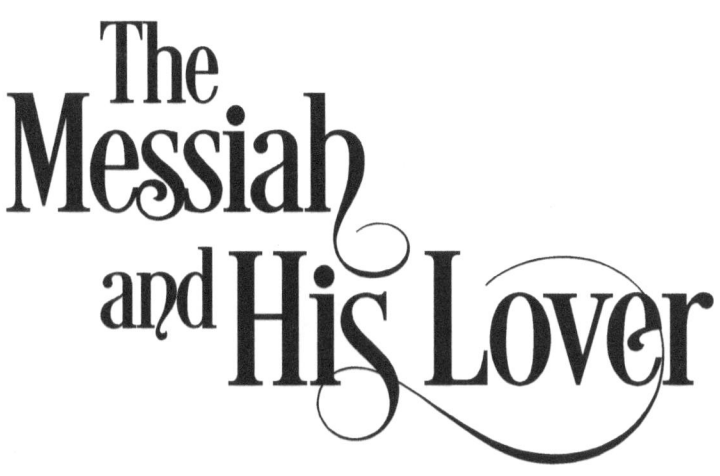

The Messiah and His Lover

David Hoffman

The Messiah and His Lover

ISBN: 978-0-9997645-0-3

To Jane, Always and Forever, Jane

PART 1
Patient X

1

Three burly MPs descended on Patient X's room. He appeared to be expecting them. "The Commander says we're not supposed to talk with you," the shorter of the men with the shaved head and tattoos announced. "He don't want none of your voodoo tricks spookin' us," he laughed.

X had the lean athletic body of a pole-vaulter. His blond hair was straight and long, touching his shoulders, eyes alert. He said nothing, gathered his few things, looked around the room and turned off the lights.

They walked down empty hallways under electric bug killers dangling from ceiling fixtures; a fluorescent light flickered with an annoying hum. Outside, they placed him in a white Land Rover, a soldier on each side as if he were a prisoner, and drove through the gates of the base along an empty asphalt highway to a three story red brick building that once housed a cannery, its front entrance manned by guards carrying assault rifles, a sign overhead identified it as a military hospital.

After some paperwork and the confusion of admitting someone without name, rank or serial number, he was escorted down a flight of stairs to the basement, through swinging double doors to a large open ward with injured soldiers in twenty beds, ten on each side. They eyed him warily. A female nurse studied the clipboard with his papers, frowned and looked up at him several times, then pointed to an empty bed at the far end of the room. The ward smelled of alcohol, urine and old wounds. There were no windows and the air was stale with sweat. A single ceiling fan spun ineffectively. He was left alone with his one bag and some books the psychiatrist had given him.

He lay there staring blankly at the ceiling like a ship unmoored. He didn't remember dozing off, but he woke in the darkness and found a tray of food, gone cold now, by his bed. He tried to eat, but had no appetite. To his left, a boy of about eighteen, wrapped in bandages, missing an arm and a leg, was staring at him. "As-salamu alaykum," Patient X greeted him. The boy continued to stare, unblinking, saying nothing. Patient X turned back and resumed his vigil staring at the ceiling.

Finally, the boy answered, asked him what he was there for. X explained his strange loss of memory, how he had been found stark naked on a hill on the edge of the city with absolutely no idea who he was or why he was there. He had spent the last two weeks at the American base in the psychiatric ward. His memory had not returned. He did not tell him the rest.

He asked the boy what had happened to him. A roadside bomb had shred his lower half, the boy said, matter-of-factly. They talked for two hours. The young man recounted everything: how he joined the army, what he had seen, how he missed his family, especially his girlfriend. He cried when he spoke of her. He could see no future. He would have no wife now, no children. He would be a burden to his family. If only he had died in the roadside explosion, he repeated like a prayer. X moved over to him, held him in his arms while the boy wept quietly into his chest.

Someone across from them woke with a start, calling for the nurse. But none of the nurses were on the floor so X brought him some water. Soon others woke up. Able to walk around, he moved to each of them in turn, listened to their inconceivable tragedies, and comforted them as best he could. Young men all—blind, burned, maimed, ruined, cast aside. He experienced each of their private sufferings as his own. They would not let him go. Those with arms and hands clung to his shirt. A babble of voices begged him to stay, but quieted when he spoke. He told them stories—he had no idea where they came from—of soldiers and beautiful princesses, of genies and jinns. They laughed together and cried tears of joy. They talked like this till morning when the nurses came on duty to serve them tepid tea. X returned to his bed, overcome with exhaustion, exhilaration and despair.

2

Two weeks earlier, Dr. Peter Solomon, a US Army psychiatrist, closed the leather-bound journal on his desk, fidgeted with his pen, and looked up at the clock above his door. He was eager to interview the man they had found earlier that morning. Amnesia rarely happens, but it always fascinated him.

Short and thin, his curly black hair had begun to recede from a bald spot on top, turning grey at the edges which, like his beard, he kept closely cropped. He removed a set of rimless glasses and folded them carefully before laying them next to his leather journal.

A knock at the door. "Come in," he said, clearing his throat. The door swung open and two military police officers ushered in a tall man with seawater-blue eyes, dressed in khakis and a grey sweatshirt. They closed the door behind him.

"Hi, I'm Dr. Peter Solomon," the doctor said with a slight stutter, extending his hand. He motioned to a well-worn brown leather couch against the wall. "Please sit down."

They both sat, the doctor's hands folded in his lap. He nodded towards his guest in a gesture meant to turn the conversation his way.

"I don't know my name," the man shrugged, anticipating the doctor's question. "I don't remember anything before they found me."

He appeared relaxed and at ease. After a few moments he let his slippers slide from his feet and sat back on the couch. The psychiatrist guessed he might be thirty at most.

The room was cool, the lights dim, the yellow paint on the walls had begun to peel. There was a fresh scent from a bouquet of white lilies on a small table next to the psychiatrist. The tall blue-eyed man glanced at the framed certificates on the wall behind the doctor, at the Ansel Adams print on the opposing wall and admired a plant in a bamboo container in the corner. "It's a Sansevieria Trifasciata," the doctor remarked—pretentiously, he realized.

The patient's eye contact was steady and uninhibited. He smiled easily. But this apparent comfort in his body and in the silence between them made the shrink feel oddly self-conscious. It was usually the other way around.

"So, you don't remember anything? No idea how you ended up where they found you?" the doctor asked, still fidgeting with his pen. The patient shook his head. "Do you remember what you had to eat last?"

"No, but it must have been quite a while ago," the patient said with a grin.

His voice was soft and round, a soothing, melodious voice. "Don't worry. We'll get you something as soon as we're done here. We won't be long."

"Thanks," the patient replied.

Solomon looked him over carefully. There was something unusually attractive about him. Partly it was his eyes, a child's eyes, innocent and curious, and a quiet alertness about him. But he had the vulnerability of someone injured, as well.

In a moment of silence, the patient took the measure of the psychiatrist without blinking. "Doctor, you've seen patients with amnesia before," more a statement than a question. "What could have caused this? What can I expect?"

"I'm not sure. We usually see this with bomb blast victims. Their memory disappears along with their hearing. But yours seems fine and, besides, you don't appear to have any obvious bruises or burn marks. I'm going to order an MRI to see if there are any neurologic issues, but I would be surprised if there were. We'll check your blood for any poisons or drugs. You aren't aware of taking anything, are you?"

"I wouldn't remember, if I did."

"How are you feeling otherwise?"

"I'm really fine, thank you. I mean physically, anyway. Emotionally, I don't know. It's all so weird. You know the feeling you get when you walk into a room and you forget why you're there? It's like that all the time for me now. Could it be some sort of Alzheimer's?"

The doctor shook his head. "No, I don't think so."

Dr. Solomon craved a cigarette. The patient's confidence unnerved him. Yet there was something fragile and innocent about the man that made the doctor want to protect him. He leaned forward.

"Any headaches, any pains?" he asked.

The patient shook his head.

"Memories of people or places from your past?"

"Nothing. I feel like the *Man Who Fell to Earth*."

Dr. Solomon looked up, surprised. "You mean the movie, with David Bowie?"

"Yes, I suppose so." The patient raised a finger to his lips, thinking. "I guess I do remember facts and things; but I can't seem to grasp where they come from."

"Interesting. Can you recall any other movies?"

He shook his head. Neither of them said anything.

'Someone whose frontal lobes have been compromised, wouldn't have such poise,' Dr. Solomon reflected. The patient showed none of the drugged fogginess he was used to seeing in such cases.

"Why don't we try some word association, if you're up for it? Sometimes that can jog memories."

The patient seemed to like the idea.

"This could be fun. Are you ready?"

The young man sat forward, resting his hands on his knees, and nodded.

"Tell me the first thing that comes to your mind when I say something." A pause.

"Home," said the shrink.

9

"Roof," responded the patient without delay.

"Baseball...bat."

"Movies...Hollywood." The patient's smile broadened.

"Friend...school."

"Girl...boy."

"Mother...Naomi."

Dr. Solomon stopped, stiffened and leaned back in his chair.

"Who's Naomi?" he asked.

"Your mother," the patient responded matter-of-factly, tilting his head to one side.

The doctor's heart raced, his ears throbbed. "How'd you know that?" he asked, taken aback, lips quivering slightly.

The patient squinted his eyes, perplexed. "I don't know. I just..." He paused. "I just guessed, I suppose."

Shaken, Dr. Solomon didn't know what to think. He tapped his foot nervously. They continued the word association exercise, but there were no new surprises.

"Can I get you anything, some tea?" he asked when they finished.

"No, thank you." There was an awkward silence. They could hear the clicks of the second hand on the clock.

He had frightened the doctor, he realized. The benign self-confidence the patient first exhibited seemed to disappear. The seriousness of his situation had begun to sink in. This was not how ordinary people acted, he realized. 'What am I doing? How did I get this way? What the fuck's going on?' he asked himself.

He tried to take stock. But concentrating as hard as he could, he could remember no one he knew. He had no inkling where he'd been, what he'd been doing. He remembered facts, things, places he must have been; but he didn't see himself in any of the pictures. The only experiences he could recall were what happened to him in the past two hours. 'I'm barely two hours old,' he thought.

He tried to think of some rational explanation. The amnesia was likely caused by trauma, either physical or psychological. But this clairvoyance? How had he known the doctor's mother's name? He stood up and paced to the door and back, trying to imagine who he might have been: a thief, a soldier, a spy? He could be anything.

Noticing the patient's growing anxiety as well as his own, the doctor removed a cigarette from a pack in the inside pocket of his brown corduroy jacket and offered one to the patient who shook his head. "Do you mind if I smoke?"

"Of course not." He sat down on the couch again.

"It's a bad habit, I know," the shrink admitted, taking a lighter from his jacket pocket and lighting up. "I planned to cut back and only smoke at home, but today I'm cheating."

"What happened to your vaporizer?" the patient asked. He saw the surprise on the doctor's face.

Dr. Solomon felt the room shrinking in on him again. He turned his head to exhale. 'How's he know this stuff?' He worked to maintain his composure, but the patient's apparent clairvoyance had him rattled and confused.

'This is no ordinary man. I feel completely exposed in front of him. He sees through all my boundaries.'

"Doctor, I'm sorry I'm freaking you out. I don't mean to. I guess we're here to talk about me; there just isn't a whole lot I can say about myself. But I should stop talking about you."

"Not at all," Dr. Solomon responded. "Go ahead. It's fine to talk about me. What would you like to know?" he asked, disingenuously.

The patient hesitated. "Well, to be honest, I'm curious to know why someone like you would leave his private practice to come to an army base on the other side of the world in the middle of a war. You weren't drafted."

The doctor sat back in his chair and exhaled deeply. He realized he'd be violating standard protocols sharing his life with a patient, but he was too intrigued by this stranger to hide behind formalities. He thought back to that period of his life in Philadelphia and was about to answer when the patient added, "Was it the work or because of Melinda?"

It seemed for a moment that his heart stopped. His mind raced, searching for some explanation as to how this stranger knew so much about him. 'Is someone playing a joke on me?' But, he was sure the man was sincere. He could read the innocence in his face. Dr. Solomon began to tremble, took a final drag on his cigarette and crushed it in an ashtray on the table.

"It was more than Melinda," he stammered, aware that he had never discussed this part of his life with anyone before. "I had been thinking of coming here for some time before she and I broke up. Many of my patients were veterans of the war and I was treating most of them for PTSD. I felt I needed to see the war for myself to get a better understanding of what they'd experienced."

He went to light another cigarette, but thought twice and put it back. The patient's expression remained unchanged, but his eyes were full of sympathy.

"I talked to Melinda a lot about this," the doctor said. "When she left me," he paused, swallowed, and then continued. "When she left me, I had no reason to stay in Philadelphia anymore."

"But you still miss her a lot, don't you?" the patient asked with genuine empathy.

Dr. Solomon felt his throat tighten. *Always remain unruffled;* he heard the voice of his mentor, Dr. Coulson, in his head, a mantra repeated often throughout his psychiatric residency.

The doctor was bent over in his chair. He looked up at the stranger's face, full of compassion. "How do you know so much about me? How did you know my wife's name?" he pleaded in a small voice.

"I don't know, doctor. It doesn't make any sense to me either. It's weirding me out. I know nothing about myself, but I seem to know everything you're thinking and feeling. I can't explain how. It just comes into my head as if they were my own thoughts."

They were silent with each other for a long time, like witnesses to a crime. "It seems natural for me to read your mind, but I can understand how frightening that is for you. I'm sorry," he added.

The doctor sat up, gathering his courage. "Tell me more about myself then," he said, testing him, fearful, yet anxious to know the extent of the man's telepathic powers.

The patient wasn't sure what to do. He liked the doctor, but could tell that his clairvoyance had obviously scared him. He waited for a long minute, before finally answering. "I know you just turned forty-four, that you celebrated alone in your apartment, that you have no kids, but wished you had, that you play softball for the psych ward team, that you once loved a woman named Cecilia, who later committed suicide, and that you berate yourself for not practicing your violin as much as you should."

The fear that had been simmering inside Dr. Solomon threatened to erupt. He stared at the patient, stupefied. He felt the beating of his heart. No one knew all these things about him. Struggling to maintain his composure, he thought he should say something, but nothing came out. Somehow, though, the look of compassion on the patient's face eased his fear and he felt himself surrender like a swimmer washed onto shore.

"I'm really glad we found you," Dr. Solomon said at last. "I don't know what you would have done out there on your own without a name, an ID or a place to go. I'm going to admit you to the hospital here while we try and find some answers. We'll call you 'Patient X' for now, 'X' for short. We'll run some tests later. You'll have a room just down the hall from here. The cafeteria should be open now. Just sign my name. Let's keep what we discussed today to ourselves, though. We can talk a lot more tomorrow. You'll need all the rest you can get." He picked up the phone and the two MPs returned and escorted the patient to his quarters.

As soon as the door shut, Dr. Solomon waited for his heart rate to settle, then hurriedly wrote a few notes in his journal. *Patient X, as I will call him, appears to be utterly unselfconscious, unusually empathetic and without fear or ego. His ability to read minds...* Dr. Solomon stopped mid sentence. 'I can't write this down,' he thought.

He scratched out the last words and put down his pen, feeling drained, but curiously uplifted, as if he'd just been witness to a miracle. Confused and distrustful of what he had experienced, though, he again heard the voice of Dr. Coulson, this time warning his fellow residents to be on guard against their own fantasies. *When you're around so many delusional people, you can forget your own reality. Insanity can be infectious.*

3

X slept off and on, fitfully, through most of the next day and woke when dinner was served. He was unable to tell what the meal consisted of, but ate it anyway. It was flavorless, greenish brown in color, the consistency of gruel. He forced himself to down two glasses of bleach-smelling water in a dented tin pitcher that sat on the table next to his bed. Flies buzzed over his plate. The conversations from the night before weighed heavily on him. He felt condemned to a destiny he didn't understand. Whatever comfort he took in knowing the relief he provided these sad, broken young men was outweighed by the burden it placed on him. 'Why me?' he pleaded to an unknown power. 'What do you want of me?'

He nodded off again. Awakening from a dream, the weight of his despair broke like a fever. He couldn't quite remember it—something about scales falling off his body—but the feeling of being reborn remained with him. When he opened his eyes he was surprised to find Dr. Solomon there watching him, seated in a metal chair just a foot from his bed. They remained silent for some time.

"How are you?" the doctor asked.

X sat up, wrapping his arms around his knees. "Fine, doc." He paused. "It's good to see you."

"Look," stammered the shrink, "I tried to stop this. They wouldn't listen. I tried..." X raised his hand to cut him off.

"It's OK Peter," he said, the first time he has called him that. "I know how hard this is for you."

The muscles in the doctor's face winced slightly. He could see his patient had changed.

Their eyes met, faces relaxed. X swung his legs around to face the doctor, their knees almost touching.

Solomon stared at his patient. "I'm trying to get you released, but it's not simple. The lawyers won't allow it until we've established your identity. There were rumors flying around the base that there was some kind of a prophet or fortune teller holed up on the ward or that I was experimenting with a new drug that could let people read minds. The base commander lost it. He ordered me to transfer you to the locals. To be precise, he said, you 'could stay there till the Second Coming,' as far as he was concerned.'"

Solomon tried to make light of the situation, but his concern was acute. "I'm looking for some program in the town where you could work without proper papers; make use of your skills. We could still see each other off base."

The patient smiled, as if he knew something the doctor didn't, but waited for him to finish. "I had a dream just now," X told him, "a kind of deliverance."

Solomon's eyes widened.

17

"I can't recall what happened exactly, but it was a revelation." His kind, soft eyes met the doctor's intense gaze, disarming him. "I'm glad I'm here," he said. "It's helping me find myself. I'm beginning to understand what this all might mean." He waited a moment, letting his words sink in. "At least I can see some purpose to my life." The doctor sat passively as X explained the insight that had just come to him.

"I was up all night listening to these brave young men. They've lost everything. But they gave me back something even more important. They shared with me their deepest truths, their pain, their sadness and despair, their lost hopes. They told me about the people they love—their mothers and fathers, children, family, friends. They love them with all their hearts, but they feel guilty and impotent. Their remorse is endless."

He paused for a minute. "And me? I, who have no idea who I am, stood silently. Their pain was unbearable and I thought I might die listening to them. But I realized there was no me there to die, just a body with skin and bones. As I looked at each of them and listened to their stories, I felt myself identifying with them completely, recognized them as myself, literally. That's who I am. I'm each of them, I realized." He paused for a moment. "I'm not this body, not what's bound inside me. That's an illusion. I'm you and you are me. When we see, God sees. When we love, God loves. When we realize our true selves we become divine."

He considered the meaning of his words. "It's been obscene for me to feel sorry for myself. I've been tormented these two weeks feeling like I was some kind of freak. But last night when I saw how helpful I could be to these wretched men, I understood what a gift I'd been given. If I have a soul, it began to be born then."

X felt the blood rise to his head. His eyes were on fire. A look of radiant compassion filled his face. The doctor opened his mouth to speak, but could not.

4

X awoke the next morning feeling more alive than he had his entire life, the little of it he remembered. He was almost giddy with a lightness he had not experienced before, like a bird about to fly. The moment he opened his eyes, Sami began chattering to him. He had been waiting patiently for X to wake up, watching him sleep for the last hour, anxious for this moment when he could talk to him.

"As-salaam 'alaykum," Sami said eagerly.

"Wa alaykum as-salaam," answered X.

The young man's eyes opened wide with excitement. "Did the patient sleep well? Who was the man who had visited him last night? What were the books all about that sat by his bed?" The questions came pouring out of him, one after the other.

X laughed at his exuberance. He could not remember laughing like that before.

Sami could not quite believe that this man, who seemed so learned, whose stories had bewitched all the other patients, could not even recall his own name. He peppered him with more questions. "What about your mother? What is her name?

What does she look like? Where are you from? What made you lose your memory? Do you have a wife, children?"

Each time Patient X laughed and shrugged his shoulders. For Sami, the reality of such total amnesia was the most fascinating thing he had ever encountered. He was utterly charmed by this otherwise healthy patient who seemed to recognize in him the fullness of his being. It reminded him of the way his fiancée would look at him, as though he were the only person in the world.

"Please, Mr. no-name, tell me anything about yourself. What is your favorite food?"

X could not resist teasing him. He knew that Sami was thinking of the white fish with pomegranate and dates that his mother made him back home, so he described the dish to him.

Sami's eyes widened even more with childish delight. "That's my favorite!" he squealed. "We are brothers. What about games?" Sami demanded, and X replied "foosball," the very thing Sami pictured in his mind. Sami's mouth opened in wonder. X smiled back impishly. "Who is your favorite singer?" the young soldier asked and, once again, X answered without hesitating. "Yeeks! You are a sorcerer, a jinn!" he exclaimed, half in jest and in fear. "How did you know what I was thinking?" he begged.

X laughed again, a big full-bodied laugh that seemed to wash away all the anxieties and despair that had tormented him since the day he was found. He pointed past Sami to a magazine that sat on the tray next to him with a cover featuring Asala, the Arab diva Sami adored.

Sami giggled with uncontrollable glee. "OK, here's a harder one. Who is the most beautiful woman in the world?"

X answered immediately, without thinking. "A'ishah" he responded, the name of Sami's fiancée.

But this time Sami did not laugh. He stared at X with a frightened look of incomprehension. X realized he had gone too far with this game. He could have lied and said that Sami had yelled out her name in the middle of the night, but he respected him too much for that.

"Sami," he said, in a conspiratorial whisper. "I will share with you a secret, but you musn't tell anyone else. OK?" The young man nodded his ascent. X explained that when he lost his memory he somehow became able to read peoples' minds. The doctors didn't understand how this worked and it had gotten him in trouble at the American base. He didn't understand it either; it just came naturally to him. Sami stared suspiciously at X, afraid that he was making fun of him, unsure whether to believe any of this.

He struggled to sit up. With both an arm and leg missing, he had to squirm uncomfortably to right himself. He sat straight as if trying to make himself taller. His expression was stern now. "What number am I thinking of?" he asked, challenging him.

"362," responded X.

Sami put his hand over his mouth to stifle a scream. "What is the name of my brother?"

"Khaled, though you call him Makin, after your uncle's cat."

Sami's face froze, stupefied. X did not smile. They sat silently staring at each other.

Finally, Sami spoke. "What will be the winning number for the lottery?" he asked.

X held up his hands in prayer. "I can only read minds, not the future." They both laughed gleefully.

"OK, but you could play cards and know what was in the others' hands, couldn't you?"

"I suppose," said X. "But it would be unfair to do that."

Sami pondered this. "Please Mr. No-Name, you have not met her yet, but when Ghaada, the young nurse—not the fat one with the mole the size of a walnut, but the beautiful one with the hair down to her waist—when she comes to dress me, please tell me what she is thinking." X agreed to do so.

As he drifted to sleep that night, he was filled for the first time with a sense of belonging.

5

A sound woke him in the middle of the night. At first he thought he was dreaming, something to do with a speech he was late for; but then he realized it came from outside of him, a moaning, muffled cry of pain. He sat up and listened, assuming it was coming from one of the patients on the ward. But it came from further away. He lay down again, hoping to get back to sleep. But the screams persisted, someone crying out in pain. Knowing he wouldn't be able to ignore them, he got up to see what he could do, put on his shoes and tipped-toed through the room and out into the dark hallway.

Slowly his eyes adjusted to the dark. He walked towards the sounds, running his hand along the wall, guided by the cries, which grew closer. He reached the stairwell one floor below ground level. The screams were coming from deeper still. He could not turn back. Opening a door marked "bomb shelter" he walked down another set of stairs. The sounds were now more distinct. It appeared to be a man crying out in pain, pleading to die, praying. X descended the stairs silently, afraid of what he might find and turned down a tunnel towards the sounds. The cries were more urgent now, filling up the empty spaces. Two floors down, the air was cold and clammy. He turned down another tunnel towards a yellow light coming from a large metal door that was slightly ajar. Something told him to turn away, to not look at what was behind there. But he was unable to.

He stopped just outside the threshold. Against the plaster wall facing him was a man hanging by his feet from a chain suspended from the ceiling. A soldier stood next to him smoking a cigarette, his leg bent with his foot resting against the wall. Another soldier sat on a metal chair at a small green table with a light dangling over it. They had attached electrodes to the man's testicles and to his teeth. Wires ran to a mechanism on the table. His body writhed in agony as the soldier applied electricity. They threw water on the prisoner, causing his torso to convulse uncontrollably. The light above the table flickered.

X heard the man's screams from outside him; but the cries were also his own, coming from within. 'Oh God, help me,' he heard a voice inside him cry. 'Take me now, please! Oh God.' The prisoner's suffering had become his own. The pain, hot as lightning, arced from his mouth to his balls, searing him. His limbs quivered, jangling like live wires. His eyeballs were singed. His mouth tasted of burnt ash. He could think of nothing as the sound of these screams obliterated all.

Suddenly the soldier leaning against the wall noticed the patient standing there frozen in the doorway and strode quickly towards him, slamming the door in his face. In the moment before it closed, X's mind flipped to the soldier's, comprehending him in an instant. The soldier was ashamed to be seen like this; but he blamed the prisoner for making him into a torturer, blamed him for all the wrongs done to his family, to his tribe, for his blasphemy against God. His power over this pathetic infidel washed away all the humiliations of his life. He was strong. The prisoner was weak, repulsive. He deserved to die.

All of this flashed in a split second, like the taking of a photograph. The metal door shut with a clang. The torture reverberated within X. He felt as if he had been fatally poisoned, his brief remembered life sundered. He knew he should run, but he stood riveted to the floor.

He tried to open the metal door, but he could not. 'What good could I do, anyway?' he thought. He was helpless and frightened. 'God, tell me, what can I do?' he pleaded. He was surprised to talk this way to God. 'I don't believe in God,' he reflected. But he couldn't seem to help himself. 'Why have you brought me here? Why have you revealed this to me?' He sobbed, his body trembling, his face now wet with snot and tears. His despair nauseated him. He turned finally and ran through the darkness, racing for air. He didn't stop at his floor, but continued up another flight, emerging at the entrance where the MPs first brought him in. A guard on duty was sleeping in a chair. He pushed open the front doors and rushed into the cool night air. Above him was a sea of stars.

6

The first hint of daylight pierced the horizon. He walked slowly through the still sleeping streets, lost in a jumble of thoughts. The only lights still on were at the frequent checkpoints stacked with sandbags, which he avoided. A truck filled with burlap sacks of flour rumbled by. Startled by the rattling of metal shutters opening at a bakery, he walked faster followed by a hungry, mangy dog.

He was lost without a destination, without a past, a home or any idea who or what he was. It left him empty as an echo. A wind came up, blowing plastic bags haphazardly down the narrow street. Haunted by what he'd just seen, unable to separate himself from the wretched hanging man and his body of pain, he kept repeating in his mind the prisoner's thoughts, how much he wanted to die, how badly he wished he could see his wife, Maria. 'Maria?' X wondered if he could find her, but what would he tell her? That her husband had been burnt like a piece of toast?

He realized his despair was rooted in his impotence. 'What could I have done?' he asked himself. He wished he had acted, had walked into the room and confronted them, with an open heart, without judgment.

But such delusions of grandeur were madness. 'Who the hell do you think you are?' he berated himself. The clarity he had felt the night before disappeared like fog. 'You're no saint, no savior. Even if you were, they would have killed you, would have strung you up by your heels.' He wanted to run, to obliterate the images of torture that tormented him, but he knew it would attract too much attention. He walked faster. His breathing quickened. But the memories continued to cling to him. He could not escape. He recalled the very feeling of the current in the man's mouth, how his gums bled, how the pain shot through him to his toes.

Around him were signs of life as the city began to wake from its sleep. A merchant swept the pavement in front of his shop. A man pushed a cart loaded with watermelons. A rooster crowed indignantly.

Ahead of him a lone street lamp flickered on and off. There was a bench nearby under dusty and decrepit palm fronds. He sat down, held his head in his hands and started to cry.

'What kind of God allows such evil?' he demanded. But he knew there was no God. That was part of his loneliness.

'I'm nobody's victim,' he reminded himself. 'No one is torturing me. I torture myself.' He lifted his hands from his face and looked around. Across from him a woman was unloading boxes of fruit from her car and carrying them into her store. A boy on a bicycle pedaled down the street balancing a heavy bag. He perceived how the sun painted the roofs of the stores and houses with rose-colored light.

PART 2
Jonathan

7

The sun had now risen above the one-story shops that lined the road leading towards the center of the city. The odors of rotting garbage, donkey shit and kerosene began to give way to the smells of a city coming alive. A bus chased him onto the sidewalk. Street urchins, vendors and beggars took up their places like actors in a play. Horns blared, people talked on cell phones and the sounds of hip hop and Arabic love songs filled the air. He passed several bombed out buildings, a government office and a bank that were surrounded by high concrete blast walls. Ahead of him, he noticed a waiter moving tables and chairs onto a wide sidewalk under a large faded red and white striped awning.

He paused for a moment, then walked into the café and sat at an empty table towards the back. The restaurant smelled of tobacco and coffee. Three older men and two women in hijabs sat on stools at the coffee bar eating croissants and drinking mint tea. Armored in chrome, an elaborate espresso machine sat proudly in front of a large antique mirror whose reflective coating had started to peel off. Some students with backpacks ordered cappuccinos next to him. Across the room two men in black T-shirts gazed at him with hard looks, whispering to each other. But they were too far away for him to be able to read their minds. Closer to his table, two women were holding hands and laughing, a young woman with long thick black hair wearing dark pants and a red blouse and an older woman whose head was covered with a black scarf.

As the waiter walked over, X suddenly realized he had no money. "Just a glass of water for now," he said in the local dialect. The waiter, a skinny young man with a slight cleft pallet, looked down at the loose grey pajamas the Westerner was wearing, then met his gaze, turned back to the bar and returned with the water.

X thanked him, stretched out his legs and sipped the water. He was thirsty and hungry, too. He'd been so preoccupied with the torture he witnessed that he had not stopped to consider his situation. He had no money, no ID, no friends, no place to go. He could return to the army hospital he just left, but he was afraid the torturers might find him there. Dr. Solomon would help, he was sure; but he preferred not getting him involved, if he could help it. After a few minutes, he noticed the two women near him had stopped laughing, their expressions grim as their gaze shifted back and forth between X and the two men in black shirts.

Sipping his water, X considered his options. Sooner or later he'd have to eat and find a safe place to sleep. He could go to one of the Western embassies, he considered, though they'd want proof of his nationality. Should he tell them what he saw? They'd contact the Americans, but they just got rid of him. They would not want to take any responsibility, he realized. His leg twitched nervously. He tried to think of a way to use his mind reading ability to get some money quickly, but a voice inside him insisted he must never use these gifts for his own advantage.

One of the students got up and placed a coin in the jukebox. A Western pop song came on. The others moved over to a pinball machine and lit up cigarettes. Tossing some coins on the table, the two men in black shirts walked out, turning to glance back at X as they exited. A moment later the young woman with the long black hair and the older, grey-haired woman pushed back their chairs and walked over to him. "May we speak with you a moment?" they asked. Their expressions were grave. He stood, gesturing for them to sit. The younger of them had intense green eyes, like a tiger's he thought. He recalled Blake's poem:

Tiger, tiger, burning bright
In the forests of the night,
What immortal hand or eye
Could frame thy fearful symmetry?

"Please excuse us," said the young woman, scanning the cafe as she spoke. "But we must warn you. You are in grave danger." She pretended to smile for anyone watching. The older woman stared intensely at him. "My grandmother is deaf and mute, but she can read lips. The two men who just left,

35

who were sitting over there, kidnap foreigners, Westerners, and make their families pay ransoms. But afterwards they kill them anyway."

The threat of danger he felt in the dungeons of the hospital returned like a cold wind. He was defenseless. There was no place to run. He was like an animal caught in a trap. But he lacked the normal flight or fight reflexes. He didn't know how to act in this situation. "No ego, no fear," Dr. Solomon would say. "What should I do?" he asked them flawlessly in the local dialect. "The truth is I have no money, not a dirham or a sou, and I don't have any family here who could help, none at all. The kidnappers would be wasting their time."

He saw the disappointment in their faces. They were not sure he believed them. They started to leave. "No, please stay," he pleaded, reaching for the young woman's arm. She pulled it away and stood abruptly. Her eyes darted wildly around. He should not have touched her. "I'm very sorry. Please sit a moment and let me try to explain."

The older woman took the girl's sleeve and pulled her back to her seat. She recognized the kindness and the sincerity in his face. It had been many years since anyone had looked at her with such understanding.

"I don't know where to begin," he said. He was vulnerable, yet strangely unafraid. The young woman was struck by his innocence. Instinctively she wanted to protect him, but this stranger could cause them great harm. She should not be talking to him at all, a man who is unrelated to her, let alone warn him of a threat. They could be killed for this. But the older woman was riveted. She could not turn away from him. She read his lips. He looked at her while he spoke. He took a deep breath. "Something happened to me," he began. "I don't know what it is. Something caused me to lose my memory, all of it." He looked at the green-eyed woman to see if she believed him, but she remained suspicious. The older woman was not.

"I've been in a US Army hospital for almost two weeks since I was found. They haven't been able to identify who I am. Finally, they transferred me to one of your own military hospitals. I ran away from there last night," he stopped, trying to decide how much to reveal. "I saw something I shouldn't have seen," he paused. "I had to escape." The young woman glanced down at his hospital clothes and his worn slippers, then looked in his eyes. He did not blink. His eyes were soft but strong. Something told her she could trust him, despite the many alarm bells ringing in her head urging her to flee and not get involved.

She looked at the glass of water, realizing that, indeed, he seemed to have no money, then looked back up at him.

"I don't know my name," he said, reading her thoughts.

"I'm Leila," she said. "This is my grandmother, Hanan." She stood suddenly. "Come, we must go quickly." Hanan followed behind him as they walked to the door to hail a cab.

'How ironic,' he thought. 'A woman who can read lips saving a man who can read minds.'

8

Leila handed the cab driver an address and climbed in the back seat beside her grandmother and X. After a few short blocks, she abruptly told the cab driver to stop and hurriedly handed him a large bill. They walked through the sullen city in silence. She signed to her grandmother, explaining that there were checkpoints along the way and the taxi was likely to be stopped. She was terrified they would be asked for their papers. It was one thing for this unknown foreigner to lack identity papers, quite another for them to explain what they were doing with him. She told him to follow at a short distance.

They navigated their way through a warren of narrow alleys and passages, some only shoulder width across, past piles of rubbish and foul-smelling debris. They cut through neighborhoods specializing in one trade or another: auto repair, clothing, metal works. They passed several Shawarma restaurants where lamb was slowly roasting on vertical rotating spits. Some of the buildings were pock marked from bullets and shrapnel. Finally they emerged out of the shadows into a bright leafy street on the edge of what used to be the municipal zoo. Several tall but dilapidated apartment buildings sat forlornly next to empty lots across from the part of the zoo that once housed lions. Hanan, the grandmother, who has lived here since the war started, still remembered the sound of them roaring in the early mornings.

Leila turned to tell X to remain silent when they entered the apartment building. "If anyone asks, you are my brother-in-law from Brighton, married to my sister Aisha." He nodded his assent. They entered the dark foyer of number 37, past rows of empty metal mailboxes and climbed six flights of stairs in the dark. No one saw them. There was a scent like old photographs, of unopened closets. At the landing, Leila took out a brass key ring, methodically unlocked three deadbolts and pushed the door open.

The apartment was spacious with the tall ceilings of a long-ago era, mosaic tiled floors and an enormous Persian rug in the entryway to the living room. Leila moved to close the large double shutters of a floor-to-ceiling wrought iron and glass doorway that opened onto a small balcony facing the apartment building next door. As the room darkened, she turned on a light switch to no avail. "Shit!" she exclaimed, shaking her head in frustration. Electricity was intermittent, when it existed at all.

Hanan removed her headscarf, placed it on a hook next to the front door and took a seat in an old green upholstered chair. Leila flipped off her shoes and moved towards the kitchen. "I'm making some tea, would you like some?" she asked him.

"Yes, very much, thank you." Reading Hanan's mind, he picked up a red leather hassock from the corner of the living room and moved it close to her. It was something Leila routinely did. She placed her feet on it, looked up at him and grinned broadly. 'She believes I'm an angel,' he realized and smiled back at her.

Leila came in carrying a large silver tray with tea, cookies and dates. "Please, take a seat," she said, gesturing to a chair that matched the one Hanan was on. She put the tray on a low coffee table in front of them, poured a cup of tea for her grandmother and placed it carefully on the arm of her chair.

He looked around the room. The two walls next to the entrance were covered in shelves crammed with books. Framed photographs hung on either side of the balcony doors. Leila pulled over an ornately carved mahogany chair from a corner for herself. He waited for them to start, though he was now ravenously hungry.

Leila stared carefully at him, quietly, like a biologist examining a specimen. 'He is not easily intimidated,' she thought. She was usually taller than the men she met. She noticed he was several inches taller than her. She searched for any weaknesses. She didn't want any surprises. As she studied him, she considered all the problems they could run into.

He was comfortable looking back at her in silence. He had been attracted by her beauty at first sight in the café, but had not thought about it since. Her eyes were almond shaped with long lashes, he now noticed, her skin the color of fresh bread.

Finally, she spoke. "OK, Mr. runaway amnesiac, let's start from the beginning."

He told her what he knew, though saying nothing about his unusual powers: how he had been discovered on a hill on the outskirts of town, how the army tried to find out his identity, but couldn't, how the commander had him transferred to the local army hospital.

"And what did you see that you weren't supposed to?" she asked.

He paused for a moment, considering. "A man being tortured."

She didn't say anything, but he could tell she wanted to know more. "I heard someone screaming in the middle of the night. It woke me. I wandered down into a sub-basement, a bomb shelter of some sort, and came across a torture chamber. I'd rather not describe it. I ran away, as you can see, with nothing. And then you found me." Again, silence. She examined him, searching for clues that would tell her more.

"It's a very short story, don't you think?" she said. "Do you know anyone? Do you have any friends?"

He told her about Dr. Solomon and how hard he worked to help him, and Sami, whom he had come to love. Her eyes softened as he described this.

"It doesn't seem like a good idea for you to return to the hospital with the torture chamber," Leila concluded. "They know you're missing now and there's a good chance the men you saw torturing a prisoner are not too happy about it. I'm surprised they let you escape." She stood and paced, tapping the fingers of both hands together in thought. "It seems like the only option you have is to call this Dr. Solomon and see what he can do."

"You could hide out here for a day or two, I suppose," she thought out loud. "But if any of the neighbors see you here, a white foreigner…" she switched to English, "We'd be fucked."

Her grandmother did not react. Clearly she didn't understand English. But he found Leila's cursing quite appealing. He smiled.

"You'll need some kind of fake identity card, I suppose," she continued.

Her stream of consciousness, her habit of thinking out loud, was rather ironic, he thought. There was little reason for him to read Leila's mind.

Turning suddenly to face him, as if just realizing he was in the room, she asked, "What can you do? What skills do you have?"

She made him laugh. It felt good. His world had become far too serious. He began to respond by saying, "I can read minds," but stopped himself. "I can play music," he announced proudly.

"What instrument?" she asked.

"Um, violin, or anything really."

She frowned, doubtfully. He loved how expressive her face could become. She hid nothing. Walking to her bedroom, she pulled a long black case from under her bed.

"I haven't played this since high school," she said, handing it to him.

Delicately, he opened the case, looking up to meet her gaze. She was testing him, he knew. He pulled out an old alto saxophone and wet a reed in his mouth. It was like a game they were playing, but the mood was light. He started to play, squeaking and squealing like a train braking. She covered her ears with her hands and moved to take the sax away, when suddenly he broke into a riff on John Coltrane's "Nancy." The tone was sweet, luxurious, melancholy. She sat and stared at this stranger in wonder.

Her grandmother began to clap. They turned to her laughing. "I thought she can't hear," he said.

"That's why she's clapping," Leila joked. "But seriously, she can tell by my reaction how good you are." Hanan signed. "She thinks you're an angel."

"I'm no angel," he answered.

"I know," Leila said. "You're just lucky." She paused for a minute thinking. "Well, Mr. Lucky, you'll need to be called something, a Western name. Not a Larry or a Bob, something a little more sophisticated. How about Calvin or Joshua or Geoffrey with a G?" She stared at him, trying to divine some essential truth in him. "Somehow, I think you are a Jonathan, though I can't say why. How does it feel to be a Jonathan?"

He smiled. She sees that this has moved him. He opened his mouth to respond, but said nothing. She has bestowed something on him, something precious, something that had eluded him. A name, any name. "You can't imagine how much this means to me."

He returned the sax to its velvet-lined bed and closed the case. "Now you know pretty much everything you can know about me," he said. "What about you, Leila? What's your story?"

She reached for her cup of tea, raised her eyebrows to Hanan, as if to ask permission, then began. "I come from a small village, about 50 kilometers east of here. My mother died in childbirth. My father and Hanan," she nodded towards her, "raised my brother and me. We had olives and dates and a few sheep. It was enough. We were never without. The village was very beautiful. When the war started I was just finishing high school. I won a scholarship from a British foundation to study business at the University of Cardiff and left my family and my village for the first time. My father moved my grandmother to this apartment for her safety and went off with the other men from our community to fight. He never came back. I wanted to return home but my brother, who was now the head of the household, wouldn't allow it. I was offered another scholarship to go to graduate school to get an MBA at Cambridge or to the Wharton School in the US, but then my brother was also killed. So, I came back immediately to take care of Hanan. She is all I have left. I got a job as a photojournalist. It suits me much better than business. I love my job, but the longer I stay here, the more I'm losing what faith I had left in humanity. Whatever brought you here, mister, you've come to the end of the world."

He looked at her with utter compassion. The silence was painful. "What was Amir like?" he asked and immediately realized his mistake. She was alarmed. She was sure she had not mentioned her brother's name before. 'How does he know?' she asked herself. She locked eyes with Hanan, but her grandmother did not catch what just transpired.

Ignoring his error, he pushed ahead. "What was your brother like?" he asked again. She stammered, describing him, but she was more wary now of this stranger.

9

"What about you, Hanan?" Jonathan asked, turning to the grandmother, hoping to divert Leila's attention. "Would you share your story with me?"

Hanan's eyes brightened. She loved telling her story. "I'm an old woman now, 90 years old," she signed, eyes twinkling with pride, as Leila translated into voice. "I have nothing left in my life but my memories."

"I'm jealous," he said. "I seem to have lost all of mine."

Hanan read his lips and laughed, an infectious laugh that made her eyes water with delight. This stranger had charmed her completely.

"My family came from a small village in Turkey," she began. "I can't even remember its name now. Close to Armenia, I think." She scrunched her face in frustration, looking to Leila for help; but Leila said nothing. The frown on Leila's face after Jonathan mysteriously named her brother slowly began to disappear. "We had a large family," Hanan continued. "When the fighting in the big war came near us—the world war, the first one—" she smiled ruefully, "my grandfather decided to pack everything and leave. The whole family left, abandoning their land, houses, animals, everything."

"My mother, she refused to go, but my grandfather made her. She was very beautiful. Everyone said she was the most beautiful woman in our village and for miles around. That year when she was 18 she fell in love with the son of an Imam from another village, a boy named Nidham. But their families would not let them marry. He was already promised to someone else. My mother wanted to run away with him, but back then it was impossible. Maybe now. But even now," she shook her head, disapprovingly. "Are you sure you want to hear all this? Old stories from a deaf and dumb woman?" she signed.

Jonathan remembered to wait for Leila's translation before answering. "Yes, please, go on. These stories are precious for me."

"Nidham, my mother's lover, stayed behind when my family left Turkey and married the woman he was promised to. My mother, it was said, cried the whole way here and for two months afterwards. She wanted to kill herself. My grand-parents were very worried about her. She was so headstrong, but she finally agreed to marry someone else from our village, a distant cousin, my father Jamal. It was a good marriage. He was a handsome man and owned many olive trees. They had the biggest wedding anyone in our tribe had ever seen, people say. I still have my mother's wedding dress. It is covered in jewels, so heavy you wouldn't believe it. I have kept it for Leila for the day when she gets married, Insha'Allah."

Hanan looked sternly at her granddaughter and waited for her to translate before continuing. "My father, Jamal, may he rest in peace, was a very proud man and very strong. He loved my mother very much, but she never stopped thinking about Nidham, I'm sure of that. Twenty years later, when Nidham's wife died, he travelled all this way just to visit my mother. They both still loved each other, but my mother was very faithful to my father and would never hurt him. However, she told Nidham—this I know because she told me so the night of my own wedding—'If I can't have you, then you should have my daughter, Hanan, for your bride.' And that is how it was arranged that I became engaged."

"You married your mother's lover?" he asked. Hanan looked at Jonathan, cackling with impish delight.

"Of course, he was much older than me, but he was very attractive. That's where Leila gets her good looks."

Jonathan followed the conversation by first reading Hanan's thoughts, then listened again as Leila translated. He noticed Leila skip this last line.

"I suspected something was up between them. I saw that my father was acting very strangely at the wedding. I was very close to him and could tell that the presence of Nidham disturbed him, and not in the normal way. They were the same age, too."

She rocked back and forth in her chair, delighting at the telling. "The night of the wedding," Hanan continued, "the mother of the bride must dance with the groom. When they moved around the floor in each other's arms I could see in their eyes there was something between them. Later, after much celebrating, I forced my mother to tell me everything. Everything. But I didn't care. I was 18. I wanted to be married, to get out of my house and see the world. Nidham was all I could ever have hoped for. And I'm sure he was very happy to have such a young wife, one that looked just like his first love when they were each 18. I gave him everything he wanted," she giggled, "and he gave me two beautiful children, a son, Isa, and Leila's mother. He died twenty years ago."

Leila picked up the story, signing as she spoke. "My grandmother was a real feminist before her time. She was the first woman in our village to smoke cigarettes and the first to drive a car. My grandfather didn't know how. At the end of one summer Hanan got it into her head to drive the whole family to the Haj. No woman in our country had ever done so. She bought a car, a four-door silver Renaut, and drove the four of them, all by herself, with my grandfather sitting in the front seat, across seven countries. There was a war going on at that time in Egypt, but nothing stopped her. When they got back she had become a local hero. Everyone in our village still loves to tell this story." Hanan clapped her hands twice and held them to her chest, beaming proudly.

Leila stood, as if at intermission. "You must be starved," she said addressing Jonathan. "Have you eaten anything today?" He pointed to the empty silver platter. "Let's have some lunch then," she said and walked towards the kitchen. Jonathan also stood, offering to help, and followed her from the living room, leaving Hanan with her cup of tea, her eyes still sparkling.

Leila lead the way down a narrow dark hallway papered with faded gold and silver silk wallpaper that was threadbare in many places. There were more photos of old family members, mostly dashing men with oversized moustaches wearing fezzes, one mounted on a white horse clutching a long barreled rifle. The women were largely in the background, holding children. One photograph, in an ornate brass frame, showed a woman in an elaborate bridal gown adorned from neck to foot in jewels, with more jewels in her hair and bracelets covering her arms. Too heavy to carry them all by herself, she was supported by two veiled women on either side of her. The bride was undoubtedly Hanan. She looked incongruously young, with an expression of bewilderment captured in the light of a flashbulb, a vision of innocent youth and beauty.

The kitchen sat off to the right with windows that looked out to the apartment building next door and a playground below. It was a small kitchen but efficient. There were pots and pans hanging from a wrought iron potholder suspended from the ceiling in the corner. On the floor was a gas cylinder with a rubber tube that snaked up and attached to the back of a two-burner stove on the counter. Next to that was a gas lamp, which sat on a small wooden shelf above a deep sink. Rows of spices and canned goods lined the walls. A refrigerator sat under the counter next to the gas canister. Leila explained that with the uncertainty of intermittent electricity they tried not to store any fresh food for more than a day or two.

There was barely enough room for the two of them to fit. Jonathan breathed in the odors of cumin, cardamom and turmeric. She handed Jonathan an apron with a floral design, making them both laugh out loud. Unwrapping some mutton she'd bought earlier that morning, a rare treat, she passed him an onion and a knife. She poured olive oil from a blue ceramic pitcher into a cast iron pan and lit a flame under it. "So, Mr. Jonathan, now you know my wild feminist grandmother."

"A good role model, I can see," Jonathan answered. "What about you?" he asked. "What are you going to do with your life when she is no longer here?" Leila turned around and looked at him sharply. He could tell she didn't like the question, worried that her grandmother would not be around much longer.

After a long pause, she said, "My grandmother has pancreatic cancer. There's nothing the doctors can do, so we just wait. But I can't think about what comes next. In this city you take life a day at a time. I love my job. I love being a photojournalist. Perhaps I'll always do that," she said, wiping her hands on her apron.

"It must be very dangerous work, I would guess," Jonathan responded.

"Everything is dangerous here. Just living is dangerous. But, yes, my job is to get as close to the action as I can and I suppose that puts me at risk. Some of my friends accuse me of being a 'danger junkie.'"

"Is that what attracts you to it? Is it the adrenaline rush?"

She thought for a long time before answering. He saw the scenes of violence and destruction that rushed through her mind. "That's probably what everyone thinks about me. Maybe there's an element of truth to that; but believe me, what I crave above all is to live in our quiet village again hanging out the laundry. I want nothing more than for the drama to stop. No, what makes me love photography is how close you can come to the truth of something."

He saw her in a different way now, attracted to her passion and intelligence. She had beautiful, expressive eyes, uncompromising eyes, 'eyes that could take whatever they wanted,' he reflected.

"But isn't photography just a way of being a voyeur?" he asked, challenging her. "Aren't you actually playing it safe looking through that lens instead of taking sides, watching the drama, but not being a part of it?" She was not used to being confronted this way, but enjoyed the repartee.

She put down her knife on the cutting board, turned and faced him, arms on hips. "You're wrong." She stared hard at him, collecting her words. "I take photographs to capture the madness of this war, to expose the raw reality of what humans are capable of. A voyeur gets pleasure from watching others. Believe me, what I see is very painful to me. But I know there's nothing like images to move people to action. Pictures are far more powerful than words. I do what I do in the hope that my photos will provoke people, provoke them to do whatever it takes to stop this violence. Our greatest fear is that the world will forget us. I'm trying to do what I can to prevent that."

For the first time in his short, remembered life, Jonathan felt himself drawn to a woman. He didn't know how to relate to what was happening. It was all so new. He felt nervous being near her, a feeling like vertigo, so close he could smell her perfume, close enough to touch the softness of her skin. He felt vulnerable, was irresistibly drawn to her. But he knew he must restrain himself. He must not take advantage of her kindness. She had taken risks, great risks, to protect him, to let him into her house and share with him the intimacies of her life. He must not abuse this trust.

Still, he wanted to take her in his arms, to hold her close to him. Her beauty, her courage, her passion and the poetry of her ideas enthralled him. He felt himself caught in an emotional whirlpool, his heart beating to a rhythm of desire and despair.

And he realized, with painful clarity and a foreboding sense of disappointment, that Leila did not share such thoughts. He read her mind, desperately hoping to find the slightest sprouts of attraction, but she was thinking only of tomato sauce and rice, and not of him.

10

A light bulb flickered overhead and the refrigerator came to life with a whirl. "Hamdulillah!" Leila exclaimed, throwing up her hands. Quickly, she plugged in her cell phone and followed a well-practiced routine to capture the scant electricity that drove the air conditioner in Hanan's bedroom and a digital recorder her grandmother used to watch her favorite television series. Jonathan remained in the kitchen stirring the mutton, feeling confused by unfamiliar emotions of longing and rejection.

Hurrying back to her cooking, she turned the conversation to practical matters. "So, Mr. Jonathan, what are you going to do? Where are you going to live? How are you going to pay for your living expenses?" Questions without answers. He must not return to the hospital, they agreed, and, without papers or even a known nationality, it was probably best he stay off the streets for now.

"We need to build you a new identity," she told him. "I may have a contact who can get you fake identity papers. We know how to do such things here," she smiled. "For the time being, you will need to stay here, with us," she thought out loud. "I could ask several people I know to take you in; but as a foreigner, a tall white one at that, you'd attract immediate attention and suspicion. It's better that you stay here until we can get this sorted out."

"I wish I knew how to thank you," he admitted. "You don't even know me. I don't even know me. How can I accept such generosity?"

She studied him, hands on hips, as if weighing his worthiness. In her mind she was thinking how vulnerable he was, how innocent. Yet he made her feel comfortable, unusually so, and he was so kind to her grandmother. He read all this and met her gaze with tenderness. "What am I to do, throw you out in the streets in your hospital pajamas? Which reminds me. We'll need to get you some real clothes. My brother's may fit you. He was also very tall and skinny."

"Skinny?" he asked. They both laughed.

He helped her carry plates of food out to the living room. The television blared loudly. She turned off the volume, but Hanan never noticed, reading the captions for the hearing impaired. She and Jonathan sat cross-legged on the rug by the coffee table in front of her.

"You must have been into yoga in your former life," she said. "I don't know many Westerners who can sit comfortably like that." They ate in silence for some time until Leila remarked, thinking out loud again, "I wonder how it is you speak so fluently, without any hint of an accent. You must have lived here for some time." He threw up his hands. So many unanswered questions.

He decided not to tell her about his paranormal powers to read peoples' minds and feel their emotions, to know the things they know and speak their languages. He was afraid she'd see him as a freak. He wanted her to see him as a normal human being, as a man. But it was not easy for him to hold anything back from her. She had given him her trust and he wanted to be totally transparent with her; but no, it was too early to share his inexplicable abilities with her. The amnesia was strange enough.

When they finished Leila took their plates and retreated to the kitchen. Jonathan followed, volunteering to do the dishes. She looked at him, still wearing the floral apron, handed him a dishtowel and excused herself. She liked having him here, she realized.

It was hot outside and sand swirled up in gusts as she walked out to the terrace to place a call. "Khaled, is Muna there?" Khaled was Leila's first cousin, from the same village, in his early thirties, a lawyer and an activist for prisoners' rights. Muna was Leila's best friend. She came to the phone with her hair wrapped in a towel.

"I just stepped out of the shower, what's up?" Muna asked.

"You won't believe this," Leila said. "I just invited a man to live with us."

"What? Are you crazy! Who? What are you talking about?" Muna screamed into the phone.

"Muna, it's a weird story. We were having tea at Farouk's, as usual, and this Westerner was sitting alone when Grammy read the lips of two lowlifes at the table next to us plotting to kidnap him. I know better than to get involved, but Grammy insisted we warn him, so we did."

Muna interrupted. "So you fucking brought him home? Have you lost your mind? Who is he?"

"That's the problem," Leila laughed. "We don't know."

Muna held the phone up in the air above her head and covered her eyes with her other hand. Khaled looked at her quizzically. She put the phone to her mouth again. "Is this a joke? What have you been smoking? How old is this guy?"

"I don't know," Leila responded, suppressing a laugh.

"What's he doing here?" Muna asked.

"He doesn't know."

Muna held the phone away from her again, looking at it as if it were toxic.

"Leila has lost her mind," she told Khaled, loud enough for Leila to hear. But Leila was enjoying the torment she caused.

"OK, look, it's really insane, I know," Leila said, calming her. "But this foreigner was running away from an army hospital. He had total amnesia. He didn't know who he was or where he came from or anything." There was a long silence on the other end. "He's very kind, very innocent, like a puppy. He speaks like a native. I suspect he grew up here." Again, silence, like a cry of disapproval.

Leila continued. "He's young, our age more or less, very tall. He plays the sweetest saxophone I've ever heard. Grammy thinks he's some kind of angel."

Muna responded with a note of disdain, "You're in love."

Leila insisted she was not. "He's not my type. I want a man who's got his shit together, an Alpha male, not a puppy with no idea who he is. Give me a break."

"You're crushed out," Muna said, annoying her.

"Look, Muna, let's not argue. I need your help. I need your advice. What should I do? I can't let him out of here without an ID, without a place to go. Can you and Khaled quietly see what you can find out and help me assess the situation? Why don't you come over to dinner this week and size him us for yourself?"

Muna held her free hand to her forehead, thought for a while before finally relenting. "OK, but we can't make it tomorrow. How 'bout Thursday night?"

"That'll be perfect. I'll make fish couscous, your favorite."

"Just be careful. You don't know what you're getting into. Tell me what else you know about him."

"Well, he's bright. He's a great listener. In fact, it's almost spooky. He seems to know what I'm going to say before I do. But there's so much I don't know about him, nor does he. For some reason the Americans kicked him off their base and sent him to one of our army hospitals, the glorious Fourth Corps I'm assuming. He claims he accidentally came across some torture chamber in the dungeons there and ran away."

"Leila, you are crazy!" Muna screamed. "You know better than to be talking like this on the phone. Have you lost your mind? You're going to get yourself killed. This is insane. You just can't stay away from danger, can you? You're addicted. But this is too much, too much." Khaled moved next to her and put his ear near the phone to overhear.

Leila persisted. "Just come here Thursday. Come around 8. Don't bring anything. And make sure Khaled can come. He'll know what to do. In the meantime, I'm going to try and meet the doctor who took care of him at the American base and see what I can learn," she said.

"Leila, this is Khaled. I don't know what's going on, but be careful."

"I will," Leila answered and hung up.

11

"Dr. Solomon? I'm Leila Al Alami." Wearing high heels, Leila stood a good half-foot taller than the doctor. She offered him her hand. "Thank you so much for seeing me on such short notice."

She was striking in a smart red dress, black hair hanging in a long braid over one shoulder. Dr. Solomon led her over to the couch and sat across from her in a leather chair, legs crossed.

"I was so relieved when you called," he stuttered. "Frankly, I've been worried sick about him. When I went to the hospital this morning, they told me he had gone AWOL." He took his glasses off and cleaned them with a cloth, his hand shaking slightly. "Where did you find him?" he asked.

She told him about their unlikely meeting at the café earlier that day, how his life seemed in danger, how vulnerable he appeared. She repeated what Jonathan had told her about his loss of memory. "Doctor Solomon, your patient—I call him Jonathan—mentioned he was in your care and that you were a friend he could trust. I thought I should meet you and find out what I could about him. As I mentioned on the phone, I'm in a very compromised situation with him staying temporarily in my apartment alone with my grandmother and me. He kept to the apartment all day yesterday with my grandmother, so no one else saw him, but we'll need to find some other arrangement for the long term."

Solomon took out a pack of cigarettes and offered her one. "Do you mind if I smoke?" She shook her head no. Normally, he wouldn't break a patient's confidentiality, he explained, but in this case safety took precedence over privacy. He told her about the unusual circumstances of X's discovery, naked without any visible signs of trauma. "Usually, with people who suffer total amnesia, there are multiple psychological issues that present themselves. But Patient X—" he paused to smile, "that's what I call him—seemed calm, alert, fully in control of his faculties. In fact, he may be the sanest person I've ever met." He stopped for a moment, collecting his thoughts. "There is nothing about this case, frankly, that is in any way conventional." He took a long drag on his cigarette.

Leila's face contracted. "I can see you're as concerned, as I am," Solomon continued. "He has that effect on people. Usually when someone loses their memory, they keep the personality they had before. But Jonathan—I like that name—acts like he's just been born, a man-child without an ego." He waited for his words to sink in, tapping the ashes of his cigarette into an ashtray on the small table by his chair.

"Ms. Al Alami, Jonathan is no ordinary man. His empathy and compassion are truly Christ-like." He waited to see her reaction. "I'm Jewish and you are probably Muslim, but I think you know what I mean. I gave him all the standard tests. We searched every database we could to discover his identity. I spent many hours with him trying to find a clue that might explain his condition or suggest a cause for his loss of memory. But nothing. He is a complete mystery. He could easily be an alien from another planet or the product of some genetic engineering experiment that caused his unearthly powers." He took a long drag from his cigarette.

Leila's face froze at the mention of "unearthly powers." She tilted her head. Her eyes widened. She was beginning to think she shouldn't have come here, shouldn't have gotten involved at all. 'This doctor is over-the-top,' she thought. 'This is all too weird.'

Sensing her discomfort, Solomon stopped talking.

"Please go on," she said, her eyes forming a question.

He leaned forward and, stuttering, asked, "Have you not noticed that?"

Leila shook her head, "I don't know what you mean."

Solomon, sat back, crushed his cigarette in the ashtray and removed another from the pack. "Are you sure you don't want one?"

"No thank you, doctor."

"When I first interviewed him, he seemed to know everything about me, details of my past that no one else knew. I soon realized he could read the thoughts of anyone near him, could speak their language as well as they could."

Leila's mouth dropped open, a look of incredulity, of amazement, perhaps fear, on her face. She hadn't expected anything like this. Her hands moved to cover her mouth.

"I've been amazed how perfectly he speaks our language," she acknowledged, "as if he were born here."

"Even Tagalog," said Solomon. "In the cafeteria he chatted with the Filipino mess sergeant who served us lunch. The sergeant later tried to convince me that he had to be a Philippine native. He showed other extraordinary aptitudes too. One day we stopped at the library and spoke with Master Sergeant Harris who was working on a math problem for an online doctoral course—Harris is the brains of this unit—X, Jonathan, suggested a simpler, more direct approach to solve the equation. We left the guy sitting with his mouth open, stupefied."

Solomon leaned forward. He felt he was talking too much, but he couldn't stop. "In one of our interviews he picked up my violin," pointing to the case on the floor by the door, "and played the piece I was learning like a concert violinist."

Hearing this, Leila felt panic rise inside her. She stood up and paced around the room, holding her hands to her head, then turned suddenly, addressing the doctor. "I had the same experience." Her breathing was hard. She felt a rush of adrenaline coursing through her, a feeling that was part terror, part awe. "When I talked to him about work and asked what he could do, he mentioned that he could play music, any instrument, he said. I handed him a saxophone and he played like John Coltrane." She sat down like a weight. "Doctor, I think I'll take you up on that cigarette, if I may."

He reached for the pack sitting by the ashtray and handed her one. Her hand was shaking as he lit it.

Leila felt her heart racing out of control. "He also feels whatever someone's feeling," Solomon went on. "A week or so ago, we were walking around the perimeter of the base just before dinner indulging in our usual philosophic speculations when we passed near two groundskeepers who were arguing. Although they appeared close to blows, Jonathan walked right up to them, spoke in a flawless accent and rather soon both men began laughing, tears rolling down their cheeks. They tried to keep him from leaving, tugging at his shirt, but I finally was able to pull him away. When I asked him what that was all about, all he would say was 'just pride.'"

"He has an ability to empathize like I've never experienced before. I feel myself drawn to him, not sexually, not that kind of attraction at all. It's deeper, the opposite of charisma. He's selfless in the truest sense of the word. He not only knows what I'm thinking, but also what I feel. When I'm around him all that I am is OK. He seems to affect everyone he meets that way. Jody, the mess captain, says he feels 'cleansed' when he passes by."

He took another drag on his cigarette. "Ms. Al Alami, whether he is an alien, a scientific experiment or a freak of nature, he is the most wonderful and intriguing human being I've ever met. Knowing him has been a real blessing."

Shocked by these revelations and his obvious adoration, Leila studied her cigarette, trying to collect her thoughts. She was bewildered, had never heard a story like this, never encountered anything so strange and inexplicable. Despite his infatuation with Jonathan, Solomon seemed a reasonable, well-educated man. She had no reason to doubt him. Besides, his description matched her own—the saxophone playing, the colloquial dialect and—she suddenly realized—his knowing her brother's name. But what could explain all this? What was he?

She had earlier decided not to relate Jonathan's story of witnessing torture and escaping from the army hospital, afraid it might compromise his safety. But having met this doctor, who so obviously cared about him, she changed her mind. "Dr. Solomon," she said, clearing her throat, "There's one thing I was hesitant to tell you, though I see now that you have Jonathan's best interests at heart." She reached over and put out her cigarette in his ashtray. "When my grandmother and I met Jonathan at the café this morning, he was wearing his hospital pajamas. He had no money. It was obvious he was in some kind of trouble, was running away from something. When we got him to our apartment he told us that he had witnessed a prisoner being brutally tortured in a room deep underground, beneath the army hospital, and he fled from there and couldn't go back."

Solomon sat quietly for a moment, eyes wincing. "That must have been awful for him," he reflected out loud. "He would have felt the man's pain as his own."

Leila considered this for a moment. "I suggested he come back here to see you, but he said he didn't want to get you in trouble, that the base commander badly wanted to get rid of him."

Solomon explained the difficulty he had trying to get more time with his patient, but rumors about the man's paranormal abilities had begun to circulate and the general in charge wanted to wash his hands of the whole affair.

"Maybe that was a good thing," he reflected. "I've recently been getting enquiries from our PSYOPs people about him. I worry that our military will want to exploit his capabilities. Just imagine what the NSA might use him for. It is one thing to intercept peoples' communications, quite another to know what they're thinking. I'm glad he got out when he did. The important thing now is to keep him safe until any interest in him blows over."

Leila stood up. She felt the need to move again, to get outside and get some air. "Doctor, I'm glad I came here. Needless to say, what you've told me is hard to comprehend. It's a lot to take in. I hope we can stay in close touch. Perhaps together we can help protect him." She handed him her card. "I should go now. I have some friends coming over for dinner who might be able to help him and I need to shop before I go home."

"I'm so glad you came by," said the doctor. "I can see he's in very good hands. Thank you. When we talk on the phone, let's pretend it is you I'm seeing for treatment. I work at a clinic every Friday downtown." He wrote the address on a prescription pad and handed it to her. "We are trying to win hearts and minds. I've got the minds job." They shook hands and she left.

12

Leila wandered through the market in a daze. In a city where the unexpected was the norm, her encounter with the American psychiatrist had left her reeling. 'Is the doctor sane or delusional? Could half of what Dr. Solomon told me be true? Reading peoples' minds? But Jonathan had played the saxophone just like he did the doctor's violin and he spoke Arabic like a native. "Patient X," the very name sounds like an experiment,' she thought. 'The psychiatrist is obviously obsessed. The war can make anyone crazy,' she knew, 'but this is just cookoo. What have I got myself into? Thank goodness Muna and Khaled are coming over. They'll know what to do.'

The market was alive with people hurrying about before the evening call to prayer: lines of shoppers anxious to get home, women holding children, everyone jostling to finish another long day. The sky was tinged with oranges and reds, the smells of carrion blended with fresh herbs, fruits and vegetables. She bought the groceries she needed and boarded a number 72 bus crammed with women in black hijabs and abayas and men in sweat-stained shirts and djellabas. They rode in silence through noisy streets in a sullen mood of resignation.

As she climbed the dark and musty stairs to her apartment carrying her plastic bags of meat and vegetables, she paused on every landing hoping to glimpse the clarity that eluded her. A vague sense of apprehension weighed on her when she unlocked the dead bolts and pushed open the door. Her grandmother was sitting in the same position where she left her, talking to Jonathan with her hands. He stood when Leila entered and moved to take the groceries.

Their eyes meet. "So, you know," he said, as if she had confronted him with proof of an indiscretion. In an instant he grasped the conversation she's had with Dr. Solomon and felt her confusion and uncertainty. She handed him the groceries and he turned and retreated into the kitchen.

Leila removed her headscarf and knelt by her grandmother. Hanan's eyes were moist with tears. "What's wrong? Why are you crying?" she asked.

Hanan smiled broadly and held open her arms to embrace her grandchild. "I'm not sad. I'm happy," she signed. "Jonathan and I have been talking non-stop since you left. What an angel he is."

Jonathan came in and stood near them. Leila looked sternly at him, studying him apprehensively. "So, you speak sign language, too, or do you just read her mind?" she asked sarcastically.

He waited to answer. It wouldn't take a mind reader to see the frustration, the uncertainty and suspense on her face. He sighed, experiencing all that she was feeling. Finally, he answered. "She signs. I listen to her thoughts and she reads my lips," he says. "We get along quite well."

She saw that something important has passed between them like a secret. "So, what have you two been talking about?" Part of her was angry. She wanted to yell at him, to make him leave. How dare he intrude into her space, into the deepest part of her life? But the trespass was pure and benevolent, she understood, like the sound of a bell. She felt the compassion in his eyes. It was almost as if her heart beat in his chest. He understood her thoughts and responded with exquisite caution.

"Your grandmother told me things she has been afraid to talk about," he said, looking at Hanan. The grandmother turned to look at Leila with tender, loving eyes. Jonathan walked back to the kitchen to give them their privacy.

Hanan patted the hammock, signaling for her granddaughter to sit. "Two months ago I received a letter from Dr. Akbar with the results of my last tests," she started. He explained the cancer diagnosis and what it meant. I didn't tell you because I didn't want you to worry about me, but I know there is nothing to do and that my time is short."

Hanan signed again. "It's alright, Leila. It's my time. I'm ready. I've been so worried about you, but Jonathan made me realize you will be fine. I believe him. He will help you."

Leila wrapped her arms around her grandmother and silently wept. She wiped the tears from her face with her fingers, smearing mascara, and looked up. "I've known for two months as well," she admitted. "Dr. Akbar told me, too. I thought he was leaving it up to me to break the news to you." She took a deep breath and let it out, feeling her body relax. "I've been afraid to tell you. I wanted you to enjoy as much of your life as you could without this weight," she explained. "I wanted to carry this load for you."

"My precious Leilita," Hanan signed, using her pet childhood name, "the day you were born and your mother died I knew that her soul had passed to you. You were my own little girl, as if I had birthed you myself. Since that day—Allah is my witness— I have prayed every morning and every night that I would stay alive long enough to care for you until you married. When I learned I had cancer, that I was dying, I worried only about you. I'm not afraid to die. I can't hear. I can't talk, soon I won't see. Everything that lives also dies." She held her hand against her heart. "I'm tired. It is only for you that I live now. But Jonathan—may Allah bless him—opened my eyes. He said, 'You were like a cherry tree in full bloom,' that I could let you go, stop holding onto you. You have a life to live, a song to sing. I want you to be free."

Leila rose, embracing her grandmother again, kissing her on her cheeks and her brow incessantly. Tears made a mess of her face.

Jonathan waited anxiously in the kitchen. He worried that he had intruded on their story, altered its course for better, perhaps; but who knew? He could see and feel everything about a person; but he couldn't know the future; he couldn't know the consequences of his actions. He had tried not to interfere, but Hanan could not help herself from telling him everything. When he realized he could lift her burdens effortlessly just by listening to her, how could he not do so? He felt her pain; then he felt it leave, knew that it was right, that it was good. It was the same with the men in the army hospital. He was able to connect to their deepest fears and bring them peace. It was a blessing for him, as much as for them; but it left him with a feeling of acute loneliness, of being an outsider separated from others.

Leila came into the kitchen and saw him staring forlornly out the window. "So, Mr. Mind Reader, tell me what you are thinking about. You should be happy, but you look so sad. You have given us a gift. I'm very grateful," she said.

"I'm just a little overwhelmed," he admitted. "It's been a big experience for all of us." He noticed how she repeated his phrase "all of us" in her head, as if it were a question. "I'm sorry to intrude into your family's affairs. I had no intention to do so, but Hanan wanted so badly to talk to me about it and…"

But Leila cut him off before he finished, held her hands up to stop him. "It's OK. You did good. You gave her peace. It was a blessing. Thank you. I'm very grateful." Seeing she was OK, Jonathan breathed a sigh of relief.

Leila opened the packages from the market, turned and gave Jonathan another long look as if measuring him, searching for understanding.

"So, the good Dr. Solomon told you all about me, all the magic tricks I do?" She nodded. "Most of the time, I wish I didn't have these quote 'gifts.' They come on their own. Peoples' thoughts and feelings come into my head; but I also suffer everyone's pain and despair and seem to have no defense against them. But there are times, like today, or with Sami in the hospital or even with Dr. Solomon, when these things may do some good. But it's so draining."

She sensed the toll her grandmother's revelations have taken on him, the emotional exhaustion. She wanted to thank him and comfort him, but she held back. Looking in his eyes, she perceived the depth of his dilemma— the irony of the intimate stranger, closer than a lover, but always an outsider. He read all these thoughts and affirmed them with a nod of his head.

She realized through this last silent exchange that she could project her thoughts to him like a conversation. 'You really can tell what I'm thinking and feeling in real time, can't you?' she thought.

And he responded out loud, "Yes."

'Freaky!' she thought again in silence.

He nodded. "Crazy freaky," he answered out loud. "I haven't tried talking with someone like this before. It's going to take some getting used to."

She held her hand to her forehead. 'What is this like for you?' Before he could answer, though, she signaled for him to follow her out of the kitchen and into her bedroom. 'It's the only place where we can really talk.' Her room was covered with lavender wallpaper silhouetted with intricate white tree branches and delicate buds. The floor was made of ceramic tiles inlaid in old wood. There were no windows. An antique chandelier made in brass with crystal glass drops hung over the bed. The bedspread was white, the room neat and feminine. He noticed a book by Antonin Artaud on the table by her bed next to a silver metal reading lamp.

'It's more comfortable here,' she said to him in her head, motioning for him to sit in an overstuffed chair covered with a silver shawl in the corner. She took a seat on the edge of the bed.

"You asked 'what it's like?'" he said. "I will try my best to tell you. Please understand that, as far as my memories go, I've only been alive for two weeks. Most likely there is another me who claims to use this body, but I have never met him. So, everything is new. When Dr. Solomon recognized my strange powers, his surprise bordered on fear. For me, though, reading minds was as natural as breathing. It's not something I can turn on or off; it's just appears like my own thinking. It's the same with others' feelings. Apparently, some normal boundary that usually separates each of us just isn't there for me. Dr. Solomon says I lack any ego and normal fear responses. But I have begun to feel fear now as I begin to experience the world." She listened intently without reacting. He continued.

"All this is a way of explaining what's going on, but you asked me 'what it's like?' Mostly, it's very lonely. I don't know how I could ever fit in with normal people. That's why I didn't tell you about my condition. I hate being seen as a freak. I find myself craving simple human contact. I desperately want to belong. It was such a huge relief to meet you and your grandmother and, at least for a while, not be identified as that weirdo who can read minds. You have been very kind to me. I want you to know how grateful I am."

She looked at him now with pity. His eyes were cast down. He did not meet her gaze, though she knew he felt the compassion in her heart. She could see the depth of his loneliness. She realized there was no way to censor her thoughts. He looked up at her when she thought how much she cared for him. She told him again, thought it, that she appreciated what he'd done for her grandmother and how grateful she was for his consideration and his honesty.

'This could be an interesting friendship,' she told him, telepathically. 'To be totally honest and open with another person could be quite an adventure.' Then she wagged her finger at him like a schoolteacher warning him, thinking, 'But for this to work, Mr. Mindreader, for us to be equal, you'll need to tell me everything that's on your mind as well. Absolutely no censorship! Can you do that?' she asked.

"I can," he answered.

'And now?' she asked.

"Now, I just want to hold you," he admitted. She hesitated. Then they stood and he held her in his arms for a long time. He breathed in deeply the smell of her hair and he was fully happy for the first time in memory.

She broke off. "I have to cook!" she exclaimed out loud and headed toward the kitchen.

13

Charged with energy, Khaled and Muna arrived almost an hour late. "Arab time," laughed Khaled. He was carrying a green plastic bowl filled with oranges from their village, which he handed to Leila, kissing his cousin on both cheeks. Muna did the same, apologizing for being late. Standing behind Leila in his floral apron, Jonathan dried his hands on a dishtowel, then shook hands with them both. Khaled walked directly to his grandmother, removed a pair of rimless glasses and bent down and kissed her several times. "As-salaam 'alaykum," he greeted her. "Wa alaykum as-salaam," she signed beaming.

Khaled was in his early thirties. He had short dark curly hair, and sober, intelligent eyes, a head taller than Muna. His smile was slow and deliberate, revealing hidden dimples. Jonathan could sense instantly that he was street smart, quick witted and kind.

Muna was in her late twenties, five-foot-five, slim, with short chestnut hair stylishly cut and dyed, one side longer than the other. She was dressed in an orange short-sleeved sweater and tight-fitting jeans with rhinestones along the pockets and tall, soft leather boots. Sharp-tongued and effervescent, she talked with her hands like an Italian, always touching people and things. Two and a half years ago she had started an independent newspaper and website on current events and cultural news called *Haria* or *Hope* that had attracted a considerable following among young, Western-oriented, secular youth.

Muna kissed Hanan in greeting and then took Leila by the arm and marched her to her bedroom at the back of the apartment. "He's adorable!" she told Leila excitedly.

"It's not like that, Muna," Leila responded defensively. "Please believe me."

Muna looked at her askance, skeptically. "Well, he's still cute," she said. "Did you get to see the American psychiatrist?"

"I did, but let's wait until we can all talk about it. You'll need to be sitting down." They walked back to the kitchen arm-in-arm.

Jonathan and Khaled were talking about politics while Jonathan stirred a large pot on the gas burner. As she entered the kitchen, Leila made eye contact and directed her thoughts to him, 'Maybe we shouldn't tell them about your mind-reading. I want them to treat you like a normal person.'

'A normal person who doesn't have a clue who he is,' he smiled. 'I like them. If we're going to have a "normal" relationship, I need to be honest. Otherwise, I'll be violating their privacy whenever I'm around them. The fact is: I'm not normal. I just hope they can accept me as I am.'

Leila nodded. Muna watched this silent exchange suspiciously, surprised at the level of their intimacy.

While dinner was being served they all sat on the rug around the low coffee table below Hanan in her chair as on a throne. Leila brought in a large red clay tray filled with a mound of steaming fish couscous surrounded by crispy potato briks folded in triangles. Khaled prepared a plate for his grandmother and signaled for Jonathan to serve himself.

The talk at dinner was about the latest gossip from their village, from which Khaled had recently returned. Nothing was said about Hanan's cancer. Muna described the pressure she'd been under at work after publishing an article about corruption in the finance ministry. Because Muna and Khaled were aware of Jonathan's amnesia, they avoided the usual questioning that greeted a new guest—"where are you from, what do you do?" But Jonathan participated with ease, questioning Muna about her new website and Khaled about his work with prisoners.

Jonathan could see, even without reading their thoughts, that Khaled and Muna were fiercely independent and militantly opposed to any doctrinal, ideological orthodoxy, whether religious or political. "Have you ever thought about running for office?" he asked Khaled. The question opened up a heated discussion: Muna feared for Khaled's safety, Leila worried what this might do to his soul. Khaled said little. He was tempted to enter politics, he admitted, but hadn't made up his mind.

"It's difficult to not offer yourself to prevent suffering, if you believe you can do some good," Jonathan suggested, projecting his own dilemma. He and Khaled smiled at each other.

After a dessert of Leila's homemade halvah, Hanan excused herself and retired to her room. As soon as Muna and Leila were alone, Leila related the conversation she had earlier that afternoon with Hanan about her cancer prognosis. They'd known about the cancer, but thought their grandmother did not. "It's a relief that she's so peaceful with this," said Muna.

Khaled opened a bottle of wine and poured them each a glass. When he served Jonathan, he said, "Leila tells us you're suffering from total amnesia. That's pretty rare. It must be awful."

Jonathan nodded, "It sucks," he said and let out a large sigh. He could tell they were genuinely sympathetic.

"Sometimes I feel like a science experiment, a freak of nature. Everyone else has a personal story to tell. I'm just the dull boy at the party," he said. "But on the other hand it's also very enlightening. People think their stories are their true selves; it's who they are. On some level this all seems kind of silly to me, as if everyone is running around like actors in a play, but a play whose meaning they don't understand. Does that make any sense?"

Khaled smiled broadly. "I know what you mean. We're all so pretentious, each with our little egos and our masks, but what's it like when you don't have any of that? Does it make you feel superior, above the battle, so to speak, or what?" he asked.

"Mostly, I just want to belong somewhere," Jonathan said and looked at Leila.

She was thinking, "You are fitting in pretty well right now." He smiled. Muna, ever perceptive, watched them with increasing interest.

"Leila told us something else, that you ran away from an army hospital after seeing someone being tortured," Khaled said. "Is that true? Can you talk about it?"

Jonathan looked at each of them and then shared the story of his encounter in the basement of the army hospital. "There was nothing I could do. I ran away."

"You were lucky," Khaled said. "We've always suspected they tortured prisoners in that hospital, but no one has ever come out of there alive to tell us."

Jonathan read Muna's thoughts and asked, "Do you want me to testify to what I saw?"

Khaled shook his head. "No, a man who doesn't even know his name wouldn't make a very credible witness, I'm afraid. Anyway, they'd kill you, if you talked. But it's helpful to know what we suspected is true and to know where it was happening. I'm grateful."

"What are you going to do, now? Muna asked him. "If you can't pick up your old life, you'll have to start a new one. You'll need to create a whole new identity and find a way to support yourself. You're like an immigrant who lands in a new country with no money and doesn't speak the language. At least you speak like a native." She looked to Khaled and to Leila for their advice.

Khaled asked, "What can you do?"

Before Jonathan could answer, though, Leila said, abruptly, "He can play the saxophone and read minds." They looked at each other in puzzlement.

"What do you mean?" asked Khaled. Leila laughed and held her hand out, palms up, towards Jonathan, gesturing for him to explain.

"It's very, very weird," Jonathan began. "Even weirder than the amnesia. Whatever happened that caused me to lose my memory also did something else. When I'm near someone, like we are now, I can…" he paused before continuing, took a deep breath and exhaled. "I can read what you're thinking, and what you're feeling, as if it were in my own head."

He waited to see their reactions. Muna was skeptical and worried that he might be an escapee from a mental hospital. "Muna, I'm not an escapee from a mental hospital," he said. She practically jumped backwards.

Khaled somehow half believed him and wondered what could explain it. "OK, I'll think of a number and a color," he suggested, testing him. "Blue 1183," Jonathan responded immediately. Khaled's eyes bulged. "Holy shit!" he said in English.

No one laughed. They looked at each other with shock, the fear of the unknown, a breathless feeling of anxiety. Only Leila was relaxed, enjoying their astonishment, proud of her amazing discovery. Muna remained incredulous. 'There's got to be some trick,' she thought. So Jonathan repeated, "There's got to be some trick." Her mind sought a tougher test and she thought to herself, 'Who was my first grade teacher?' and he answered, "Mrs. Gandoura." Her mouth dropped open. Leila squealed with delight. "He's a jinn!" exclaimed Muna, her eyes wide with amazement.

Jonathan tried to calm them. "Enough of these party tricks," he said. "I know it's spooky. I wish I could turn it off, but I can't." Khaled, who had been focused on Jonathan like a laser, suddenly erupted in laughter, breaking the tension, and soon everyone was laughing uncontrollably. When they finally calmed down, Jonathan explained in greater detail the extent of his powers, his "disabilities," as he called them. He told them how he could speak the language, even the dialect, of anyone he talked with; how he became adept at music, mathematics and probably anything else that the person he met was involved in. Most importantly, he felt whatever that person was experiencing. "I'm overwhelmed with unlimited empathy. It's embarrassing to say this, but I'm left in awe of this power. It is so much bigger than I am, whoever I am or whatever I am," he added. "But it is also a cruel gift in a way, for me that is. I don't want any of these powers. I didn't ask for them."

There was a long silence when he finished. Leila reached over and put her hand on his arm to comfort him. Khaled stood up and paced around the room rubbing his fingers through his hair, agitated. He turned to face them.

"Jonathan," he said, his hand now clenched, "You are indeed lucky, incredibly so. I'm amazed that the Americans didn't keep you there. These powers you have could give a country a strategic advantage over its enemies. Imagine how effective you'd be as a spy. Or imagine the American President taking you along as an aide to a summit meeting. This is no trivial 'party trick,' as you say. This is a matter that could affect the highest national security interests of powers great and small. You must be very careful," he said. "Your life could be in danger."

"So, what should he do?" Leila interjected.

Khaled sat back down on the rug and said, "I think he should stay here for the time being, at least until we can get him a fake ID and proper papers. We can do that, but it may take some time."

"And what about the long run?" asked Muna, turning to Jonathan. "What will you want to do?"

Jonathan looked at each of them in turn. "I feel I have an obligation to use these powers for some good. I appreciate what Khaled was saying. It's potentially an awesome power that could be used for good or for evil. But I'm in the same boat as Khaled, as all of you, in fact. Khaled doesn't want to be a political leader, but he feels that may be where he can do the most good. Leila, you take pictures of war to provoke the world to stop it. Muna, you started a newspaper and website to raise peoples' political consciousness. Whether it's a random accident in the universe or part of some greater design, these are very powerful gifts, as Khaled said. So, the question for me is how can I use them for the greatest good?"

Leila turned to Khaled and Muna, "I visited with Dr. Solomon today, the American psychiatrist who cared for him. He told me he thinks Jonathan has messianic qualities." She turned and said to Jonathan, "But we know what happened to the last one. You don't want that."

Jonathan shook his head disdainfully. "The last thing I want is anyone putting me on any kind of pedestal."

"I have an idea," said Muna. "What if you were to write a blog for my website. Walk around the city and get into peoples' heads, then write what people were actually feeling and thinking, ordinary people. We could get you a fake passport and pass you off as a foreign correspondent. I can get you press credentials working for my paper. No one would have to know how you do it; but if you can capture peoples' stories, it might be a kind of collective therapy, a catharsis. Would that interest you? Can you write?"

Jonathan smiled. "It's an interesting idea," he said. "Let me think about it. I don't know if I can write. I've never tried, that I know of. But if I can play the violin and the saxophone, I probably can pick it up. Maybe I just need to sit near you when I work," he joked. Muna smiled. Leila laughed to herself. Jonathan read her mind and said. "She wonders if I could learn to cook."

14

—*Days of Joy and Sorrow, Blog Number 1,* Crowdsourcer at the Market

As I was walking through the fish market today I passed by a young man without legs. He was smiling for no apparent reason and seemed happier than all the others who were pushing and shoving their way to the front of the queue. I watched him for a long time. Finally I approached and asked him his story.

The loss of his legs, it turns out, was not the result of the war, as one might expect, but an early car accident when he was four. His mother was killed and he was raised by his grandmother in their ancestral village, the name of which I will leave off. There was nothing exceptional about his life, other than being a double amputee. He went to school, had plenty of friends and did what he could around the house to help. But he had a singular talent, an uncanny ability to sing like a soprano. He sang at weddings and at all his village celebrations and was treated like some kind of special angel. Indeed, his beaming countenance was truly angelic. I asked him if he would sing something for me and without any hesitation he began singing "La donna e mobile" to the delight of the shoppers who broke into sustained applause when he finished.

It was oppressively hot today, but this was like a fresh breeze.

15

Jonathan pulled on his new running shoes and headed out through the dark stairway into the brightness outside. It was early in the morning. The sun, hanging low on the horizon, cast long shadows across the former zoo grounds. He jogged down a flight of metal stairs in a cadence of rattling noise and headed to the ball fields and the cinder track in the empty park across from their apartment. He hungered for these morning runs.

His long legs glided effortlessly around the track in a smooth cantor that turned into a sprint whenever he neared the finish line. His breathing was deep and slow. After endless frustrations trying to regain his memory, his pounding heart brought him back to the present.

His breathing was hard now. He focused on the track receding below him. He sped up ever faster, relishing the added pressure in his chest. Overhead, a flock of crows circled, black dots against a pink sky.

Realizing he was a stranger even to himself, he wondered what kind of person he was to have landed in the middle of a war zone. 'What if I don't want to be that person?' He laughed at the irony. What confused him even more, though, was that he lacked normal boundaries. He had trouble knowing where his self stopped and others began. He thought of Dr. Solomon. When he had spent his days dialoging with him he wasn't sure who was who.

He liked Dr. Solomon, but the shrink thought his situation was something miraculous. "There's a purpose for everything," he liked to repeat. When X told him he worried that his condition might be the result of some unbearable tragedy or some science experiment gone horribly wrong, the doctor replied, "Or, some higher calling we don't understand. Think of what good you could do with these powers."

'But all I want is a cure,' he thought. 'Why do people always need divine explanation for things they can't understand?'

His breathing came too fast to form sentences anymore. As his mind quieted, he rounded the final curve of the track sprinting hard into the straight, legs pumping. His upper body heaved forward as he crossed the finish line, breathing hard. He clasped his hands above his head.

His breathing calmed. He remembered a dream he had. It came like a memory. He was in a sprinter's crouch, leaning over his outstretched fingers, head lifted, poised to race; but he couldn't see his face, couldn't make out where he was or what the race was all about. 'I guess that's me. I keep waiting for something to happen, for the story to begin.'

He began to jog again. Slowly thoughts returned. His freakish abilities tormented him. 'Just please let me be normal,' he pleaded to no one in particular.

He sped up again, punishing himself, working his anger into a rage. He veered out of his lane, legs wobbly.

He was thinking about Leila when, suddenly, a thought struck him that he might not be the only victim of this amnesia. 'Whom might I have left behind?' he wondered. 'Do I have a lover, a wife? Is she frantically searching for me? Could there be children waiting for their daddy to come home?' He tried hard to picture this. But no images came to mind. 'Christ, it's been a month. At least I know I'm alive, but there may be someone out there who is seriously grieving.' The thought pierced him. His pace slowed. His loneliness was like poison. It enveloped him like a shroud.

The realization that he might remain a man without a past, a freak of nature who could read peoples' thoughts and feelings, was frightening. He had no memory of feeling fear before, but now he was like a man drowning in it. 'What's the meaning of all this?' he asked. 'There's got to be some purpose to this madness.' But it was a metaphysical hall of mirrors with endlessly receding questions and no answers.

16

Leila opened the door to her apartment and smelled smoke. Jonathan was in the kitchen cooking. She rushed in and turned down the burners on the gas stove. "I've made you dinner," he exclaimed with pride.

"I see," she said. The table was set and candles were burning. Hanan had already eaten and gone to bed.

"I spent the day reading your cookbooks. I don't remember what most things taste like," he said. "I thought I'd better learn."

"It's a feast," she told him.

But he read her mind. "Maybe I'll get better at this with more practice," he said. They both laughed.

She put down the bags she was carrying. "Muna called," she told him, switching back and forth from thinking to speaking out loud. "She's so excited. Your blog's a hit. They had 50 comments so far, as many as they've ever received before. She wants more and she can pay you. People love it."

"Hamdulilah!" he said, hands spread open in thanks.

"I like it, too," she told him.

'I stopped on the way home to see Dr. Solomon again,' she transmitted silently. He has an office at a clinic in town where he volunteers seeing local, civilian patients on Fridays. He badly wants to see you. I think he could be helpful. He has an offer I think you should consider.'

"What is it?"

"He thinks he can get you a part-time gig at this clinic. It might be a way for you to make good use of your skills and get paid doing it. He has some money in his budget to hire an intern, but he hasn't found anyone suitable. He's seen how people react to you. The nurses at the army hospital told him the effect you had on the patients was nothing short of miraculous. Between reading peoples' thoughts and feelings and having unconditional empathy, you'd make the ultimate therapist, he thought. You could do a lot of good. Of course we'd have to be super careful to protect your identity. What do you think?"

Jonathan's mind went to Sami and the other patients at the army hospital and the charge he got in being useful. It only took a moment for him to decide. "I like the idea," he said, nodding his head up and down like a chess player seeing an opening. "I like it very much. It may be exactly what I've been looking for."

Leila was thrilled. In a way, having him in the house was like having a live-in therapist. He'd be perfect for the job. She liked having him around. She felt she could count on him to always be emotionally steady. She was slowly adjusting to living with someone who could read her every thought. It would be impossibly unnerving, if any judgment followed. But with Jonathan there never was any judgment.

After they ate, he cleared the dishes. She invited him to the roof to look at the stars. It was cooler there. Entire families camped out on rooftops on these hot summer nights, she explained.

"Great idea!" he said.

'Let me grab a blanket,' she thought. 'I don't think we'll have to talk to anyone. It's dark already. But if we do, I'll introduce you as my brother-in-law, married to my sister in Manchester.'

"I didn't know you had a sister."

"I don't," she smiled." Don't worry, though; we'll be alright up there."

They climbed two flights of stairs and turned down a dark corridor. The smells of many dinners being prepared in the apartment building seemed to converge. A slight draft of fresh air led them to an opening in the ceiling where they could see the dim lights of the nighttime sky above. They heard the soft murmur of conversations as they climbed a stairway to the roof.

Leila found her way to a corner that was empty, passing by parents whispering bedtime stories to their children. It was still stiflingly hot, but the air felt less constrained and there was an occasional subtle breeze that at least held the promise of cooler moments to come. Colored lights from outdoor signs and traffic reflected off satellite dishes and antennas on the roof. The sounds of the city below were muffled. Leila spread out

the blanket and they sat with their backs against a ledge looking at a sky brilliant with stars.

'It's beautiful tonight,' she thought to him. 'I feel so peaceful here above everything. It reminds me of my childhood in
the country, of the long summer nights where we slept outside
like this and dreamed of castles and love.'

He envied these childhood dreams and told her so. "Did
you watch for shooting stars?"

"Yes, of course."

"Looking at the sky like this, I can understand the Arab
love of poetry," he said. "It is easy to imagine your Bedouin
ancestors staring at a starry sky, writing love poems in the dessert. I spent a lot of time today reading some of your poetry
books. They're wonderful."

'Which did you like?' she asked in her mind, enjoying the
intimacy of their silent communication, wishing she could also
read his.

"Maybe Qabbani, Nizar Qabanni," he answered, and re-
cited in a whisper,

In the summer
I stretch out on the shore
And think of you
Had I told the sea
What I felt for you,
It would have left its shores,
Its shells,

Its fish,
And followed me.

She found herself being drawn to him and wished she could hide such thoughts, but she couldn't. She must not let herself get involved that way with him, she reflected. It was already dangerous for her to have him here. She realized he was listening. 'Neither of us know who you really are, what you have left behind, what trouble you might be in.' She looked directly at him. 'No, it would be impossible, she thought. 'You're a good man, Jonathan. I can see that. I hope we can remain friends.'

He smiled, acknowledging their fate, but in his eyes she could see his sadness. He told her he understood. He would leave their apartment as soon as he could, he said. He didn't want to put her in harm's way.

But she didn't think it wise for him to leave just yet, nor did Muna or Khaled. "In any case, I have a present for you," she told him. "I bought you a name." She handed him a British passport with the name Jonathan Laufer.

17

—*Days of Joy and Sorrow, Blog Number 2*, Crowdsourcer with the School Teacher

Gridlock downtown, car horns blaring, hot, hot, hot. School is out. The young woman is walking home alone, fanning herself ineffectively, stopping to see the fashions in the windows along the way, clothes she can't afford. She looks at her reflection and at the red dress on the manikin that stares blankly back at her, but she turns and walks on. Another day completed. In her briefcase she carries the essays her students turned in. Marking them will be like eating a bad meal, she thinks. If only she could release their imaginations. The boys think only of war and the girls of marriage. But is she any different, she asks herself? Her brother is missing, probably blown to bits somewhere, lying in an unmarked grave. Her boyfriend abandoned her for the sister of her best friend. 'Good riddance,' she tells herself. 'He would never have amounted to anything anyway and, besides, his personal hygiene was deplorable.' She wears her loneliness like a heavy shroud. A truck drives by with a loudspeaker spouting political slogans. She puts her fingers in her ears. Tonight she will cook for her mother and pray that electricity comes on to cool her apartment. She wants desperately to escape from the city and from the country itself. The poster of Switzerland on her bedroom door beckons her. She will dream tonight of salvation and love.

18

—*Days of Joy and Sorrow, Blog Number 3,* Crowdsourcer at the Argument

At a Starbucks on Suleiman Street, two old men are arguing. They have known each other since childhood, suckled by each other's mother, shared like hand me downs. They were together at the police academy during the fight for independence. One of them lost an arm in the war, the other a wife. The one with one arm continues to work as an auto mechanic. The other is a clerk at the national land registry. Their children have all left and rarely see them. Their lives are a tedium of work and sleep with little play and less joy. But today is a feast day and they are expected at the mosque for evening prayers. The mechanic with one arm refuses to go, though, refuses to be in the same room with the Imam whom he blames for the violence. The other is devout, performs his oblations everyday without questions or doubt. He accuses his friend of blasphemy, tells him he has gone astray, of abandoning God. But the one-armed man says it is God who has abandoned him. His liver hurts. He wakes each night in a sweat, filled with fear and foreboding. His dreams are all in sepia. He wishes his daughter would come and bring the child whom he has never seen. The two old friends argue politics and history. The clerk has learned that the mechanic's daughter and granddaughter have died in a roadside blast, but he cannot bring himself to tell his friend, not now, not when they are fighting. "If only he would come with me to the mosque," he thinks.

19

"What a glorious day!" exclaimed Jonathan as they stepped off the bus by the Flower Market. It was cooler and the early morning air felt fresh. There was even a hint of dew on the grass that surrounded the flower stalls.

"This is my favorite part of the city," Leila told him. "I like coming here at daybreak and watching them unload the trucks. It's another business day for them, but for me it's like watching artists paint."

"Let's explore," he said.

Before them an elderly couple was unloading clutches of yellow chrysanthemum's and orchids, orange ranunculus and armfuls of long-stemmed white and yellow daisies. The man stood on the flat bed of the truck and with some difficulty bent over to hand aluminum buckets filled with flowers to the woman who carefully positioned them on a wooden stand. She considered her arrangement with the practiced eye of a Flemish still life artist, turned to the man on the truck and pointed to a row of tulips in a range of colors. Next came purple iris and red and white roses. Leila and Jonathan stood silently watching them. 'We should applaud,' she thought to him, but they walked on invisibly by other merchants displaying their wares.

"Come," said Leila, "there is a café that opens early over there on the corner where we can have tea and coffee and watch the show." He followed behind her as they made their way along rows of flowers, passing familiar fragrances of jasmine, violets and lilies and arrived at the café just as the waiters were setting up their outdoor tables and chairs.

'It's OK for us to sit together in this neighborhood,' Leila assured him. He smiled, thinking how she too could read minds. He ordered a latte and Leila a pot of tea and an assortment of fresh pastries that were still warm when they came out.

"When I was child it was a big deal to come to the city, though it wasn't very far," Leila recounted. "My father would bring me here to this café and I'd order a hot chocolate. The pressurized can they used for making whip cream fascinated me. One day when my father told me I could order anything I wanted, I said I'd like a cup of whipped cream, just that, and hold the hot chocolate, please. And he did!" she recalled with glee.

Jonathan laughed, picturing a little Leila, filled with joy and promise, as the waiter handed her a cup of cream like a servant bent before a queen. "Shall I order you one?" he asked.

Leila held her hand up to stop him. 'No, no,' she thought. "It's funny, though, isn't it, how when we were children we thought that when we became adults, we could order whatever we wanted? Then when we grew up, we discovered we're even stricter than before."

"I don't recall. But I do love hearing your stories," Jonathan said. "Without any memories of my own, your stories mean even more to me." He paused for a moment. "If you don't mind, tell me about the boyfriends you've had."

Leila blushed slightly. "I'd need all day," she teased. "Actually, there were very few. Mhamed was my first great love. He had eyes like a camel's and hair blacker than ink that smelled from some scented gel he got from America. He planned to be an airline pilot. He was very brave, but he got into too many fights over me. He wanted to marry me and got very angry when the other boys talked to me."

"How old was he," Jonathan asked.

"Six," said Leila and they both laughed.

"Who else?"

"Well, there was Hamid. We were both 15. He was the only boy in our school who was taller than me. Oh, I was head over heels for Hamid. He ignored me, wouldn't show me any attention, wouldn't talk to me; though I'd notice him staring at me when he thought I wasn't watching. I finally realized he was just shy. I liked that about him. I made up my mind that if I ever kissed a boy, it would be Hamid. One day we were on a school field trip to visit some shrine. I had walked far ahead of everyone and decided to hide in some tall grass and surprise them; but when they didn't see me, I let them all pass. Hamid came back looking for me. I jumped out to scare him, but he didn't flinch at all. He just stood there quietly looking at me not saying a word. Finally, I just took him by the shoulders and kissed him right on the mouth. You should have seen the look on his face!" she laughed with embarrassment. "Something between terror and ecstasy. But then he wrapped his arms around me, pulled me towards him and kissed me passionately, just like in the movies."

Jonathan relived her memory like it was his own, his eyes widening. He bit his lip. "Go on," he encouraged her. "There's not a lot more to tell, actually," she said. "It was strictly forbidden to mix with the boys after school, so we hardly had any chances to get together. Then, one day Hamid's family moved to the city and I never saw him again. I was crushed. By the next semester the war had started and I began applying to schools in Britain."

"What about when you were at Cardiff? Did you have any grown-up loves?" he asked.

She looked at him suspiciously, her head slightly cocked to one side. "Are you searching for what I think you're searching for? Is this some kind of virginity test?" she asked. Jonathan's face turned beet red. They knew they shouldn't laugh too loudly in public or it might attract the wrong kind of attention, but it was difficult to stifle their laughter.

"Jeffrey," interjected Leila, "Jeffrey Sanderson. We were sort of unofficially engaged to get married. He graduated a year before me and took a job with a brokerage firm in London. He'd commute to Wales on weekends to see me. It wasn't easy being a Muslim woman in the UK after 9/11 and the London subway bombings, and even harder being a biracial couple. I sensed he was uncomfortable in the role, though he insisted he was not. But I could tell from the way he changed his voice when he introduced me at social events that he was. I had real doubts it could work and when my father died and I had to return home, I knew I had to break it off."

He was pleased to read her thinking that she had no regrets. "What about places you've been?" he asked. "What are your favorite memories of travel?" He wanted to record her memories, hungry as a miser.

"Do you really want to know or are you just trying to change the subject?" she asked him.

"No, I'm interested. I just thought you had run out of boyfriends."

She laughed. "I guess I did. Favorite places, though. Let me think." Many scenes flashed through her mind.

"This is like a slide show," he laughed. London, Paris, Barcelona, Tangiers, and a ski trip to a town on the French-Swiss border.

My favorite is Barcelona," she said finally. "The city is so whimsical. I love the Gothic quarter, its narrow meandering streets. I went there at Easter with Jeff. He had plenty of money. We rented an apartment in the Gracia district with a balcony that overlooked the whole city. It was magical."

Some hint of memory fluttered at the back of Jonathan's mind at the sound of the name Barcelona and the Gracia, but it quickly disappeared like smoke. Another feeling pushed it aside, a nervousness in his stomach, an unfamiliar emotion like lava wanting to erupt. They paid their bill and walked back through the market, which was now swarming with customers and the sounds of commerce. Remembering his pledge to tell her whatever was on his mind, he stopped and said, "Leila, I promised to share whatever I'm thinking. Well, I think I just felt jealousy, for the first time in my short, sheltered life."

She turned and continued walking. "It's good for you," she said, picking up the pace.

20

Muna arrived at the restaurant out of breath. "Sorry," she said. "Fucking checkpoints. I got off at Ali Baba's and ran the rest of the way here."

Leila always found Muna amusing. "Relax," she said. "I only just got here myself."

The restaurant was on the floor above a second hand store that sold used designer clothes. They sat out on an open balcony that was perched cantilevered over the busy street. It was loud and sometimes dusty there, but the food was authentic and the atmosphere unpretentious. A waiter in a spotless white shirt arrived and cleared their table from the previous customers with quick efficient movements, sponged off the yellow print oilcloth and deposited menus and a large decanter of water with lemons and two glasses seemingly in one movement.

"So how are you?" asked Leila.

Muna took off her sunglasses, hung her purse from a hook on the edge of the table and exhaled in a puff. "Tired," she answered. "I haven't been sleeping well. Khaled twists and turns all night." She fidgeted with her utensils. "Usually, I can fall right back to sleep; but if I think of work for even a second, I don't have a chance. I'm constantly receiving death threats, and Khaled is always overwhelmed with too many cases and too little to fight with." She paused for a moment to catch her breath. "We're both stressed out. We come home late each evening and end up grabbing a quick snack instead of a real meal and then work on our computers sitting next to each other in bed till it's time to sleep. We haven't made love in weeks. I'm worried what will happen to us, if we don't break out of this routine."

Leila shook her head. "You two desperately need a break. Why don't you take off a few days and go up to the cottage? I need to check on things there myself soon and I promised Jonathan I'd take him to see the village, so maybe we could all go together."

"Let's do it!" Muna exclaimed without hesitation. "How about this weekend? I'll see if Khaled can take off Monday and we could stay for three nights."

"Excellent," said Leila.

The waiter returned ready to take their orders, but they hadn't glanced at their menus yet. He stared off in the distance, impatiently. Leila looked up at Muna. "How about the house Lebanese platter, like we usually get?" she asked.

Muna snapped shut her menu. "Two, please," she said and the waiter disappeared like a ghost.

"How is Grandma?" asked Muna.

"It's hard to tell," Leila responded. "She'll never complain, but Jonathan says she's thinking about death and the after life most of the time. She's not eating much and you can see she's losing weight." She poured herself a glass of water, drank some of it and continued. "She's also sleeping a lot during the day. When he's home, Jonathan takes good care of her. She loves telling him stories. It must be a blessing for her to have someone new who hasn't heard them a thousand times before." Muna smiled. "She's also getting a little delusional, I think. She keeps talking as if Jonathan is my husband. I don't correct her anymore. I think it makes her feel better thinking I'll be OK after she's gone."

The waiter returned with a basket of pita bread and a plate of hummus, babaganouj, kawarma and shanklish, floating in olive oil. Muna attacked the food hungrily. Leila watched her with bemused detachment. "You eat as fast as you talk, Muna" she said, laughing. "But we're all crazy. We're like hamsters in a wheel." She took a large spoon and composed her pita sandwich, reflecting. "Lately I've been thinking I'm ready to bail. I was up early this morning to cover another car bombing. It's déjà vu all over again, the usual grotesque scene of body parts and blood and wailing women." Muna's eyes darkened. "The most frightening thing is I don't feel it anymore. I used to wretch when I saw such carnage. Now I don't even react. I just snap my pictures and shake my head."

Muna put down her bread and stared at her friend. They were quiet as mourners. The sounds of horns blaring and hawkers filled the empty space. Muna reached over and held Leila's hand.

Leila shrugged in resignation. "I'm sorry," she said. "I don't want to ruin our lunch, but watching you so frantic and out of breath made me realize how both of us are running around in endless circles, not really getting anywhere. When grandma dies, I want to move back to the village. The cottage will be mine. Maybe I'll get married and have babies before my biological cuckoo clock chimes."

Muna wiped her mouth and put down her napkin before responding. "Cuckoo's the right word. You'd be bored to death. Besides, your work is really valuable. Images are what keep the world engaged. What you're doing is so important."

Leila scooped some babaganouj onto a piece of pita bread and ate it. "I used to believe that, but I don't think it's true anymore. Pictures may have awakened the world to famine in Ethiopia and helped end the wars in Yugoslavia; but now even videos of children killed with chemical weapons don't move anyone to act. Disaster fatigue, the whole world is suffering from PTSD. No one cares any more," Leila said.

They ate in silence. The waiter came back with a plate of steaming stuffed cabbages soaked in lemon juice and moussaka in a creamy béchamel sauce. "Let's talk about something else," Muna suggested.

"Yes, let's," said Leila.

Muna served her a large portion of the cabbage. "How's Jonathan?" she asked.

Leila smiled. "He's fine. He's always fine. Nothing ever gets him down. Everything comes so easily to him, except his cooking. He's been a joy to be around."

"He never comes onto you?" Muna asked.

"No, not really," said Leila. "We actually talked about it once. We both understand we can't get involved with each other. It's impossible. He doesn't even know who he is. He might be married and have a family somewhere."

"But that's your head speaking," Muna said. "What about your heart? Are you attracted to him?"

Leila took two bites of the moussaka and didn't respond.

"Come on, answer me," Muna begged her. "You're blushing."

But Leila waved her off. "It's not so simple."

"What's not so simple? Either you're attracted to him or not." Leila shook her head. Exasperated, Muna pulled the plate of moussaka away from her. "Nothing more to eat until you confess. Come out with it!"

Reluctantly, Leila answered. "Muna, you're so pushy. I can't believe you're asking me this." She paused. "Don't share what I'm going to tell you with Khaled and please don't make this into something bigger than it is. The truth is that when I'm close to Jonathan, like when I'm in the kitchen with him and we're in such a confined space, I can hardly stand it. I even love the way he smells. I'm afraid he can tell that I get excited when I get close to him. Knowing he can read my mind, I sing a song to myself so he won't know how turned on I get. I can't stay in the kitchen for more than a minute. That's why I've never taught him how to cook." She blushed deeply. "Yes, I'm attracted to him, on a lot of levels, not just physically; though he does have a great body. I wish I weren't. It's awfully complicated. I'll miss him when he moves out, but it will be so much easier on both of us."

21

Khaled sat on a bench in a small park that surrounded Lions Gate, the point of entry for the invaders who periodically took their turns conquering the city—Ottomans, Persians, a variety of European colonialists. A group of boys were playing with a football made of rags, dreaming of glory. A cluster of little girls stood around a playground swing set gossiping. There was no grass to be seen. A large roundabout encircled the "gate," as it was called, which used to connect the east-west and north-south roads that led in and out of the city. But as the urban area gradually expanded to the west, it marked more of a boundary with the past than any hub of the present. Khaled had chosen to meet Jonathan here because it was on a bus line convenient for both of them and it was much quieter than in the center of town.

Jonathan recognized him as soon as he got off the bus and waved. They hugged each other when they met and kissed on both cheeks. Spotting the book in Khaled's hand, Jonathan exclaimed with some surprise, "*Crime and Punishment*? Dostoyevsky?"

"It's work related," laughed Khaled. "Speaking of work, how are you liking the clinic?" asked Khaled.

Jonathan took a seat on the bench and surveyed his surroundings. "Actually, I love it," he said, turning to face Khaled. "After spending so much time having nothing to do, it's a blessing to have meaningful work." He stopped to watch a little boy chasing a pigeon. "Being able to read minds is remarkably useful in this line of work. I may have found my niche," he smiled. "But I seem to have no defense against other peoples' suffering. I experience their pain as if it were my own. Ironically, my patients often leave our sessions feeling great relief, but I feel like I'm left in a fetal position on the floor in emotional agony."

Khaled examined him closely. It seemed that Jonathan's eyes had aged. "But you know their worries are not your problem, right?" he said. "Can't you separate yourself from their points of view?"

"Of course I do, in my head," Jonathan responded immediately, "but there's a physical reaction I haven't learned to control yet. Maybe I will with time.

Khaled shook his head. "But you like it, huh?"

"I really do. It's fascinating. I find people so interesting."

"People want to know that you care. They want to be heard. You're great at that," said Khaled.

Jonathan reflected for a moment. "What people say in therapy is often very different than what they think. After fifteen minutes they believe I'm some kind of a genius because

I'm able to hone in on what's really bothering them no matter what nonsense they might say."

Khaled laughed. "I should take you with me to court."

Jonathan smiled. "Today, I had a big breakthrough with a woman who's been in and out of several different psychiatric hospitals for the past twenty years. Her family and her doctors have been unable to get her to talk or even to move. She sits in a chair night and day with no interest in what's around her. It's been some years since a therapist got her to speak. But her family keeps trying and Dr. Solomon thought I might be able to make some headway."

"Although she showed no sign that she even heard my questions, no change of expression, I could read her mind clearly. If you had watched us, you would have sworn that my questions were disappearing into thin air. But she answered all of them candidly. I began to get a picture of a person who felt imprisoned in her body, unable to communicate with the people she loves. She wanted desperately to speak, but the signal from brain to vocal chords wouldn't work. I learned that her condition started after her uncle, who lived with her family, sexually abused her almost daily. She was a young girl of six or seven—she's no longer sure. When she tried to tell her mother, she was beaten. At some point when her uncle was hurting her she tried to scream, but nothing came out. Eventually, she stopped trying."

Khaled rested his chin on his hand and shook his head. "Was she aware that you were reading her mind?" he asked.

"Yeah, that was the breakthrough. Towards the end of our 'conversation,' she moved her eyes, which had been fixed on a spot on the floor in front of her, moved them up to meet my own. It was a real 'Eureka' moment, a flash of comprehension between us, like a lightning bolt. I felt it, too, and I could see, ever so slightly, that her head nodded. It was a beautiful moment. Dr. Solomon thinks it's like a miracle. He told me he wished he could quit his army commission and work full time with me."

"This must be so gratifying for you," Khaled remarked.

"You can't imagine. I'm finally able to put these paranormal powers to some use. I just wish I could do this on a larger scale. I wish I could teach other people how to do what comes so naturally to me."

After a moment he turned the conversation around. "And what about you, Khaled? How's the prisoners' rights movement going?"

"Too many prisoners and two few rights," Khaled answered. "I'm kind of like you, looking for a way to take things to scale. The moment I help one person—today I got a 13 year-old boy moved to a juvenile facility—10 more prisoners get screwed. I can never get ahead of the problem."

"So, what are you going to do?"

"I'm thinking about running for political office. Muna, of course, hates the idea. She thinks I'll get myself killed. But if I keep doing what I'm doing, I'm just spinning my wheels."

Neither of them said anything for a moment, collecting their thoughts. "People are fed up, but what really drives change the most? Politics, religion, the media?" asked Jonathan.

"I think people are oversaturated with information," answered Khaled. "What they lack is political leadership. The country is torn in two by sectarianism. We need political leaders who can rise above their tribal identities and unite everyone as citizens."

"Preach brother. Lead us out of slavery," Jonathan teased him.

'You're good for me, Jonathan,' Khaled thought to himself. 'My life gets way too serious. I need to laugh more often.' "Let's go for a walk," he suggested. The boys' rag ball rolled close to them and Khaled kicked it back with finesse. The sun was low in the sky and the air had cooled from the furnace it was earlier in the day. The pace of life seemed slower out here on the edge of town as they strolled along wide streets.

"Besides the gig at the clinic, how's the rest of your life going?" Khaled asked.

"Pretty well. There's an apartment in Leila's building that should be available to rent soon and with my blogs and this Friday clinic I ought to be able to afford it."

"Things are lining up pretty well for you," Khaled remarked. "You've found some meaningful work, no thugs seem to be chasing you and soon you'll have your own place."

"It'll be good to sleep in a real bed. Sleeping on the couch at Leila's is ruining my back," Jonathan admitted. "Overall, though, my life is going well and I'm very grateful, especially to have found friends like you and Muna and Leila and her grandmother." He kicked a stone in front of him. "I still fret about my memory, although it's a different kind of worry. I used to obsess about it. I wanted to regain my memory more than anything in the world. But after I met Leila and you all, it became less and less important. I have memories now, a whole month's worth, and they're very precious to me. Now my worries are the opposite of what they were. These days I worry more that I will remember who I was and it might not be so pretty. I have nightmares sometimes where I discover that I'm an escaped killer who gets returned to jail. I'd much rather cast my lot with the present and the future than go back to some unknown past. Frankly, it freaks me out."

"Your world is upside down," remarked Khaled, shaking his head. "The rest of us are always anxious about the future and you only worry about the past."

A shadow passed over them and they both looked up. A rare grey cloud tried to assert itself against a crystal blue sky. Jonathan said, "I'd give anything to just be like everyone else, to have a memory and not know what people are thinking and feeling. These powers prevent me from ever falling in love, from having a normal relationship with someone. What's more important than that?"

Khaled didn't answer. He seemed to understand Jonathan's predicament. Without knowing the past, it was impossible to make any plans for the future. *And what about Leila?* he thought.

Jonathan read his mind. "I think she's wonderful," he said. "She's smart, beautiful, kind, courageous and fun to be with.

But she knows as well as I do that it would be crazy for us to get involved with each other. She's put up a wall and I respect it. I do the same. It's a shame, but that's reality."

"It must be frustrating for you living in that apartment with her then," Khaled responded.

"It is, very," said Jonathan. "But we'll be neighbors soon and good friends and I'll consider that a real blessing. Who knows what the future will hold?"

22

They picked Jonathan up at the clinic at noon. Muna insisted he ride upfront with Khaled. Climbing into the back seat of the 15 year-old green Dodge Caravan, she slid the door shut behind her. They headed east out of the city behind a long line of trucks spewing dark noxious exhaust from their tail pipes. Khaled turned on his citizen band radio to listen to the chatter of truck drivers who offered an early warning system of insurgent checkpoints and IED attacks. "So far, so good," he said.

Once they escaped the center of the city the traffic began to thin. There was a festive mood on the streets. Colored bunting adorned many of the shops along the road in preparation for a weekend festival. Girls in blue school uniforms walked in double file holding hands; a donkey laden with bags of flour trudged mournfully, prodded with a stick by a boy dressed in burlap; and women in black chadors carried babies on their arms, smiling. Inside the van Khaled hummed a song and Muna soon picked it up and sang along.

They talked about their work. Khaled described a new draft law he'd been working on that will limit a judge's discretion in sentencing and how the Islamist parties were trying to block it. Muna was struggling with a decision whether to accept financing for *Haria* from a progressive businessman. She needed the capital to expand her operations, but she feared losing control. Leila was uncharacteristically quiet, at peace with herself.

"How's it going with the patient who can't talk?" Khaled asked Jonathan, recounting to Muna and Leila what Jonathan had told him at the Gate. "She made her first sound," said Jonathan excitedly, "and her eye contact is increasing. She thinks she'll be able to talk again someday. She feels hopeful for the first time in years. Even Dr. Solomon can detect a glint in her eyes. It's quite amazing."

In the other lane coming at them a truck pulled out to pass a slow moving tanker and appeared not to have the speed to overtake it in time to avoid a head on collision. The road was elevated, leaving no shoulder to swerve onto. The angry blast of the truck's horn filled the air with fear. Khaled jammed on his brakes and the truck managed to pass miraculously. It took a few minutes before the rush of adrenaline subsided.

"Are you alright to drive?" Muna asked.

Khaled nodded his head, but his legs continued to shake. "I've read that there are fifty times more deaths from road accidents than from improvised explosive devices," he said.

"Thanks for sharing," Muna responded.

Soon, they were again travelling alone on a two-lane highway, with no traffic in either direction. Gaiety returned. Muna sang an old folksong with a clear, lilting voice. After a half hour they turned onto a narrow unmarked dirt road that led up to the foothills and the mountains beyond. A few yellow sunflowers and purple thistles provided the only color around. The land, dry as bones, turned more verdant as they climbed up the mountain. The air smelled sweet. Khaled turned the air conditioning off and they opened the windows to smell the fresh air and listen to the quiet of empty spaces. "I feel myself healing already," said Muna.

Meeting Leila's gaze in the rearview mirror, Jonathan smiled.

"I'm getting hungry," Muna said.

"Me too," said Khaled. "We brought tons of food, but when we get to my uncle Isa's house, they'll have a banquet waiting for us."

The road began a steep, bumpy climb. They turned right at a fork and climbed higher still, leaving the plains behind them. Sheep grazing along the side of the road signaled their approach to the village. The air was considerably cooler here. The sound of a mockingbird broke the stillness. Crossing a stream on a short wooden bridge, they saw the first structures of the village ahead of them. "I could live here forever," exclaimed Muna.

A series of houses and barns came into view. They waited while a few cows lazily lumbered up the road; then they parked by a two-story cement and stone farmhouse with a large wrap-around porch. A flock of geese scattered as they got out of the minivan. Khaled and Leila's family quickly surrounded them in a scrum of hugs and kisses. There was much news to catch up on.

The tall blue-eyed white man was welcomed warmly, a rare guest in this tiny village and the first foreigner who spoke like a native son. Jonathan gracefully managed to work his way around all their questions. Feasting on goat feta and figs, fresh vegetables and lamb brochettes, Leila and her party promised to return early the next morning to make the leavened bread to be carried to the communal oven for baking. But now they were in a hurry to get to the cottage and they bid their farewells.

The cottage came into view at the end of a mile-long narrow lane sitting by itself, separated from the village by fields of overgrown grass and occasional fig trees heavy with fruit. An old orchard and a large garden area left untended for years stood on one side. On the other was a brook that ran down from the mountain, which rose steeply behind the cottage. The house itself was small, made of large stones and rough, hand-hewn wooden planks with a thatched roof that looked badly in need of repair. A porch ran across the front. A large, oval shaped wooden door with large wrought iron latches guarded the entrance. There were divided glass windows and shutters, mostly closed, around the whole of the single-level cottage, which altogether had the elegance and grace of a beautiful old woman.

"This is idyllic," said Jonathan, "It's how I imagine paradise to be."

Leila smiled. Muna ran around the outside of the house like a child, skipping with joy. Walking up the two stairs to the porch, Khaled removed a heavy iron key from his pocket and opened the front door. He swiped away the cobwebs that had formed and carried in a load of groceries. At the rear of the cottage was a large picture window that framed the mountain. In the center of the room an antique cast-iron pot-bellied wood stove stood with two rocking chairs nearby. Jonathan followed with other bags. Stepping reverently up the stairs, filled with a deep joy, Leila pet the railings with her hand as if the house were a living thing, a gesture to peaceful days that had long ago passed.

After they brought in their sleeping bags and clothes and put away the food, Leila silently invited Jonathan to walk with her up the mountain. 'Muna and Khaled badly need some time alone,' she thought for Jonathan to hear. 'I told her we'd give her at least two hours. Are you OK with that?' she asked silently. He nodded, then turning, asked out loud, "Leila, would you like to go for a walk with me?"

"I'd love to," she responded. "Let me just grab some water and a blanket."

Leila and Jonathan walked out the backdoor and began to follow the foot trail that meandered along the brook. Steadily, they started to climb. Leila walked ahead of him in silence. As they navigated around an escarpment, the view suddenly opened to reveal a river below sparkling in the sun. It looked to Leila like a jeweled snake wandering through the great plain to the city far off in the distance.

"It's wonderful to come up here in the evening and see the glow from the city," she told him. They left the footpath and continued walking along an animal trail when they saw, perched on a rock outcropping above them, several wild goats, which scurried higher up the mountain at the sight of them. "Hanan used to raise them before she moved to town. They've gone feral now."

Leila and Jonathan followed the trail higher and higher, breathing hard. They lost sight of the goats, but Leila told him they'd almost reached her favorite spot on the mountain. As they turned a corner, Leila suddenly held out her hand to stop him and put her finger over her mouth. He looked up to see what she saw. Not more than fifty meters ahead of them, grazing on some grass, was a white deer, a young buck with antlers. Jonathan had no idea such an animal even existed. Leila's heart beat fast. 'It's an albino deer,' she told him silently. 'They are extremely rare. I've heard about them being here, but never saw one before. It's a great omen,' she thought. The deer sensed them, turned and scampered away. Leila and Jonathan hi-fived each other and pumped their fists. "What a gift!" she said out loud.

They continued their climb and finally arrived at the spot that Leila was aiming for. A view of the full mountain range revealed itself majestically before them. There was a flat spot among the rocks and shrubs covered with grass. "This is where I would come when I ran away from home as a little girl," Leila said panting. She handed the water bottle to him, threw the blanket on the ground and sat down on it with her arms wrapped around her knees, staring at the mountains. Jonathan sat next to her.

"Did you run away often?" he asked. She threw back her head and laughed. "Too often, I'm afraid."

They sat next to each other not saying a word. She was thinking about her grandmother, sorry for all the grief she'd caused her and knowing how much she would miss her when she was gone. But Jonathan sensed some other anxiety below the surface. "I'm glad we have this time alone together," she said, turning to face him. "There's something important I've been wanting to tell you." Jonathan felt her nervousness, but she started talking quickly before he could tell what was on her mind.

"Last week I wrote to my cousin Aliya, Khaled's sister, in Vancouver, British Columbia. I told her I needed a change in my life; that I wanted to escape from all the violence around me. She wrote me back, inviting me to stay with her and her husband. She works at the Graduate School of Journalism at the University of British Columbia and she's pretty sure she can get me a job as an adjunct professor there."

Jonathan felt his heart sink, felt a rush of adrenaline like he did earlier in the car. "Leila, that's wonderful news," he managed to say. She looked deeply at him wishing she could tell what he really thought, but she could sense his disappointment.

"You'll be alright, Jonathan," she comforted him. "I do worry about all the suffering you take on from everyone around you, but you've got the makings of a life now. You don't really need me any more. You'll be fine on your own now." He forced a smile. He owed her everything. He knew that. He wanted only to support her.

"When will you leave?" he asked.

"Well, I can't leave before my grandmother dies. I'm really dreading that, but I know it's coming soon. Part of me wishes I could just stay here in the cottage. It will be mine when she passes. But I know that's unrealistic. I will miss Muna and Khaled horribly, and you; but I've got to change the course of my life. I can't go on much longer like I am."

Jonathan nodded. "I think it's a smart decision. You deserve it. You've been taking care of your grandmother for years and now you need to take care of yourself." But inside he felt dizzy and slightly nauseous. "That albino deer is an important omen. It means something great is about to happen to you." Jonathan said.

She looked at him with uncertainty, asking herself, 'How did you want him to react?'

"Look, Leila, I have to be honest with you. I don't want you to go. But I can see that it's the right thing for you."

She felt confused, vulnerable. He looked so innocent. She wanted to protect him; or was it that she wanted him to protect her? He was beautiful she thought. She hadn't expected to feel this way. She wanted this to be the beginning of a separation, but now she felt herself drawn to him, to his nature, to his body, to his very soul. He took in all this and felt the same. But he could not break her trust.

Tears fell from her eyes. He reached over to wipe them from her cheek. "I don't want you to go," he said.

She felt his breath near her, could stand it no longer and pulled him to her, pressing her mouth against his. He opened his mouth and kissed her fully, pulled her down on the blanket and wrapped his legs around her. He rolled on top of her and held her tightly under him; his tongue entered deep inside her, his hand grabbed her hair, pulling her closer still. Then he stopped suddenly and lifting himself off of her, looked down at her, not wanting to hurt her, not wanting to do anything to hurt her.

"Don't stop!" she cried. "Don't look back, Jonathan. Please don't stop."

He bent down and kissed her again and slowly, excruciatingly slowly, with unbearable patience, he learned what it is to love.

23

Dearest Aliya,

We buried Grandma today. I know you would have liked to be here, but we had to bury her before the next sunset, as custom dictates. It is late now. We're back at the apartment after a day that seemed to last forever.

I don't know how much Khaled told you on the phone, so excuse me if I'm repeating things you already know. I was going to email you, but it felt wrong to put this in an email, as if it were just one more thing among all the trivia of our lives. It helps me to actually write to you now the old fashioned way. We can talk later.

On most mornings, Grammy was up early waiting for me with a cup of hot coffee, my "personal barista." When she wasn't there in the kitchen this morning, I tried to rouse her. I found her lying on her bed with her hands folded on her chest and a look of pure peace on her face, the image of an angel. I knew immediately she had passed. I will never forget it. She looked free of any weight. I didn't even feel like crying. In fact, I didn't cry at all until we placed her in the ground.

When I realized she had died I woke Jonathan. Muna and Khaled came over immediately, then Muna and I washed her and wrapped her in five pieces of white cotton, which she had left folded in her closet under her Quran. It feels trite to say this, but I was pretty certain she was present in the room. Washing her brought the reality of her passing home to me. The body without her soul was just a body, like a suit or something we just rent for a while. I don't believe in an afterlife, but I can see now that the continuity of our lives is what makes the present so precious. Hanan continues to live within me, as she does in you and your brother and others she's touched.

After we washed her and sprinkled rose water on her body, we drove to the village and Khaled and Jonathan helped your father dig a grave in back of the cottage in the orchard next to where her parents are buried, perpendicular to Mecca in the traditional way. She was laid on her right side in the earth without a casket facing the Qibla, her head resting on her Quran.

I finally lost it at that point and once I started crying it was hard to stop. It's difficult to imagine life without her. She was always there for me, whenever I was sick or afraid, made fun of or hurt by one of the other kids. Even when I got in trouble, Grammy never got angry with me, never. I felt like she was always on my side. I don't think she ever understood the modern world we live in, but in her eyes I could do no wrong.

When I left for Cardiff after the war started, I didn't think I could survive without her. But she wrote me almost every day and reminded me of the times in her own life when she overcame much greater obstacles than any I faced. A born rebel, she wasn't afraid of anything; and this allowed me to take risks in my own life that I couldn't have done without her. She was an inspiration to so many young people, especially women. I'm so proud of her.

Life changes too quickly. I've wanted to write you all week to share some other big news, but it's been all I could do to keep up with everything that's been happening. When I called you and said that I wasn't sure I could come to Vancouver in time for fall semester and told you all about Jonathan and me, I had no idea that my life would turn upside down.

I asked Jonathan to stay with me in the apartment and not move into the one upstairs that was soon to be vacant. Living with him here the last two months has been the most wonderful time of my life. However, after quitting my job I've been more determined than ever to move back to the cottage. I planned to do this after Grammy died. But what could I do with Jonathan who's become the center of my life? There's no way I could live with him in sin in the village, or even have him visit. So, guess what? I proposed to him!

Well, that's not exactly true, not literally. I was going to ask him, but before I could get the words out, he could tell what I was thinking and asked me first. I told him I'd think about it, but I was just teasing him. I threw my arms around him and smothered him with kisses and tears of joy. I knew that he was afraid of making such a commitment when he did not know what surprises from his past might surface. But he told me that no matter what, he had decided to make his life with me and nothing could ever change his mind.

When we told Grammy the news, she looked confused. "I thought you two were already married," she confessed.

We didn't want a religious ceremony. We wanted to keep it simple. We were married downtown at the city administration building. Muna and Khaled were there and Jonathan's psychiatrist friend, Dr. Solomon. Grammy hadn't been able to get out for the last month or more, so she stayed at home. The whole thing was unbearably bureaucratic. There were no windows in the room, just a single light bulb hanging from the ceiling with paint peeling on the walls and there was a metal table and three chairs from army surplus.

After the so-called "service" we went out to eat at Chez Louis where everyone could have wine and champagne. I think it was the happiest day of my life. We stayed until they closed. There was a piano—the owner used to be a professional jazz musician—and when all the other guests had gone, Jonathan played for us. He was awesome. The food was fantastic. Then we all went to Muna and Khaled's and smoked some hash and told stories till almost dawn. Jonathan and I finally pulled away and went back to our apartment and made crazy, passionate love.

So, in just two months I decided to quit my job and leave my country, fell in love, got married and lost my mother/grandmother. My emotions run the gamut from intense grief to infinite joy. I feel like my heart's been thrown into an electric blender—at its highest speed! It would all be too much except that I have Jonathan. He is the absolute rock of my life.

I can't wait for you to meet him, this handsome husband of mine. He's the most extraordinary person I've ever known. They've asked him to work five days a week at the clinic because he's having such remarkable success. The patients all love him. Everyone who meets him has the same impression. He cares about them as if it were himself. But his gift of unconditional empathy also takes a lot out of him, so he's decided to work four days a week every other week after we move to the country. That means that we'll have thirteen straight days of bliss together alone in the cottage. I can't wait. We'll probably hold onto the apartment for now, but live mostly in the village. Between his job at the clinic and the money he's earning with his blogs—which continue to get larger and larger audiences—plus the modest inheritance I'll get, we should easily make it.

I feel as though Jonathan and I may be the first human beings to ever love like this—so completely, so unconditionally. There is nothing about him that I'd ever want to change. We are totally transparent with each other. There are no secrets. We share our every thought. I'm crazily turned onto him and he's an amazing lover. In the midst of all the chaos in my life and all the violence around it, Jonathan's love is the one certainty I can count on.

I'll let you know about Vancouver once things settle down here a bit. A lot depends on Jonathan's fake passport. It worked getting married, but we don't know whether it'll work travelling overseas. Everything's still up in the air.

I'm going to sign off now. It's very late and I need to sleep. We'll talk soon.

Your dearest cousin,

Leila

24

Two weeks alone in the cabin had been uninterrupted bliss. Time vanished.

They ran down the trail along the brook laughing and wet, caught in an unexpected morning shower. Jonathan still held a bouquet of pink and blue cornflowers they had discovered up on the ridge. By the time they reached the porch, the sun had already reappeared. There were no rainbows to be seen, though the sky was tinged with color. Jonathan put the flowers in a tall blue glass pitcher and grabbed a towel from the bathroom to dry their hair. "Let's take a shower," Leila suggested and they disrobed together and turned the water on.

"That was awesome!" Leila said. Through a small window they could see puffs of clouds hanging in the valley illuminated by a rising sun. Leila stepped into the shower, threw her head back and let the water run down her back, her eyes closed. Then she shampooed her hair, Jonathan taking turns getting his head wet. He took a bar of olive-oil soap and lathered her body front and back. She groped for the showerhead with suds in her eyes and he guided her under its stream, took the shower head off its hook and rinsed her torso, her arms and her legs, and ran his fingers through her hair, removing any remaining shampoo. He got out first to dry while Leila indulged herself under the hot water.

Finally, she stepped out, Jonathan waiting with a large yellow terry cloth towel. He massaged her head with both hands and methodically dried her shoulders and back, her butt and the back of her legs. She turned and faced him with her arms stretched above her. He admired her body, smiling mischievously, then slowly, patiently, pat each inch of the front of her until she was completely dry. She put her arms around his neck, drew herself up to him on tiptoes and kissed him hungrily.

"Come with me," he said and took her by the hand to their bedroom.

Their lovemaking was unhurried, cat-like, ecstatic. He lay on top of her, eyes open, watching the rapturous agony on her face as he thrust deeper inside her, waiting for her to meet his gaze. When she did, eyes wide with wonder, they were one together. He rolled off her and they lay quietly next to each other in silence and awe.

Leila opened her eyes and realized they had both fallen asleep. She tried to sneak out of bed, but Jonathan woke as well. "Thanks, that was beautiful," he said.

"Let's have some post-coital bacon and eggs," she suggested and they walked to the kitchen together.

"Can life get better than this?" he asked.

"I'm really happy here with you," Leila answered. "I love how our days unfold. I never know what time it is or even what day it is. I treasure being quiet with you, lying next to you in bed reading or going for walks or dancing like we do. I wish it would never end." She looked at him and wondered, 'But can you be happy here for long? Is this enough for you?'

Reading her thoughts, he answered, "I'm very content here, but sometimes, I'll admit, it feels a little selfish."

Leila put four slices of bacon on a flat frying pan and lit the stove with a wooden match. Jonathan got out an egg poacher and some eggs and began to dice some potatoes.

'I worry that you'll get bored here', Leila continued.

"Boredom won't be my problem. I never get bored when I'm with you. But I do worry sometimes that I should be making better use of these gifts I've been given. It's been so helpful to the people at the clinic. I know that. But is it enough?"

Leila flipped the bacon over and threw Jonathan his floral apron. "Wait, don't move, let me read you something." She searched through her desk in the bedroom and came out with an old leather notebook. "I love to save quotes," she said, as she leafed through the dog-earned pages. "Here it is, by E.B. White."

Every morning I awake torn between the desire to save the world and an inclination to savor it. This makes it hard to plan the day.

"Hard, indeed" said Jonathan, laughing. "For now, though, I couldn't be more content. I hope this can last forever."

They cooked in silence. Leila loved these moments when they were quiet. They could go hours like this. Because he could read her thoughts, he was ever attentive to her needs, as she tried to anticipate his own. But there were times, like this moment, when it was difficult to surprise him.

He learned, though, when she sang to herself she was usually trying to keep something from him. "What are you hiding from me?" he asked.

She hummed out loud, sang the national anthem, sang even more loudly a medley of Beatles songs, while he stood there in his apron patiently waiting for her to stop. Finally, she relented. "Can't I ever keep a secret from you?"

"You're late with your period," he announced, "and you're worried you're pregnant?" He said it like it was a question, but it's what she was thinking. She already knew what he thought.

"Of course, I'm scared," he said, still reading her mind and taking her in his arms. "I worry that my weirdness might be a genetic mutation and I certainly wouldn't want to pass that on to anyone. But, really my love, nothing could make me happier. I'd love for us to raise a family together and live happily ever after. Maybe that's what we were put here to do."

They ate their meal in silence. After he cleared the dishes, he walked outside to finish turning the soil and weeding the garden. He loved physical work, the smell of the fresh earth, the feeling of strength in his back and arms, loved getting out of his head. But he couldn't help thinking about Leila being pregnant. It could change everything, he feared, just when everything was perfect. Mostly, though, he feared the unknown genetic abnormalities he might carry; and try as hard as he might, he still worried what the past might hold, what unpredictable fate might await them.

The soil was hard. He stabbed at it with the shovel, turning the brown and fertile earth. Bending down, he grabbed a handful and smelled it. A worm poked its head out, making Jonathan grin. The harder he worked, the more he felt confident about having this child. With every shovel a feeling of certainty grew within him, a joy like he had never felt rose warm within him, an all-encompassing love for Leila, a mysterious unconquerable passion to make a life with her. Without realizing it, he was drenched in sweat and breathing hard. He turned and saw Leila, standing on the top of the steps watching him, her eyes wide open in prayer and longing, a pregnancy test stick in one hand. He ran to her and lifted her off her feet.

25

The sign for the clinic door was discrete. Only a small name by the buzzer identified it as the "Center for Therapeutic Medicine." The door clicked open invitingly and Jonathan climbed the two dark flights of stairs and walked through the double glass doors to the brightly lit waiting room. The receptionist jumped to her feet, blushed slightly and bowed her head in greeting. "Good day, Doctor Laufer." He forgot for a moment about the false passport he carried. He returned her greeting with warmth.

"Doctor?" he thought. "That's a familiar sound. I wonder if I were a doctor in my previous life?"

In the receptionist's mind Dr. Laufer was like a demi-god. His ability to bring relief to the most difficult cases was already legendary among the staff, though he'd only been helping there part-time for a few months. The word "miracle" entered into most discussions about his effect on severely depressed and disturbed patients. Even the doctors were amazed at his influence. And it was not only the patients who came to him for help. The staff experienced a similar release of anxiety in his presence, as if "intoxicated by his love," as one nurse put it. Jonathan read these thoughts in their minds as he greeted each of them and tried not to show how much it disturbed him, how it separated him and put him on a pedestal from which he couldn't descend.

He entered the office that had been designated for him; the one Dr. Solomon used on Fridays, and breathed a sigh of relief. On his desk was a clipboard with summaries of the patients he would see today. Stacks of folders in a neat pile held the complete records. He was glad to be back at work, but it was hard leaving Leila and the slow motion routine of life in the country.

He skimmed the list of people he was to see. There was a note from Dr. Solomon regarding certain aspects of each of the cases he wanted Jonathan to pay special attention to and prescriptions he wanted them to take. One of the patients was a young girl, a senior in high school, who seemed to be anorexic. Another was a man of 36 who had been deeply depressed most of his life, a patient Dr. Solomon worried may now be off his meds and possibly suicidal. There was an active-duty soldier who had a severe concussion from an improvised explosive device that killed two of his friends and destroyed his tank, who now suffered from terrifying nightmares. Dr. Solomon noted that the young man was so afraid of sleep that he wouldn't take sleeping pills and so sleep deprived he could be on the verge of a psychotic break. Finally, there was the owner of an auto-parts store who was experiencing random paranoid delusions. "Something about this man makes me nervous," noted Dr. Solomon without further explanation.

Jonathan picked up the folder on his first patient, most likely the intense teenage girl in a brown hijab he noticed sitting anxiously in the waiting room. As he read through the file, he found it a little hard to concentrate, his mind wandering back to Leila, imagining her sewing curtains for the cottage or weeding in the garden. He looked around him at the bare office and made a mental note to get some plants as a gift for Dr. Solomon.

He worked his way through his appointments, managing to create a rapport and a sense of trust with each patient that took others on staff months to build. Partly, this came from his extraordinary empathy that disarmed his patients' fears and mistrust. But his ability to read minds, which none of the other staff were aware of, allowed him to know the underlying truths that our conscious brains were so adept at disguising. It was how he uncovered the young girl's fears that her father would harm her mother during one of his alcoholic rages or how the 36-year old man planned to kill himself, as Dr. Solomon suspected he might. With the soldier, it was Jonathan's empathy that allowed the young recruit to cry, as he hadn't permitted himself to do before, sobbing and wailing in an exorcism of grief. By the time the soldier left, Jonathan was emotionally drained. But he still had one patient to go.

Hussein Abdo is a 43-year-old mechanic and owner of an auto-parts store, he read in Dr. Solomon's report. *Referred by his physician, Dr. Tariq Allawi, he came to the clinic suffering from recurrent paranoid delusions. There is no previous history of mental illness and no sign of recent trauma or neurological regression. Mr. Abdo complains of debilitating fears of death from natural causes of all kinds, though being struck by lightning is the most* prominent. *The patient will sometimes stand at a crosswalk for thirty minutes, powerless to cross on the green light. At other times he will refuse to get under a car raised on a hydraulic lift, which he needs to do for his work. Lately he has been unable to drive a car at all.*

Mr. Abdo is consumed with fear, Dr. Solomon noted. *Initial interviews uncovered little about the source of these fears. The patient appeared to invent stories of persecution as he pleaded for medication that might relieve his anxieties. I prescribed a 2mg/day dose of Ativan, but have included here another prescription at 4mg.*

On a Post-it note attached to the report Dr. Solomon added, *This patient frightens me for some reason. Reminds me of death-row inmates I treated in the past. Might have bi-polar guilt mania. But why?*

Jonathan rang the receptionist and asked her to bring Mr. Abdo to his office. A moment later there was a polite knock at the door and Jonathan invited him in. Abdo was a stocky man of medium height with short balding hair, a square jaw and heavy, downcast eyes. Jonathan introduced himself and held out his hand to shake, but the patient made no eye contact. Abdo's hands, Jonathan noticed, were big and strong and his knuckles were badly cut and bruised. They sat across from each other, Jonathan in Dr. Solomon's chair and the patient on the couch.

"I read Dr. Solomon's notes," Jonathan began. "It must be very frustrating for you, I would imagine." The man looked around the room as if searching for anything that might be dangerous. He nodded. "Did you ever have periods of fear like this before?"

The patient turned to look directly at him. "Never. I've never feared anything or anyone," he said with some annoyance. Jonathan could see, though, the memory of an older man removing his belt, probably his father, and was tempted to ask him about that; but it would not be prudent to challenge this man so soon, he decided.

"How have you felt this past week? Did you notice any change since you starting taking the Ativan?" asked Jonathan.

"Maybe, maybe a little, but it's not strong enough," the patient responded. Jonathan could read that he had no interest in therapy, only going through the motions to get the medicine he wanted.

"That's no problem. I can give you another prescription for double the dose."

The man smiled and prepared to leave when Jonathan asked, "What do you think brought on these fears? What's changed in your life?"

The man thought before answering. Scenes of war flashed through his mind, images of body parts and blood, of babies killed. "It's the television," he said. "The war. Everywhere you turn there is destruction." But Jonathan could tell these were first-hand experiences he was recalling.

"Were you a soldier?" he asked.

"No, never. I hate war. It's a game for losers," Abdo said with disdain. Like everyone else, though, he sensed the tall, young doctor across from him understood him, saw him, saw all of him, and accepted him without judgment or reservations. Yet, this made him feel even more vulnerable, unable to hide the terrible secret that was driving him insane. Jonathan read all this.

"Mr. Abdo, you have nothing to fear from me," he told him directly. "The medicine I will give you may help you feel less anxious, but unless you can name what you really fear, it will come out in other ways." The patient said nothing and, after a moment, Jonathan continued. "It must be embarrassing for you to come here, Mr. Abdo. You don't strike me as a man who is easily frightened. On the contrary, I can see that you are a man of unusual courage. There must be something awful that weighs on you, something you feel powerless to prevent."

The patient felt alarm bells go off inside him, as if a train were bearing down on him. He choked off a terrible desire to cry. His hands shook and his face turned red. He felt trapped, but unable to move. He realized he couldn't hide this anxiety from the young doctor.

Jonathan stood and walked to a small table with a pitcher of water and brought him a glass. "Here, drink this," he said. Then, to lighten the tension, he asked innocently, "What happened to your hands?"

"I'm a mechanic. This is normal," he said, with a grim smile, opening his hands wide and turning them over. But Jonathan perceived something else, images of a young man being beaten, pummeled by these fists.

Jonathan reached over and took one of the big hands in his, turned it over to examine it and measured his own hand against it. Abdo's hand was larger. "You should have been a boxer or a surgeon," he said, still holding the man's hands in his own. The patient laughed, breaking the tension.

Not letting go of his hand, Jonathan looked him directly in the eyes and asked, "What is it you really fear, Mr. Abdos?" The patient looked away, unable to meet his gaze, determined not to answer him. But in the heavy silence that followed, the curtain of his secret opened, revealing its terrible truth to Jonathan. Hussein Abdo, he realized in an instant, was the fixer and engineer who arranged logistics for a network of radical Jihadist suicide bombers. He prepared the suicide vests and their detonators, filled them with ball bearings and plastic explosives and scouted the location that would bring the maximum mayhem. A fighter for the cause, one of the toughest and most ruthless, he was now consumed with guilt, guilt that was devouring him like a demon, guilt that tormented him every waking second of his life.

The patient removed his hand and stood to leave. "Perhaps I need an Imam more than a psychiatrist," he said.

Jonathan stood with him, went over to the desk and handed him the new prescription. "It is never too late to stop," Jonathan said.

Hussein Abdo held out his hand to shake Jonathan's goodbye. "It may be," he said tragically and in that moment Jonathan learned that his patient had planned a suicide bombing at the Flower Market on Friday at 10am. Abdo walked out the door and closed it behind him.

26

Jonathan paced frantically around the room, not knowing what to do. 'I should never have let him leave,' he thought. 'But what could I have done, held him against his will? Even if I could, what would I have told the police, that I had read his mind? They'd laugh at me.' He held his head in his hands concentrating on his options.

He paced some more, nervously looked through Dr. Solomon's desk for a cigarette, but couldn't find any. 'Somehow I've got to stop this,' he repeated like a mantra. There were voices, very small ones in his head, arguing that he should stay out of it, that nothing he could do would stop the cycle of violence, that he would end up endangering Leila; but he dismissed these out of hand. 'I've got to stop this somehow,' he repeated to himself.

He considered calling Dr. Solomon, but remembered that the doctor had gone to Aqaba on vacation and would be offline, referring all emergency calls to another doctor. He dialed Khaled. His extension was busy and no one answered the main number. He looked up at the clock. It was already half past six. After several fruitless attempts, he ran out of the clinic and hailed a cab to Khaled's office, which was not far away.

The Institute for Prison Reform was housed in the offices of the Center for Investigative Journalism in a run-down office building close to City Hall. Luckily, someone buzzed him in and he ran up the three flights of stairs, encountering Khaled at the top as he was preparing to leave. Khaled was startled to see him, especially so unnerved. Jonathan's usual unwavering calm had been replaced by a look of panic, his shirt and face wet with sweat. "What's wrong?" exclaimed Khaled, thinking immediately of Leila and the baby.

"It's not them," said Jonathan. "Can we talk somewhere privately, someplace we can't be bugged?" Khaled led Jonathan through the office and into the rear of the building where they climbed through a large window onto a fire escape. The sky was turning rose color in the setting sun. The sounds from the street were muffled as another day slowly came to its end.

"What's going on?" Khaled asked.

Jonathan explained what had happened in his office with Hussein Abdo.

"Probably not his real name," Khaled speculated.

"I feel so responsible," Jonathan said. "I should have prevented him from leaving, no matter how."

"Look," Khaled responded. "I see how upset you are, but I doubt you could have stopped him. And if you did, you would have ended up in a big mess yourself, probably arrested. The fact is you're very vulnerable. You're working for a psychiatric clinic without any kind of certification, let alone training. You have fake identification papers and you pretend not to know who you really are. You ran away after being committed by a US Army psychiatrist to a local hospital where you claim to have witnessed torture by uniformed army personnel. On top of all that, you believe you are able to read peoples' minds." He shook his head doubtfully. "Sounds like you're a mental case. It's more likely they'd lock you up rather than Abdo, and you'd probably get Dr. Solomon and Leila and even me in trouble." He took out a string of coral-blue worry beads from his pants' pocket and worked them with his thumb.

Jonathan sat on the iron steps of the fire escape and hung his head on his knees. "So, what should I do?" he asked with resignation.

"Look, I'm not the most loved guy in the police department, more like enemy number one. But I do have some contacts who trust me. I won't be able to tell them how I came across this information, but I think they'll believe me when I swear I'm 100% certain about my source. They'll want to try and trace it back, but they won't be able to."

Jonathan raised his head and looked up at Khaled. "Thank you. I don't know how I could live with myself, if people get killed there tomorrow and I didn't stop it when I had the chance. Please do your best. You're my only hope." He handed Khaled a Post-it note with Abdo's name and address, "for what it's worth," he said. "All I know is that he's planned a suicide bombing for 10am tomorrow at the Flower Market. That's all I know."

Khaled took the note and climbed back into the office. "I'd better hurry. There's not much time." Jonathan followed him. At the top of the stairs Khaled turned and faced him. "Go home and try and get some sleep. I'll call you when I hear something," and added, "I wouldn't mention anything to Leila. It will just upset her."

Out on the street, Jonathan felt some relief. It was good to walk, but the crowded sidewalk slowed his stride. Turning down a side street he headed towards the university, his mind racing. He felt the world closing in on him. He entered through the elaborate wrought-iron portal that marked the entrance to the College of Engineering. Unhindered by pedestrians, he walked in great loping strides. 'I could have prevented this,' he endlessly berated himself. 'I should have confronted Abdo with the truth. He might have freaked out, but he would have had to deal with me. At the very least I might have forced him to postpone the attack and gained some time.' He prayed that Khaled could do something. 'But what if he can't? It will be my fault. How can I live with that?" Panic seized him.

The scene with Abdo endlessly replayed itself in his mind. 'What did he say when he left?' he tried to remember. "Maybe I need an Imam more than a psychiatrist,'" he recalled. 'What did he mean by that? He must have realized that his problem was more spiritual than psychological. He needed someone to forgive him and absolve him of his sins. That's what I should have done.' He stopped and thought, 'But perhaps it's not too late.'

Turning, he raced to the entrance of the university. A cab stopped to let a passenger out and Jonathan got in hurriedly and told the driver to go to 141 Istafan Street, the address Abdo gave for his auto repair shop and his home.

He felt the panic rising again as the taxi stalled in traffic, but there was nothing he could do. He bit the knuckles on his hands. '*Hurry, hurry,*' he pleaded to himself, urgently hoping to head him off. "Please, here's twenty dinars, if you can go around this traffic and get me there any faster," he told the driver and threw a bill onto the front seat. The taxi maneuvered down side streets, accelerating whenever it could. At last, after what seemed an eternity, they arrived at the address and Jonathan leapt out.

But there was no auto shop. The address was for an old apartment building above a coin-operated laundry. Jonathan asked anyone he could find, if they knew of a Hussein Abdo. He knocked on every door in the building. Nothing. After a half hour of fruitless searching, he walked away drowning in despair, hoping Khaled had been more successful.

Three blocks away was a bus stop. He took the next bus that came along and transferred to a number 71 that went by his and Leila's apartment in the city. Climbing the stairs, his legs felt heavy and wobbly. He wanted to cry, but it was an indulgence he believed he didn't have a right to. He had never experienced such helplessness before. He carried his guilt like an anchor. Fear, an emotion he hadn't known before, now consumed him.

Finally reaching the 6th floor, he took out the heavy ring of metal keys and stared at them. The most intricate of these was the antique iron key to the cottage. 'My talisman,' he thought. He removed it from the ring and held it against his heart, then touched it to his lips. A sudden realization struck him with iron clarity that the idyllic life he imagined with Leila, raising their family in the cottage among the peace and beauty of the country, was only an illusion. Endless war was the reality. He slumped to the floor and began to cry.

Suddenly, though, he was startled to hear someone in the apartment. He stood quickly and listened. It was Leila singing. 'What's she doing here?' he wondered. He put the key to the cottage in his other pocket, wiped his face with a handkerchief and tried to hide his despair as he unlocked the dead bolts and entered.

"Where have you been?" she asked. "I was beginning to worry about you. Khaled called you six times. Why are his undies in such a wad?" she asked. "What's up?"

He told her that Khaled had been helping him with a difficult case that involves the police, but quickly changed the subject, faking a smile.

"What are you doing here?" he asked. 'Why aren't you at the cottage?" She told him she caught a ride in with Uncle Isa and was able to move her appointment with the obstetrician up to tomorrow. "What's the rush?" he asked. She wiped her hands on her apron. "I keep getting these strong cramps. It's probably nothing, but I thought I should check it out. Besides, I missed you."

He put his face against her belly, then took her in his arms and kissed her passionately, lifting her off the ground. "Be careful," she admonished him coyly.

As soon as she returned to the kitchen, he went into the bedroom and called Khaled. Khaled told him that he had reached a senior police official at his home who promised to enhance security at the market in the morning when it opened. Jonathan worried this wouldn't be enough, but Khaled explained it was the best anyone could do. He told Khaled about going to Abdo's address.

"All we can do now is hope for the best then," Khaled said and they hung up.

27

Jonathan spooned Leila until she fell asleep, then rolled onto his back and stared through the dark at the ceiling. Over and over again he replayed the scene with Abdo in his office and imagined what he might have said that would have made him pause. Had he exposed the fact that he could read the man's mind, would it have caused him to call off the bombing?' He blew it. He knew that. The weight of this crime was now his to bear.

There was no question about sleep. At dawn he quietly slipped out of bed and dressed. He wrote Leila a note and left it on the kitchen counter under the jar of coffee. *Couldn't sleep. Off to get you a surprise. Back later. Eternity is too short a time for me to love you.* He was glad he hadn't shared the dilemma he was in with her, despite their agreement to hide nothing from each other. She would try and convince him that it wasn't his fault or his responsibility. He closed the front door with the quiet of a cat burglar.

The stairs squeaked as he descended. Outside, the sky was turning pink with the dawn. A garbage truck stopped down the street, breaks squealing. Two men in green uniforms leaped from its back and threw large black trash bags into its gaping mouth. The truck groaned forward. There were no taxis at the stand on the corner. Jonathan began to jog. It felt good to move, to feel his body, to fill his lungs with air.

When he got to the Flower Market only a few trucks were beginning to unload their goods, small blotches of color on an otherwise grey canvas. He headed over to the café on the corner, sat at one of the green metal café tables and ordered an omelet, toast and a latte. For now this was the perfect spot from which to scan things. There was nothing that seemed out of the ordinary, no sign of Abdo casing the place and, frighteningly, no extra police presence or warning to the public. He tried to calm his heart rate but failed.

After some time he paid his bill and began to wander through the market, which was coming to life with the sounds of voices and traffic. There was a pair of policemen on each corner, but none of the elite squad he was expecting, and the police that were there seemed too preoccupied in their own conversations to pose any challenge to a would-be bomber. A block away on each of the streets leading into the market there were concrete barriers staggered so no truck could speed past them. Each of the trucks bringing flowers was checked with metal detectors and a long-handled device with a mirror attached on one end to examine the underside of each vehicle. All of this was normal for a Saturday, though it did appear to Jonathan that there may have been more police than usual. Or, he might have been imagining this.

'They should be warning people about the danger,' he thought, but such threats have become a way of life here, something to live with like the weather. He saw nothing out of the ordinary as he scanned the faces of everyone entering the square. 'It could be a woman,' he considered, 'but unlikely.' He concentrated on the men, especially those alone. He looked at his watch. It was now 9:15am. He walked more hurriedly from stall to stall, back and forth and around the market. It was now teeming with people, mostly families, and it was harder to move around. He was becoming frantic. In each of the faces he saw the terror of his eternal damnation. Snatches of their conversations, of the most mundane thoughts, assaulted him like pin pricks. He wanted to shake them, to wake them up to the danger that confronted them; but he knew he would be carted off like a madman.

He moved ever faster through the growing crowd, urgently, with the alertness of a hunter, or the hunted. Still, no sign of anything unusual. A beautiful young woman in red bent down to smell a bouquet of hyacinths; a boy pulled on his mother's hijab; an old toothless woman smiling wrapped some long-stemmed chrysanthemums; two teenage girls holding hands talked excitedly to each other. He heard all their thoughts, all the babble of their lives, which merged into a rising chorus of humanity, rising into a crescendo of impending doom. The noises of ignorance and innocence assaulted him. Even the fragrances of the flowers made him nauseous. He couldn't think above the din, the sound of blood rushing in his ears like a metronome, his heart beating faster and faster.

9:57AM. A picture of Leila flashed in his mind and then, across the square he spotted Abdo in a group of three or four men wearing dark nylon jackets. He watched as Abdo's eyes followed a small man in a hooded grey sweatshirt and a baseball cap a hundred yards from them making his way along the outside sidewalk, alone.

'That's him!' Jonathan realized at once and saw the man turn towards the center of the market. Jonathan was about to scream for people to run; but knew if he did, the man would flip the switch that may already be in his hand. Jonathan rushed through the crowd towards him, pushing people aside, scattering flowers in his wake. 9:59AM. The man was 100 feet away. Walking towards him was a line of school children each holding a knot on a rope that connected them.

Jonathan forced his way through the shoppers that stood between them. In a minute it would be too late. He thought of Leila and prayed. The man was just a few steps away now. Jonathan had no idea what he would do to stop him, but he was close enough now to read his thoughts. He put a hand on his shoulder. "Mother wants you to turn back, don't do it," he whispered to him. The man turned to face him in a panic, his face red with fear and anger "Your sister, Farha, would suffer horribly," Jonathan told him. "These men are not going to pay her for your martyrdom. They lied to you."

The man's mouth was open, sweat poured from him. Jonathan was serene, his face full of compassion. He held the man's shoulders and kissed him on each cheek. "It is not heaven you would go to, my brother, but hell. Remember what your father told you before he died." All these thoughts were mixed together in the bomber's mind. He froze, staring at Jonathan in terror, his finger around the switch that would ignite the plastic explosives in his vest. "Nazim is not waiting for you. He wants you to be a hero for life, not for death. He knows you are not afraid to die, but asks if you have the courage to live? These men back there are not your friends. They are using you. You are better than them. Let go of the switch. Be a real man," he implored him.

The would-be suicide bomber's face froze in utter shock. He began to cry. He let go of the trigger and slumped to the ground. A crowd formed around them until someone saw his vest and shouted, "Suicide bomber!" People scattered in panic. Blue-shirted security guards rushed forward and pinned the man's hands to the ground. Jonathan backed away, turned and ran. When he looked back he saw Abdo and the other men pointing at him, speaking into cell phones. They began to run after him.

The panic that followed the shouts of "suicide bomber" spread outwards in ripples through the market. He pushed past the crowd of people rushing to get away, past the concrete barrier at the end of the street that led to the café and turned left on a narrow side street and left again, bumping into a cart loaded with bales of fabric. His pursuers followed him. He ran through packed downtown sidewalks, past hawkers and shoppers, darted up side streets, crossing red lights; but still the men chasing him closed in on him.

Car horns blared as he dodged oncoming traffic, mixing with the wail of sirens that converged on the Flower Market behind him. He ran across Suleiman Street, was almost hit by a motorcycle, held his left hand out, as if to ward off the speeding taxis, and then from his right, there was the screech of brakes and the cries of onlookers as a truck slammed into him, knocking him unconscious. Pedestrians rushed forward and carried him to the safety of the sidewalk. His pursuers stood off helplessly and watched as an ambulance arrived and whisked him away.

Jonathan awoke in the ambulance, dazed, the faces of two paramedics staring down at him. "You've been hit by a truck," one of them said in English. The other one wrapped a blood pressure cuff around his arm and pumped the rubber bulb. "120 over 80," he said. "Pretty good." They asked him to raise his arms and wiggle his fingers and then move his legs. "Does anything hurt?" He shook his head. They let him sit up. "Please, follow my finger without moving your head," the first paramedic said and he did. "It looks like you're fine."

A voice crackled on the CB radio, a cardiac arrest by the LBC bank close by. "We should go," said the driver.

The paramedic put the blood pressure kit back in its case and told Jonathan, "You can ride with us or we can let you off here. There's really no reason why you need to be admitted. It's your choice. It will just be hours of paperwork and waiting."

"No, I'm OK, just a little shaken up," he responded. In fact, his head hurt mightily, but he was, otherwise, unhurt.

"You'll be fine," they assured him. "You're lucky."

"Yes, I suppose so," he replied.

The driver pulled over to the curb. "We'll just need your name and address," the first one said.

Jonathan's face went blank for a moment. He blinked several times, trying to clear his head. "Alejo, Jacobo Alejo," he said. "1842 24th Street, San Francisco."

PART 3
Jacob

28

He climbed out of the ambulance and squinted in the bright sun. Confused, he tried to remember where he was and what he had been doing here. Fragments of memories slowly came into focus, but they didn't fit any pattern or context. He remembered travelling, pictured having breakfast at the American Colony Hotel in Jerusalem and checking into a small pension off the Blue Mosque in Istanbul; but he had no recollection why he was there or what he did after that. The signs around him were all in Arabic, not Turkish.

'Maybe I should have gone to the hospital,' he thought. 'Something serious has blocked my memory.' But more curious than afraid, he assumed his memory would return shortly, like a small cut that would heal. He strained to remember anything about the unfamiliar city he'd found himself in.

He felt in his pockets for his cellphone, but there was nothing except an antique iron key he didn't recognize. Someone must have taken his wallet and phone when he was hit. There was no recognition of the clothes he was wearing, either. The pain in the back of his head distracted him. He realized there was a ringing in his ears, but it was quickly subsiding. It was hard to think, to stay focused on anything. He sat down on a bench at a bus stop and tried to recall anything that might be a clue to what had happened. All he could remember were the faces of people staring down at him as he lay on the sidewalk and the medics in their white coats lifting him onto a stretcher. But try as he might, he could not conjure up any pictures or facts that could explain how he got there.

Cars passed by. An old man in a worn grey suit stood near him. "Excuse me," Jacobo asked in English. "Where are we?"

At first the old man didn't understand him, then pointed to a street sign, "Fawzi Street," he said in a heavy accent, smiling with pride.

"No, I mean what city is this?" he asked again, but the old man didn't understand and shrugged his shoulders, a bit deflated. A bus came and the old man got on and waved goodbye to the tall foreigner.

29

The phone rang in Leila's apartment. She had been feeling anxious ever since she woke to an empty bed. It was early afternoon and she still hadn't heard from Jonathan even though he had promised to go to the obstetrician with her that afternoon. She turned off the stove and answered the phone.

It was Muna, her voice in a panic. "Turn on the TV right away."

"What's up?" Leila asked as she pressed the power switch.

"Shhh," said Muna, "just listen." The screen came to life, the announcer talking about the "mysterious hero who stopped a suicide bomber from detonating a bomb in the middle of the Flower Market." Then a grainy video played from a security camera that would rerun endlessly that day showing a tall blond man with his hands on a shorter man in a black sweatshirt kissing him on both cheeks before the short man collapses on the ground surrounded by onlookers and police, his explosives laden vest visible under his jacket.

Leila recognized Jonathan immediately, even though his back was to the camera. "Oh my God!" she exclaimed. A molten emptiness spread inside her. She couldn't breathe. She felt sick.

"Witnesses say the unknown foreigner, who seemed to know the man, talked the bomber out of blowing himself up and killing dozens of shoppers," the announcer continued. The bomber, now seen being led away in handcuffs, told anyone who would listen that he had seen an angel from God who spoke to him.

There was no mention of what happened to the hero in the brown shirt who thwarted the attack. But the police were very eager to talk with him and the news anchor appealed to the public for any information on the identity of "the Flower Market Angel," as they had tagged him. Leila put her hand on her stomach. Someone from her apartment house or one of Jonathan's colleagues at work was sure to recognize him from the security camera footage. A sour taste of nausea turned her stomach.

"He mustn't try to come home," she said to Muna. She hung up and tried calling Jonathan, but there was no answer. The minutes passed in excruciating slowness. The cramps she had worried about stabbed at her. When she sat, the fear rose in her throat. She tried to maintain composure, but tears flowed uninterrupted down her face. Everything felt like it was closing in on her. The unending joy she had felt just hours before had evaporated into danger and foreboding.

She realized in a flash how precarious Jonathan's situation was and how difficult it would be to unravel the truth for anyone. Even if she could explain away his false identity papers and his amnesia, who would possibly believe that he could read minds. With all the mystery and media frenzy surrounding the "the Flower Market Angel," it would be impossible to know the real man. Jonathan's innocence made him tragically vulnerable. Leila worried about his safety. Why hadn't he called? Could the bomber's accomplices have hurt him? Her mind turned to her cramps, which were increasing in frequency and intensity, and to the baby growing inside her. The sweet promise of a life of love in the country with Jonathan and their child turned into an alchemy of dread.

Muna and Khaled finally arrived at the apartment to join her in waiting. Leila paced nervously. They debated whether to report him missing to the police, but Leila feared his false ID and his amnesia could only lead to disastrous consequences. "I'm more afraid of the Jihadists, frankly," said Khaled. But the debate was quickly silenced by a knock at the door. Police entered. They questioned them together and separately to see if their stories jibed.

Days turned into weeks, weeks turned into months. The police came back day after day, as there was still no news of the mysterious hero who vanished without a trace.

The man who appeared to fall to Earth from nowhere now seemed to have disappeared in the same way, leaving few traces except the seed that was growing inside her belly.

30

As the bus rolled away, Jacob pondered his predicament—no wallet, no money, no credit cards, no phone and, worst of all, no clue what he was doing in this country. Hard as he tried to remember why he was here, wherever "here" was, he hit an impenetrable wall. The sun was now directly overhead and it was unbearable to stand still any longer without shade. He looked around him for anyone who might help, but the street was deserted. On the side of the bus stop, he found a route map inside a plastic cover, long discolored by the sun that left it almost indecipherable. By studying the lines closely, however, he determined that the number 18 bus that just took the old man away had originated at a terminal in the opposite direction from which many other bus lines converged, undoubtedly near the city center. He began to follow the route on foot and soon discovered a leafy, prosperous neighborhood with large houses and late model cars parked in driveways. A woman retrieving her mail spoke English. He asked her if she knew how to find the Spanish Embassy. She turned and pointed up the hill to her right and told him it was only a ten-minute walk.

At the large iron gate that blocked the entrance to a three-story white adobe mansion a lone guard stood next to a bronze plaque engraved with the royal coat of arms of Spain and the words "Embajada del Reino de España." He explained to the guard that he was a Spanish citizen who had lost his wallet and passport. The guard picked up a phone in a metal box attached to the wall and a few seconds later there was a loud click and a smaller door within the elaborate grillwork sprang open and he was allowed in.

Inside, a soldier told him to empty his pockets and pass through a metal detector, then accompanied him to a small cubicle where a young man with jet black hair in a blue suit and narrow tie the same color and large black glasses greeted him. Jonathan explained that a truck had hit him and that someone, apparently, had stolen his passport, wallet and cellphone while he was unconscious. He decided not to tell the bored young bureaucrat about his loss of memory, hoping to apply for a replacement passport with the least complication. Though prepared to make up the details of his situation as he went along, he found that many of the routine questions he was asked elicited real facts about his life, much like a picture emerging when painting by numbers.

He told the consular officer his name was Jacobo Alejo, that he was thirty-two years old, born in Barcelona to a Spanish father, now deceased, and an American mother who lived in Half Moon Bay near San Francisco. He provided his address and his Spanish social security number. No, he had no siblings. He was a software engineer and owned a company in San Francisco called Alejo Designs.

"The purpose of his visit?"

He thought for a moment, "Tourism."

The man with the heavy black glasses looked up from his notes, eyebrows raised suspiciously. "Tourism?" he asked incredulously. Jacobo smiled benignly. The man excused himself and returned in ten minutes.

"Senior Alejo," he said, scrunching his eyes, "according to our records, your passport expired three months ago and you entered this country almost two years before. What kind of tourism exactly have you been doing?"

The information that he'd been here for two years hit Jacobo like a door slammed in his face, but he tried not to show it. 'Two years?' he thought, feeling his pulse rise. 'What the fuck have I been doing?' he wondered. He smiled, hiding the nausea that began to swirl inside him like a live animal in his gut and said with a wry grin, "I like architecture, spicy food and women." The man across from him smiled back knowingly, as if they shared a secret. Jacobo added, "I also volunteer sometimes teaching programming to high school kids." The young man nodded compliantly.

"Mr. Alejo, is there someone we can call who can vouch for you and wire funds to buy you a ticket home, assuming that is where you wish to go?"

"Yes, my mother, Julia Kensington, 510 676-1181."

The young man looked at him with alarm, took off his glasses and laid them on the desk in front of him, his mouth quivering slightly. He looked down at the printout in his hands and said, "I'm sorry, Senor Alejo, I'm sorry to tell you this, but it says here your mother died two weeks ago. I assumed that's why you were going home."

Jacobo fought off the urge to retch. There was a ringing in his head and he felt faint. He pictured his mother playing the guitar, with a red bandana around her hair, still the hippie, always a joyous free spirit. The thought of her dead was almost inconceivable. A bitterness spread inside him like poison. He hesitated answering, his mind rushing to catch up with this information. 'What to say to this guy?' Finally, he admitted, "Yes, I seem to be doing this a lot lately. My brain's still in denial and I have trouble acknowledging her death. That is why I'm going back."

Jacobo reached deeply into the black well of his long-term memory and heard himself say, "Call Cary Wilson, 1274 Vallejo Street, San Francisco, 415 645-0890. He handles all of my affairs and will take care of anything to expedite this."

The consular officer wrote down the numbers and looked at his watch. "It's about 2 in the morning there, I believe," he said. "Is it alright to call now?" Jacobo nodded.

He punched keys on a black landline phone that sat on the corner of the desk. Jacobo could hear the rings on the other end. Six, seven, eight. The officer started to hang up when a voice, drowsy with sleep, answered. "Hello?"

"Buenas noches, senor. My name is Bernardo Caprilles, First Deputy Assistant Consular Officer for the government of Spain. I'm sorry to disrupt you at this hour. I'm calling to verify the identity of Jacobo Alejo." But before he could add, "who has lost his passport," the voice on the phone screamed out, "Oh my God. Is he dead?"

"No, no, Senor. He is quite alive, sitting in front of me. Here, let me pass him the phone."

Jacobo, still reeling from the news about his mother, took the receiver and said simply, "Hola."

Cary's familiar voice was a lifesaver for a man drowning in a whirlpool of lost memory. "Jacob, where the fuck are you?" he yelled loudly, causing Jacobo to hold the phone away from his ear. He glanced down at a local English-language newspaper left folded on the desk, learning for the first time that day where he was, and answered him.

"Mother is dead?" he asked.

There was a moment of silence on the other end before Cary said, "We buried her last week and scattered the ashes at Point Reyes as she had asked. It was a huge funeral and everyone asked where you were, of course. I explained that you were completely offline and unreachable. I kept my promise to you and never tried to find you, but it felt like shit when she died."

"Cancer?" asked Jacobo. "Yes, it came back. She had a good death, though. She didn't suffer until the final days. She told me to tell you that she understood why you weren't there. 'Freedom is too precious to compromise,' she liked to say. She admired you for what you did."

Jacobo handed the phone to the consular officer, stood up and walked to the wall behind him and began to cry. Once it started he couldn't stop, his body sobbing in waves. In the background, he heard Cary and the consular officer talking about wire transfers, flights and documents. The death of his mother brought up memories of leaving San Francisco. He remembered his last day with her, walking for miles along the Embarcadero while she recounted her life, her unfulfilled dreams, her great loves; and he had had a premonition then that that might be a final good-bye. It was his one hesitation in leaving, in cutting all his ties. Mother was his best friend, more peer than parent.

He turned and faced the consular officer who held out the phone for him. After such crying, a bottomless void replaced his confusion and grief. He wondered for a moment how long it had been since he ate. "Cary?" he said, "I'm ready to come home."

31

His long frame stretched out in business class, Jacob slept most of the way home. The familiarity of the routine of flying was reassuring after the confusion of the past few hours, but it also disturbed him—too rich, too antiseptic. He thought of the primitive and exotic places he'd been since he left San Francisco—villages along the Mekong River in Laos, temples in Japan, ashrams in India and monasteries in the Caucasus. Although he was anxious to return home and pick up the pieces of his life, the sterile ambience of the airplane, the relentless conformity of modern life, made him hesitate. There was a reason he left, he reminded himself.

He had only the vaguest memories of entering the country he was now leaving, trekking over mountains across an unmarked border to get there; but no recollection what he was looking for. He wondered whether he had overdosed on some exotic drug from one of the mystic sects he had sought out, but was unable to imagine what he had been doing for two whole years. It seemed inconceivable, as if it had happened to someone else. He fondled the mysterious metal key in his hand like a talisman, hoping to divine the mystery it held. As he buckled himself into his seat, there was a part of him that wanted to stay and try to figure it out, but his mother's death was a sign to come back home.

Cary was waiting as he passed through customs and out of the security area. Seeing him, Jacob broke into a wide-open smile and almost lifted him off the ground. A foot shorter than Jacob, wonkish, prematurely balding with tufts of curly brown hair, Cary was dressed in a tan suit with a Hawaiian shirt, designer sunglasses and a small gold hoop in his left ear. He stepped back to better examine his friend.

"You've changed," Cary declared, tilting his head slightly to one side.

"And what's with the earring?" Jacob laughed. They hugged again.

"I've missed you badly, brother," said Cary. "Did you find your answers? Have you discovered the secret of life? I've been worried to death about you. I thought maybe you had died."

Jacob said nothing. He put his arm around Cary's shoulder as they walked from the terminal. "Part of me did, I think," he said, not breaking stride. "I have no memory at all of what happened to me the past two years or so."

Cary stopped and looked up at him. "What do you mean?"

"Nada, nothing," Jacob said. "Complete amnesia. I don't have a clue how I even got into that country. All I have is this." He showed him the key.

"I got hit by a truck and must have passed out or something. When I woke up both my wallet and passport were gone and my cellphone, too, along with my memory. I didn't know where I was. It was only when I called you that I learned I couldn't account for the last two years. They just disappeared."

"Fuck, Jake. I never heard of such a thing," Cary said, his face taut.

They started walking again in silence. Cary shook his head from side to side, not sure what to say. Finally, "You need to go see someone."

"Yeah."

"You were pretty fucked up when you left here three years ago, but this…" Cary looked down at his feet, shook his head some more. "Nothing Jacob? You don't remember anything?"

"Nope. Not one thing. It's like the last two years just don't exist."

They headed up the escalator and walked across to the garage. "Tell me about mom," Jacob asked.

"There's not much more to tell other than we spoke about on the phone," Cary said. "She didn't suffer much at all. She stayed remarkably lucid right to the end, telling everyone what to do with their lives. She loved life and she died with dignity. We all admired her. She talked about you all the time. If she worried about you, she never let on. She was always proud of you, even when you were at your craziest."

"And how's Deena?" Jacob asked.

"Same, same. Deena never changes. Pilates, power walks with her friends, book club, one glass of pinot at 6, never more, and practice, practice, practice. She can't wait to see you," Cary said. They climbed in the elevator and rode to the rooftop.

Cary had been Jacob's best friend since high school in San Francisco and had been his partner, accountant and financial advisor ever since. Nearsighted, talkative, politically conservative and devoted to his family, Cary Wilson was Jacob's polar opposite. Where Jacob was an idealist—all vision, willing to risk anything for an idea he believed in— Cary was the ballast that grounded him in reality, measuring the costs, tracking the details. Unlike Jacob, he was ambitious and loved the luxuries that money could buy. He constantly worried about his health and took enough supplements to stock a health food store. He was devoted to Deena, his wife, a rich Jewish violinist who sometimes played in the SF Symphony; but once a month he visited the same Asian escort service in South San Francisco that he'd been going to since he graduated from UC Berkeley.

"So, Jake, what are you going to do now?" Cary asked as they walked out of the elevator. You don't have to work. You've still got gobs of money." In fact, much of their wealth evaporated in the collapse of the dotcom bust, as he tenderly explained to Jacob, but they both remained very well off.

"Three years is a long time," Cary told him. "Shit happens. With 20-20 hindsight, I realize now we should probably not have sold the company. But you were in no shape to run anything and without you the company had no vision, no future." He saw that Jacob was hardly paying attention.

Jacob stared out the window of Cary's Lexus watching San Francisco's skyline emerge.

"When you left the hospital I thought we might make a go of it again; but you were so fucked up on Risperidone, you didn't give a shit about anything. You were the brightest mind in the valley, even if you were the least ambitious," Cary said as he pulled into the car pool lane.

Jacob turned to face him. "You used to complain that I was such an overachiever," Jacob said.

"They're not the same thing, Jake. You could never stop working, days on end, freakishly competitive; but you never had a goal. You never understood why you were doing it, what drove you," Cary responded, glancing sideways at him.

"I hated it," Jacob answered. "I hated all the money, all the hype, the kind of society we were creating. It didn't have any values. It was all 'do it faster.' We were like lemmings rushing off the cliffs."

"The truth is you hated yourself," Cary answered. "That's why you went crazy."

He thought about this. "Yea, I suppose so," Jacob answered with a reluctant sigh. "I was convinced I was like some kind of war criminal. I wanted out. I wanted an escape."

"Well, you did a pretty good job of that," Cary laughed. "All those drugs, those designer drugs you experimented with." He looked over Jacob carefully. "You tried to convince me this was the future; that once artificially intelligent machines took over, psychedelics were all humans would be good for. But it fried your brain, dude. Probably why you lost your memory, too, I bet."

Jacob didn't say anything. They rode for some time in silence. Finally, he said, "On the plane I thought a lot about coming home. It felt right. My great escape only succeeded in getting me lost. I thought I'd find myself, but I'm more confused than ever. I don't have any idea who I am."

"So what the fuck you gonna do?" asked Cary. "Sit around and mope?"

"I don't know. Get back in shape probably. Seems like the body is always the place to start."

"Speaking of bodies, I ran into Carol the other day at my daughter's pre-school. She has a kid the same age. She's put on weight. Doesn't look as good as she used to. She's married to some goofball. She wasn't about to wait for you, bro. Besides, you weren't exactly ready to settle down."

He pulled over to the far right lane and exited on Cesar Chavez. When they stopped at a red light, Cary pressed a button and the convertible top lifted, obediently folding itself behind them.

"Tell me about Mom's funeral," Jacob asked.

Cary told him about each of the people who were there, friends and relatives and their many clients who came to pay their respects. "It was quite the Buddhist affair. They held it out on the lawn by the Pelican Inn on a bright sunny day like today. There was some group playing didgeridoos, a lot of chanting, the obligatory Buddhist monks bowing and smiling and prayers from a rabbi your mother had befriended. He got everyone to recite the Kaddish together. That was quite moving, actually. I spoke. Karen Daniels, a Hospice nurse, who was a saint throughout your mom's dying, gave a beautiful eulogy about her unending quest for authenticity and freedom. She spoke about you and repeated what your mother had asked me to tell you. You would have been proud. At the end, she led everyone in singing some 60's folk songs. It was so over-the-top corny that everyone began to laugh and cry at the same time. A perfect send-off for your mom."

They were silent for a while. They rode past Mission Street and turned on Guerrero and right again on 24th. "I kept the house exactly as you left it," he told him. "It was a big waste of money leaving it empty all these years, but I never knew when you'd be back. He parked the car and the top rose and descended with a satisfying purr.

He turned to Jacob. "Tell me what happened. The man from the embassy seemed very confused."

"I wish I knew," Jacob said. "I simply don't remember anything about the last two years. The accident apparently caused the amnesia. It's very weird. It makes everything else seem so tentative. It isn't like any acid trip I've taken. It's more an anti-trip," He looked out the window. "I can remember being in Jerusalem and in Petra in Jordan and some fairly vague memories of trekking across a high mountain pass with snow around me, but then there's nothing." He pulled out the key from his pocket and stared at it.

Cary took it from him. "That's a pretty serious key," he said, weighing it in his hand. "They don't make keys like that anymore." They were silent for a minute. "Look, Jake, I have a friend who's head of the Department of Neurology at UCSF. Do you want me to make an appointment for you?"

Jacob thought for a moment and said, "Sure. I don't know how I can move ahead with my life until I can recover those years. I quite literally don't know all of who I am."

They sat in the car and talked for an hour. Cary noted a tinge of sadness in Jacob that wasn't there before. The old Jacob was full speed ahead. The man next to him was chastened somehow. There was a seriousness about him that was new. 'Maybe he's finally grown up, like the rest of us,' he thought.

"So, how does it feel to finally be home?" Cary asked.

Jacob thought about that for a long while. He looked hard at his friend. "Confusing."

32

He struggled to wake up like a man swimming to the surface of the ocean, his brain heavy, weighing him down. The sky above him was blue, but it remained just out of reach. His arms flailed ineffectively. The tide pulled him back and forth and he surrendered, sinking deeper back into his dream.

He was in his father's home in the Gracia in Barcelona on the front terrace stalking a dove. With each movement the dove turned in the opposite direction maintaining the space between them. His mother called him to come down for lunch. The bells on Santa Joan rang loudly and suddenly he was holding his father's hand walking through the Plaza del Diamonte past two priests sitting at a table laughing, smoking cigarettes and drinking espressos. They turned and saw him, but he hid behind his father's back. His mother rushed up to him, picked him up and twirled him around. But he was not in Barcelona, he sensed.

He watched himself in the kitchen of a stone cottage through a window on the outside. There were bright yellow flowers in a silver pitcher in the middle of a rustic hand-made wooden table. He looked down, opened his hands and found a large iron key.

Suddenly, he was startled to wakefulness by the grinding noise of a garbage truck outside. He tried to remember where he was. Jerusalem? Kabul? He pictured himself in a series of rooms and finally realized he was home in his own bed in the Mission in San Francisco, waking from a deep jetlagged sleep.

He opened his eyes a slit, tried to read his watch, but couldn't see without turning on the lamp next to him. The light burned. It was 3am. His lips were parched. He turned on his side and fell back into a well of unconsciousness.

At seven he woke again, remembering where he was. He had taken a whole Xanax. He sat up and looked at his room. A guitar stood in the corner next to an expensive road bike. On the wall in front of him was a super-sized map of the world. On another there were a series of framed posters in vivid colors from the Cuban revolution. The other walls were filled with shelves overflowing with books and magazines. The room was pale blue. The owner before him had painted the ceiling with stars like a planetarium.

He sat up, stretched his arms above him with his fingers meshed and yawned. 'I don't know why I'm here. Everything seems to be in its place, except me. It's like I've died and come back, but to what? I should have been here when Mother died. I wish I could have said good-bye.'

He swung his legs off the bed and stood, groggily. Everything was exactly as he had left it; even his toothbrush and razor were on the shelf above the sink in the bathroom as always. He peed a long steady stream with one hand lightly touching the back of his neck as he has done since he was a child. In the ochre and purple painted kitchen, his espresso maker waited faithfully. He poured some beans into the machine and it ground them, hissing and straining until the smell and sweet gentle sound of coffee dripping filled him with optimism.

There was no newspaper to read with his espresso, as was his habit. But his usual addiction to the news seemed silly to him now. A part of him wondered how much may have changed in the world, but another didn't really care. Not knowing what had happened to himself, though, gnawed at him like a cut on one's tongue; but he was determined not to let it cloud his future. His ability to compartmentalize had always been a strong point. He tried to reassure himself, 'I can move on, do whatever I like. I've got more money than I know what to do with. I'm young and in great health.'

He opened the refrigerator and found that Cary had stocked it with all the things he liked—goat milk and chevre, organic chicken, fresh vegetables and white wine. In the freezer was his favorite ice cream. He buttered some toast, sat on the bar stool by the chopping block finishing his coffee and stared at a bird outside the kitchen window. Setting aside the doubts and confusion he felt coming home, he put on his old running shoes and headed outside into the morning light for a run.

As he skipped down the stairs, he was confronted by something that seemed wholly out of place. Three giant buses with tinted grey windows were parked ominously along Valencia

Street like a column of invading tanks. A Mexican man holding a baby in his arms walked by him. Jacob pointed to the buses, "Que pasa?"

The man smiled and shrugged, "Esta Google and Yahoo, amigo."

Along Valencia a line of young men and a smattering of young women, most with backpacks and steaming cups of coffee, all immersed in their cell phones, waited docilely to board the behemoths. An image popped into Jacob's mind: the iconic poster depicting evolution—silhouettes of apes morphing into upright man, homo erectus—only now he pictured the descent of man bent over a cell phone.

He turned around and headed up 24th street towards Diamond Heights and Twin Peaks. The neighborhood was on the edge between gentrified Noe Valley and the heart of the Mission district. The boundary had moved several blocks east of Dolores since he left as more and more affluent Silicon Valley techies bought houses there. Old Victorians were being remodeled with bright blue, green, purple and pink facades and the old Mission, which used to feel like Latin America, had become ethnically mixed. Coffee houses seemed to have sprouted on every corner.

The change disturbed him, but he recognized the irony of his having been among the early waves of invading Yuppies. When he first purchased his house he was escaping the white middle class culture he found so boring, but now he realized he was the avant-garde of its expansion.

As he started to run, his mind wandered to the ancient cities he'd seen, of winding alleys in Arab medinas where the ubiquitous donkeys had been replaced by noisy motorcycles, of the songs of women washing their sarongs in communal harmony that were giving way to washing machines hidden behind walls of private space. He recalled travelling with a friend to the Pine Ridge Reservation in South Dakota to meet Russell Means, a leader of the American Indian Movement, and found him sprawled on the floor of his tepee in the middle of the afternoon watching his favorite soap opera.

He thought back to his decision to leave San Francisco three years before. He had cracked up. Writing code for 48 straight hours, he had eaten nothing but Doritos and guacamole and an endless supply of Frappuccino's, topping it off by snorting a line of Ketamine. He had puked his way down an alley behind his house before collapsing against a wall. The sounds and smells of the city assaulted him like demons and when he was finally lifted into the back of an ambulance he was screaming total nonsense. He was convinced he was the savior, he told anyone who would listen. Slowly the sedatives and anti-psychotics brought him back to earth. They labeled him with bi-polar disorder and told him he suffered from a grandiosity complex. He stayed at Langley Porter for a month, promising to stay on his meds and attend daily therapy sessions after his release.

But the writing was on the wall. He hated his life and was beginning to hate himself. He had devised a complex algorithm based on principles of quantum mechanics that doubled the efficiency of video compression. Soon money and contracts poured into his company. But the richer he became, the more he wanted out. He felt he was imprisoned by success. Two weeks after leaving the hospital, he came out of the grand old art deco Castro Theater in the middle of the day, having watching a matinee rerun of the film *Taxi Driver*, and felt total despair with modern, urban life. He yearned for a place where his feet could touch the earth. He felt sick to his stomach and made a snap decision, one he knew was irreversible, to make a radical break from his comfortable life.

"Success is a killer," he told Cary later. "It's hard to change the patterns that work. Failure is the mother of change." He didn't want to wait for some life-threatening event—an accident or a fatal disease—to force him to transform his life. His psychotic break had scared him, shattering his take-no-prisoners overconfidence. The future, which he had once thought was his to shape, now loomed over him like a threatening cloud. And there was nothing left to his life that held any attraction for him. He hadn't succeeded in any long-term romantic relationships. He felt he couldn't cope. He wanted out.

Cary tried everything he could to dissuade him, but he was not to be moved. They sold the company to an Israeli firm. Jacob handed Cary the key to his house and a notarized power of attorney over his life and made him promise not to come looking for him no matter what. "I have no idea when I'll come back," he said, then wrapped his arms around him in a bear hug.

"Take care of yourself, brother," was all Cary could say. He shrugged his shoulders in resignation as Jacob's cab took him off to the airport with only a small backpack.

Three years later, as he strained against gravity running uphill in the soft yellow light of another beautiful San Francisco morning, Jacob wanted to believe that he could still step off the treadmill, but another, more compelling, voice was telling him it was time to learn to live in the real world. Things around him might look the same, he realized, but he was not. The cocky young programmer who thought he could change the world was no more. He felt shaky, unsure of himself, fearful of losing his grasp on reality again. 'Got to get out of my head,' he thought. In his mind he heard his therapist's voice, "Take a look around you. How are things right now?" The sky above him was a perfect blue, he noted. The gleaming skyscrapers of the city below him shone like gems. Sweat dripped into his eyes as he pushed himself up the sharp incline of Diamond Heights Boulevard breathing hard, yearning for transformation.

In another half hour he reached the top of Twin Peaks, chest burning, lungs maxed out, hands on knees, bent over. A busload of Japanese tourists in identical red visors swarmed about him taking pictures of the view, ignoring him. He straightened himself and looked out at the city, getting his bearings.

The exhilaration of the run was intoxicating. He felt as if he could just let go and sail in the air. 'This is what I want, to fly like a bird.' He retraced his steps floating on gravity, descending.

His mind wandered back to his awakening in the strange city where he lost his memory, to the medics in the ambulance, to the man at the bus stop he asked for directions, to the guy at the Spanish Embassy. Something about these memories was holding him down, keeping him tethered. 'I need to know what happened to me there. How can there be a future, if I don't know the past?'

He turned onto Douglas past a new café filled with people eating breakfast outside, sipping their cappuccinos. As he glided past them, a voice yelled out, "Jacob!"

33

Jacob came to a sudden stop. "Dr. Cornish!"

A tall, heavy-set older man with a close-cropped grey beard, thick black glasses and wispy white hair stood to greet him. He was dressed in khakis and a short-sleeved green polo shirt. They embraced, slapping each other on the back.

"I can't believe it's you," Jacob exclaimed. "I was literally just thinking about you while I was running, having a dialogue with you in my head and then, suddenly, here you are, as if I just conjured you up out of thin air."

"You can imagine my own surprise," said the older man, who had been Jacob's professor, close friend and mentor at Georgia Tech—"my surrogate father"— Jacob would say, the man who taught him the magical power of programming. "I thought you had disappeared off the face of the earth."

Jacob joined him at the table on the sidewalk outside the small café. The waitress came by and asked if he wanted anything. He looked down at Dr. Cornish's omelet and said, "I'll have what he's having and a cappuccino, please." He looked again at the professor, examining him more closely. 'He's aged,' Jacob thought. "What are you doing in San Francisco, Larry?"

"I'm in town for Sara's graduation from Stanford. I'm supposed to meet her here; but she's late as usual and I was hungry, so I ordered." He noticed a big difference in Jacob. The force field of youthful exuberance that used to surround him, an edge of reckless audacity, seemed to have wilted.

"Sara's graduating already?" Jacob asked. "It seems like yesterday that we were at her high school graduation. Is Harriet here, too?" Dr. Cornish's face froze and Jacob could see pain etched in his eyes like broken glass.

"You don't know? Harriet died a little over a year ago. Cervical cancer. She went pretty fast." A long, painful silence encircled them. "She talked about you often. We both did. No one knew where you were."

Jacob's shoulders slumped, his eyes moistened. He reached over to grasp Larry's arm. "I'm so sorry. I didn't know." He felt like he'd been stabbed. It was not only the loss of someone he cared for, but some deep failure on his part to be there for others. He shut his eyes. He pictured his mother, not Harriet. 'I should have come home before she died,' he thought. The black hole of the last two years threatened to swallow him. "I can't imagine how hard this must have been for you," he managed feebly.

"It was. But one has to go on," the professor shrugged. "I miss her horribly. Events like this graduation of course; but also common, every day things like coffee in the morning. I catch myself all the time turning to comment to her about something I've read, only to realize yet again that she's not here. It happens over and over. You know how close we were." He looked intensely at Jacob, a window to his pain left open for a moment; but then formed a wry smile, letting him off the hook. "When did you get back?"

"Just yesterday," Jacob answered, fidgeting with the saltshaker, his face strained with pity and sorrow. Neither of them broke eye contact. "I just learned two days ago about my mother's death. I'm still having trouble believing it. And now Harriet. She was like a second mother to me. So, I've lost them both." He gathered his thoughts. They were quiet for a moment. 'Coming back, nothing has changed and everything has.'

Neither of them spoke, but the magnitude of their mutual losses passed between them in silence. "Harriet was a great woman," Jacob finally said, "always kind to me."

Dr. Cornish shook his head. "Life. Death. It's all flux." He exhaled deeply, looked around him, expecting to see his daughter, and then turned back to Jacob. "I'm sorry about your mother. Sara and I were at the memorial. It was a beautiful service. Everyone missed you." There was another long pause, almost a prayer. Then, Dr. Cornish broke the silence. "How in the hell did you get off the grid like that, Jacob? It doesn't seem possible."

"Honestly, I don't know. A couple days ago I was hit by a truck and woke up on a strange street in a strange city, not knowing where I was. I couldn't even remember how or why I got in the country. I can't recall a thing that has happened to me in the previous two years. Total amnesia." He waited, watching for the effect this would have on his mentor. Dr. Cornish nodded, acknowledging the gravity of what he was hearing.

"Before that I was on a 'life sabbatical,' Jacob continued, "trying to discover who I really was. I travelled with just a backpack: hung out with a group of Gnawa musicians in Morocco smoking lots of kif; crossed India and Southeast Asia searching for enlightenment, and then lived with Sufis in the Middle East trying to understand what Islam was all about."

"Did you succeed in discovering your true self?"

"If I did, I've forgotten."

"You still haven't got your memory back?"

"Not at all. I have an appointment with a neurologist at UCSF next week. Maybe I'll get some answers."

"How very strange," Dr. Cornish said with concern. "It's bad enough we think we know who we are, but not to know even that... must be pretty unsettling."

"It is, deeply," answered Jacob. "I used to feel like I had some control over my life. Now it's like I'm living in some parallel universe, someone else's virtual reality."

'Am I even the same person? Maybe not. Maybe someone's switched identities with me. Could there be another Jacobo Alejo out there who lived the last two years and remembers it all? I kind of feel like an imposter, stuck in some Murakami novel,' he thought.

Dr. Cornish quietly tried to take in all that Jacob had been experiencing.

"Look Larry, I don't mean to be so glib," Jacob said. "You know what it's like when you lose your camera after a trip and all those precious memories disappear? Well, it's something like that, only I don't even know what I lost. The worst part is the fear that this is only the beginning, like the onset of Alzheimer's." He paused for a moment. "Coming back here feels completely surreal, like running into you this way. My life seems all made up. If this were a novel, I'd have a hard time believing it."

Dr. Cornish shook his head. "Sounds awful. From what you say, though, I don't think you need to worry about it getting any worse. It's not a disease. It's an injury, probably some bruises to your frontal lobes. Once the swelling goes down, I suspect you'll get back your memories. Hopefully, they'll be good ones. You probably left a lot of broken hearts back there." Jacob's scowl lifted into a smile. "So, what are you going to do now?" Dr. Cornish asked.

"That's exactly the conversation I was just having with you in my head when I ran into you. So, as I was saying, so to speak, I don't need to work, I've got plenty of money; but I think I need something to keep me grounded. I went kind of crazy before I left." He looked up at Dr. Cornish who nodded knowingly. 'He's heard,' he realized. "I want something challenging, I guess. I don't care at all about money. Got any ideas?"

Cornish laughed. "I can hardly figure out my own life. Look, Jacob, if you really don't need a paying job, why don't you work on some future problems, solutions the world will need ten or twenty years from now?"

"That's an interesting idea," Jacob nodded. "But what about you, Larry? What are you up to?"

The waitress reached over Jacob's shoulder and placed a cappuccino on the table before him. Cornish looked down at his hands as if the answer to Jacob's question lay in his palms. "I've stopped teaching," he said. "I still hold a seminar at my house for the graduate students who want to learn something more than just numbers, but I've stopped lecturing at the university. The politics are too childish. I can't stand it anymore." He swiped his hand in front of him as if he were swatting a fly.

"So, what are you doing with your time?" Jacob asked.

"I'm writing a play, actually, about evolution, trying to escape the rut of academic jargon, hoping to win over the science deniers."

"How's it coming?" Jacob asked, sipping his coffee.

"Horribly," Dr. Cornish leaned back on his chair laughing out loud at himself. "I'm a scientist, not an artist. But I'm very determined." The waitress returned with Jacob's order. Dr. Cornish looked around again for Sara. "Sara will be anxious to see you. I think she was disappointed when you closed shop and disappeared. The big tech firms are pursuing her. She did a double major in business and computer science and did very well. She's better at programming than I ever was and," he stopped and stood up, "and here she is."

A long-legged slender blond in red running shorts, lipstick to match, ponytail, cell phone in hand, ran up to the table and kissed Dr. Cornish on his cheek. She turned ready to shake hands with the man seated across from him and cried out, "Oh my God. Jacob, is that you?" Clumsily, she almost knocked over his cappuccino as she reached across the table to embrace him, turning a cheek to him European style.

Jacob blushed, feeling uncharacteristically shy. He remembered her as a skinny, precocious tomboy, 'but she's a real woman now,' he thought. "Sara, it's so good to see you. I only arrived in the city a few hours ago. I just ran into your father completely by accident. How are you?"

She squinched her eyes and bit her lower lip, eyeing him carefully, as if considering the price she'd pay for a work of art.

Before she could answer he added, "I'm sorry to hear about your mom. Harriet was a role model for me on how to be a good person." He paused, worried he was talking too much, a self-consciousness he was not used to feeling. "Congratulations on school, by the way."

"And I'm sorry about your mom." She responded, eyeing him closely. "I thought you were dead," she said half-jokingly. "Dad was beside himself. What happened to you?"

"I was just explaining this to Larry. I had an accident and lost my memory. I don't recall a thing that happened the last two years, nada." He smiled like a mischievous child playing a trick.

Her eyes widened. "That is so romantic, like some old 1930's film," she cooed. "I didn't know that could happen in real life. Must be kind of confusing, though, but so intriguing, so very mysterious."

He found her smart-ass attitude sexy; or was it just the way she looked at him? The gangly geek of a teenager he helped with homework had grown up. She borrowed a chair from a table next to them and pulled it close. Her leg brushed against his knee. He was aware of a scent of hyacinths or lilacs. Carefully unkempt blond ringlets gave her a slightly wild look, a contrast with an otherwise well-considered outfit. When she smiled large dimples formed at the edge of her mouth. He tried not to stare at her exceptionally kissable lips. He heard himself say, "When did we see each other last?"

"It was the summer after my freshman year at Stanford. I remember it well. You came to my club lacrosse game. Afterwards, you told me what your company was doing. Dad explained how you applied quantum mathematics to data sampling. He thought your solutions were elegant. I went back to school dreaming of working for you."

"And now?" he asked.

She studied him. The old unpretentious confidence of a young man totally comfortable with himself, which made him the object of a mad teenage crush, had disappeared. He was more tentative, shy and vulnerable. The soft gentleness in his eyes had given way to a vague insecurity.

"Now? I've had some offers but I'm having trouble deciding. I'm afraid of getting lost in some huge institution."

"What do you want to do?" he heard his voice asking again, keeping his eyes fixed on hers. "I mean, if money were not an issue, what would you want to do with your life?"

"Money actually is a big factor for me. It would be great working for a small firm, be a big fish in a little pond and all. But I want to do something no one else can do. I'm very competitive, you might remember." She paused to watch the effect this had on him. "Above all else, I like to win."

Her cockiness he found attractive. He smiled at Dr. Cornish, who raised his eyebrows. "I'm sure you will," Jacob said. "You remind me of myself ten years ago. There was nothing in the world that could stop me then."

"And now?" she asked provocatively.

His grin gave way for a second to a frown and then he smiled again. "Now, I've learned that I can be my own worst enemy. Winning lost its appeal for me, but I haven't yet found something better to replace it. Your father suggested I work on future solutions to problems we haven't even imagined yet. That really appeals to me." He noticed her eyes widen, her interest piqued. He thought he should stop talking, but he couldn't stop. "I guess I don't care about the next big thing. I want the thing that comes after the next ten big things, something that will really make a difference in the world. I can't wait to get my hands on a quantum computer. The tools we have today will seem pitiful in a couple of years."

She was still mesmerized by him, as she was three years earlier on the lacrosse field. She loved his mind, but she was not unaware of his trim body and his chlorine blue eyes. His more vulnerable persona she found appealing, she decided, 'makes him more available.' She sat straighter and focused her attention with the same intensity she brought to everything she'd ever wanted before. "Are you taking applications yet?" she asked.

He met her gaze with equal purpose. "No," he laughed, "not yet," and watched her shoulders sag slightly. "I've been back less than 24 hours. I'm not in any hurry to get back in the game; but I think I'm done with my sabbatical."

34

They met a few weeks later at a café near UCSF. Sara arrived out of breath. "Sorry, I'm late," she said. "The traffic on 280 was insane." He stood to greet her. "It was really sweet of you to meet me, Jake. I've been dying to have you to look at this one problem I've been stuck on. Officially, I'm done; they've already submitted my grades; but I still owe them this last paper that's long overdue."

She was dressed in skinny designer jeans, a purple silk shirt and high-heeled leather boots that came up to her knees. A large white patent leather purse hung from her shoulder. If she were wearing makeup, he couldn't tell. They sat down and the waitress handed them menus. It was balmy outside, as if about to rain again. The café was crowded. The smell of coffee mixed with the smell of wet coats and cinnamon bread.

"You look terrific, Sara. How are you?"

"Kind of discombobulated," she admitted. "I'm afraid I'm a serial procrastinator. I've put off doing everything I need to do to clear out of my apartment and now I've run out of time. And my car broke down yesterday, so I had to rent one today.

I hate being so stressed." She worried she appeared too neurotic and turned the discussion to him. "So, what did you learn from the doctors?" she asked.

He smiled. "Actually nothing," he said. "They can't find a thing wrong with me, which I suppose is good news; but it leaves me with the mystery of what happened. The doctor thinks my memory will return in time, but he's only guessing, I can tell. He is pretty certain, though, that there's no worry of it getting worse."

She looked at him intently, eyes wide and mouth slightly open, as if caught between breaths. She felt self-conscious. "Is there anything else you can do to?" she paused, searching for the right word, "rekindle your memory?"

He looked up and behind her. "I tried hypnotherapy, but nothing came of it. I guess I'm just going to have to live with this hole in my life. It doesn't really change anything." He glanced at his hands. "But I can't help but wonder what happened to me."

She tried to look sympathetic, but she was thinking how attractive he was. "You were probably having a torrid love affair with a film star whose husband was trying to kill you, or something like that." She sensed she was being wildly inappropriate. "I'm sorry. I guess this is pretty traumatic for you."

The waitress took their orders. They listened for a moment to the pitter-patter of rain on the roof. Sara took out the paper she was working on and handed it to him. As he studied it, she worried he'd think less of her, that this man whom she idolized as a youngster would still see her as young and unsophisticated. She wiped the wetness on the skin above her lips with her finger. He glanced up and met her eyes, then turned the page and continued.

When he finished reading, he put down the paper and watched her for a moment with a serious expression, wondering who she was underneath the beauty and intelligence. "It's brilliant, Sara. Your solutions are elegant." She released her breath. He offered a few suggestions, but they were peripheral to her central argument. Their lunches arrived. The sounds of wind and rain blew in whenever a new customer entered along with the faint haunting bellow of the foghorn under the Golden Gate Bridge. Their conversation was quick and lively.

"It's funny doing this with you here," he said. "It reminds me of those days when you were a scrawny kid in high school and I would help you with your homework." He leaned back in his chair.

They looked at each other in silent acknowledgement of her new status. She enjoyed his attention. They talked about the loss of their mothers, how strange it was to live in a world without them. They were surprised by how much they had in common: their time in Atlanta, their love of statistics and programming, of biking and running, of classic films and modern mystery novels and, as Jacob especially noted, "the search for the Holy Grail of coffee ice cream." Her flirtatious eyes added to the electricity. They made plans to go bike riding on a Saturday, two weeks from then.

When she left, Jacob tried to make sense of a jumble of thoughts and feelings. Her interest in him was obvious. 'But

Dr. Cornish's daughter?' Could he ever stop thinking of her as an underage teenager? Something about it felt wrong, but there was no denying his attraction.

There was something else, though, something inside him, that held him back, something that had nothing to do with her. He never was very successful with women, he knew. His relationships burned bright, but he quickly lost interest. It was the hunt that drove him more than anything. Carol, his last girlfriend, told him he was a hopeless *puer*, that he would never grow up. 'Even if Sara weren't Cornish's daughter,' he thought, 'I don't feel ready for a love affair. There's a part of me that got left behind. I need to find that first.'

35

"You're fucking crazy!" Cary exclaimed. They are seated in his kitchen, 18 floors above Grace Cathedral. "A non-profit? Like garage sales and Girl Scout cookies?" He shook his head in disbelief. "You didn't just lose your memory, Jake, I think you lost your mind." He reached into the bowl of M&Ms and tossed some into his mouth. "Non-profits are for sissies and kids getting out of college who don't know what they want to do with their lives. Why would you want my help?"

Jacob sipped his espresso and smiled. "Because you need it. It will be good for your soul."

"Please, leave my soul out of it," Cary responded. "I've got enough trouble. The stock market's down 150 points and Deena just bought me a recumbent bike for my birthday."

"Oh, yeah, happy birthday," said Jacob. "I was going to get you a gift certificate to your club in Burlingame, but then I forgot."

"Not funny," said Cary. "Deena thinks I'm not as horny as I used to be since I put on weight. I need to cut down on pussy and pie. I know it. But what's life about, if not enjoying oneself?"

Jacob laughed, stood up and put another color-coded capsule in Cary's chrome and steel espresso machine. "This is a pretty cool machine," he said. "I can't picture you on an exercise bike at home. Let's start playing handball at the gym again. It will do us both good. But seriously, Cary, I need you to help me on this new venture. You've always been my partner in everything I do. I need you."

"You and your Messianic fantasies. I thought they cured you of that at Langley Porter," Cary quipped, taking more M&Ms before pushing the bowl out of reach. "OK, let me humor you. Tell me what's the purpose and why it has to be a non-profit. Don't you realize the market's the greatest force for change the world has ever known, beats charity hands down."

Jacob gave his spiel about the disruptive effects of technology and modernity on the third world, but also their potential for development. "There are new types of non-profits that can operate in the market just like any corporation, only the profits all go back into the company."

"Why a non-profit then? I don't get it," Cary asked, scrunching his face.

"Because sometimes the interests of making money and the interests of people on the ground conflict. In a non-profit your decisions are guided by what's good for society, not your own selfish balance sheet."

"Sounds like bullshit to me," Cary exclaimed. "I like my balance sheet."

"Shit, Cary, you've got all the money you'll ever need. You don't have to work another day in your life. What more do you want?"

Cary sat quietly, moving around colored M&Ms on the table as if reading tea leaves. "So, what do you want from me? I already gave at the office."

"Cary, it's still a business. I need your business skills. You know I don't have any. You don't have to put any of your own money in, just help me. Deena will think you're a saint."

Cary raised his hands in surrender. "OK," he conceded. "I'll play, if it makes me a saint in Deena's eyes. I'll be your apostle. You're a good salesman, Jake."

"I promise we'll have fun," said Jacob. He stood up and kissed Cary on his baldhead.

"Speaking of fun, how'd it go with Goldie Locks?" Cary asked.

Jacob walked over to the sliding glass doors by the balcony and looked down at the people streaming out of Sunday services at the cathedral. "It was fine. We had a great time. She's a good kid."

Cary walked over next to him, frowning. "Fine? Good kid? Huh? Are you kidding me? I met her at the funeral. She's not a kid. She's a fucking deva! So, don't bullshit me. What happened?"

"I love you, Cary," Jacob smiled, putting a hand on his shoulder. "You make me laugh. Well, we met at a café. I helped her with a math problem. That's it."

"Come on Jake, don't make me beg. Did you get it on?"

"Look, she's perfectly gorgeous and smart and quite ambitious, I might add. But I'm just not ready. I'm still trying to find out who I am, where I've been the last two years, what I want to do with my life. She's looking for a real relationship. I can't give that to her just now."

"You're fucking nuts, bro. You take her to bed and you'll quickly discover your poor lost self. She'll make a man of you. What's the risk? What happened to the old Jake?"

"I guess that's the question, Cary. I'm not the old Jake. I don't know where he is. And, even if I could find him, I'm not sure I'd like him."

Cary stepped back and examined his friend. "Just give it some time, dude. You'll get your fastball back."

36

Saturday opened like a gift, the sky a brilliant blue, the city bathed in sunlight. It seemed as if the air itself were humming. Jacob walked his bike down the stairs and saw Sara was parked across the street waiting for him in a red Miata, its top down and her bike already on the rack in back. She had on ride leggings and a matching cycling shirt. Her long blond hair, tied in the back, hung over one shoulder. "You look the part," he said. "I take it you've raced before." He mounted his bike next to hers and dropped into the seat beside her.

"A little," she laughed.

Aroused by her closeness, he thought how long it had been since he was with a woman—at least a few months and maybe a couple of years before that. She straightened, sensing his caution, put the car into first gear and pulled onto 24th Street.

"Where would you like to begin our adventure today?" she asked.

"You're driving. You decide."

She suggested they take Trinity Road off Highway 12 and then Dry Creek towards Yountville.

He glanced at the sky above. "God, I love convertibles."

"What kind of car do you drive?" she asked.

"I don't."

"Do you have a license? Or, is not having a car an ecological statement?"

"More the latter, I suppose. But I find I rarely need a car in the city. I'll call Uber or a cab when I do and I'll rent a car when I have to. It saves me a lot of money and I don't have to waste so much of my life looking for parking places. San Francisco's the worst."

She reached up and took a pair of sunglasses from the flip compartment by the visor and grabbed two baseball caps from the back seat. "Your choice," she said. She headed down Dolores, turned on Market and Franklin and out onto Lombard towards the Golden Gate Bridge. "Music?" she asked, passing her iPhone to him, her hand nonchalantly brushing his knee. He scrolled through her playlists and picked one she'd named "70's driving." Rod Stewart's voice filled the air as they left the city behind and headed north towards wine country.

After parking, they saddled up. Something fell out of Jacob's pocket, clattering as it hit the side of his bike. "What's that?" she asked.

He picked up the ancient iron key, noting again the heft of it, before placing it back in his pocket. "Something from the missing years, a mystery," he said. "It's the only link I have to those two years, a clue that maybe someday will help me unlock the past." He looked up at her. "It's become a good luck charm for me now, I guess. I'd hate to lose it."

They rode languidly on the rolling green hills, side-by-side most of the time. "You don't talk much about your amnesia," she remarked. "Is it uncomfortable to talk about?"

"Not really," he said. "It's frustrating. But I've begun to think it has a much bigger effect on me than I like to admit. I'm not the same person I was."

"How so?"

He pedaled for a minute trying to think what an honest answer would be. "I used to know, or at least thought I knew, what I wanted. And I'd get it. Everything came easily to me. Now I'm not so sure."

"Not so sure what you want or that you can get it?"

"What I want, I guess."

She rode alongside of him, matching his pace.

"I burned out, as your father probably told you," he continued. "They had me locked up in a hospital for a month, taking downers and anti-psychotic meds. It wasn't pretty. When I came out, I decided to take a break from life. I sold the company and went in search of a radically different path."

"Did it change you?" she asked.

"I don't know yet. Maybe." He pedaled harder up a hill. "I'm more cautious now. I never fully let myself go. There's always some doubt in the back of my mind about who I am. I expect that may all go away as my memory comes back."

She remained silent for a few minutes as they climbed the steep hill and then, catching her breath, said. "Maybe. Maybe not. It might not matter at all, if your memory were suddenly restored. You'd probably recall some great tourist sites, good meals, some fascinating short-term friendships, maybe even some love affairs."

Another steep climb made it impossible to pedal and talk at the same time. When they reached the top, she continued, breathing hard. "But it's probably not a good idea to dwell on it too much. When you were my father's student you were light and carefree. I remember your telling me, 'One shouldn't take oneself too seriously.' I try never to forget that. I loved that about you. Now, you seem more serious, more with-drawn. You'd probably feel a lot better if you could just put this amnesia business behind you and move on with your life. If memories comes back, great. If not, so what?"

Panting hard, she slowed considerably, catching her breath again. "What you need is a good dose of fun, permission to play, and I'm determined to give it to you."

And saying that, she accelerated ahead of him. He closed the gap, but she kept up a torrid pace, only stopping when they passed one of the luxurious homes that sat perched on hills surrounded by weeping willows and fruit orchards, each with picture perfect barns next to them. They were mostly quiet, breathing hard the whole way. When they finally got to Yountville, he suggested they make the short jog to St. Helena and have lunch on the outdoor patio of the Culinary Institute of America.

The restaurant was on one side of the former Christian Brothers Castle, a huge grey stone monument, sitting like an old dowager towering over the vineyards. She had no idea there were castles like this in America, she told him. They drained their water bottles while they stopped to admire it. A steep driveway wound its way to the entrance off the patio. "I'll race you!" she cried suddenly and took off. He tried to catch her but lagged far behind. When he got to the top she was beaming triumphantly, helmet in hand, her hair loose around her shoulders.

They sat outside on the stone patio as student waiters, one hand trained behind them, described the day's menu. They debated whether to take the wine pairings and decided to share one. The meal was served slowly in separate courses. They talked about foods they liked and about films and books they'd read. When he turned to discuss the news, she tilted her head sideways like a dog that's been asked something it didn't understand. "I don't watch the news," she admitted. "It just gets me down. What's the point?"

He smiled. The waiter came with a basket of fresh warm rolls. "Have you travelled much?" Jacob asked.

"Some. I've been to the usual spots in Europe—Rome, Paris, London, and oh, yes, to Venice. I almost forgot, my favorite, actually." She reached over and buttered one of the rolls. "Dad took me to Budapest and Prague, but it was so packed with tourists, I felt like I was in a theme park. I've been dying to go to Barcelona. Isn't that where you're from?"

"Yes. I was born there and my father as well. My mother met him when she was in her junior year abroad as a student in Granada. He was teaching math at the university."

"I guess they didn't have rules against professors fraternizing with students then," she joked.

"I guess not. But they didn't get together again for three years. He came to San Francisco for the Summer of Love in '67 and somehow managed to find her in a commune in Haight-Ashbury with a group of anarchists. The Diggers they called themselves. I should show you some of the pictures of them then. My dad had an old VW hippy bus. Just like the movies. After they married, they moved back to Barcelona."

Their appetizers arrived, a pate glazed in duck fat. "Heart attack food," she commented, but happily served herself. "What happened to him? I learned all about your mom at the funeral, but nothing about your dad."

"I don't have many memories of him. Most of my impressions are from stories I've heard and photographs and old Super 8 films. We lived together in Barcelona till I was 9. Then I moved with my mom to San Francisco and I never saw him again. He died in a car accident, I was told years later, as if it were a trivial fact of family history. I wish I had known him better. I'm told I resemble him in many ways, most certainly in my love for math. My mother can't, couldn't, balance a checkbook." He tried to picture his dad in real life, but was unable to.

"What about you?" he asked. "I know about your family, but tell me about yourself. Any great loves?"

She spread a slice of pate onto a delicate cracker made of kale. "I've had my share of boyfriends, I suppose, even a girlfriend once," she said, stealing a glance at him, knowing how this excited men. "But nothing too serious, no engagement rings. I mentioned I had gone to London. That was actually with one of dad's students, Brad Rittinger. We lived together for a while when I first came out to California, but ultimately my not wanting to have kids made him lose interest. My lovers always wanted to reify things, capture their girl and put the marriage in stone for eternity. I'm more of a go-with-the-flow kind of person. All I care about is how things are right now."

"It's a great way to look at the world," he remarked, "but it takes a lot of self-confidence. Freedom can be quite an aphrodisiac, but you've got to be willing to take risks."

"Yea, but when you're young and female, freedom and risk taking can get you in trouble." She looked down at her plate, not sure whether to share a story. "In the summer after my sophomore year, I fell for a motorcycle dude. He was young and handsome. Didn't wear a helmet. He had stopped to ask me directions and then asked if I wanted to go for a ride. Of course I said, 'no.' But he kept making circles around me laughing, insisting that I go with him. I don't know what came over me. I had never met anyone like him before. I finally agreed and climbed behind him. We had a passionate romance, but he got me into drugs, cocaine mainly. I got pregnant and had an abortion. By the time it was over I had to check into rehab. My father still doesn't know about this, by the way." She looked intently at him. He nodded.

"When I got out, I was pretty chastened. I had lost all my friends and just wasn't sure if I were the person I had thought myself to be. I completely stopped seeing anyone and just plunged into my work." She paused. "I guess I've never stopped."

He nodded again. "I can totally relate. Seems like there's a lot we share."

He watched her lean back in her chair, still serious.

"Except for that time with Joey—that was his name—I'm really not much of a risk taker," she said. "Everyone thinks I'm super self-confident, but I'm not. Underneath of it all, I'm always trying to impress people so they don't discover who I really am."

"Is that why you're so competitive?" he asked.

"Exactly. With guys I feel I can usually get my way, but with everyone else I feel like I'm posing. She let out a long breath.

He waited a moment and then asked, "So what, besides work, do you care about? What's your passion?"

"That's the problem," she said. "I want everything, but have a passion for nothing."

He admired her honesty, but this admission made her seem less exotic and desirable, something more pedestrian. And yet, he felt himself drawn closer to her, to someone who was more real, to someone who could be hurt.

There was an awkward moment of silence between them.

"You're young still," he offered. "Maybe you've yet to discover the meaning of your life."

She tried to smile. "Perhaps. For now all I can think about is getting a job. Don't get me wrong. I have a passion for programming. There's something about numbers I can't resist.

But I don't aspire to anything more creative. I just want to be a big success and make enough money to do whatever I want."

She paused a moment, took the last bite of her appetizer and continued. "Frankly, I was hoping you'd tell me you were starting up your company again, taking on those future projects you and Dad talked about. I think you'd be fabulously successful. I would have loved to work with you."

He smiled. "Well, I may do that, but not as you imagine. I've been thinking of creating a non-profit organization that would look at how all this new technology will affect the developing world and then design applications that can really work there. Some of this disruptive technology will be good, but lots of it won't be."

She held her head in her hands and examined him. His idealism attracted her, but divided them as well.

"You're leaving a lot of money on the table," she argued.

"I don't care about that," he said. "I've been there. Done that. It's creativity I crave."

She pushed back the hair that had fallen across her face. "I guess for those of us who haven't already made a fortune, it's still a dream to build something big, sell it for billions and then buy one of those wineries we passed."

They continued through their meal like this, filling in the holes in their biographies, learning their idiosyncrasies, sharing anecdotes. The waiter interrupted them to ask if they'd like to try the hot chocolate lava cake. They walked over to watch the student chefs, regal in their starched white hats, prepare the batter in the dessert kitchen. "These cakes always remind me of my mother," he told her, "the sweet hot lava on the inside just waiting to ooze out."

She reached over and gave him a chaste kiss on his cheek. They walked silently back to the table. "I miss Mom more than I ever thought I would," he said. "Not being here to say good-bye left a big hole." He turned to her. "And how has it been for you? We both are motherless children now."

She took a deep breath. "I don't know that I'll ever fully get over it," she conceded. "I was definitely 'Daddy's girl,' but whenever I needed help, whenever I needed to cry, I would rush to see Mom. Dad was my inspiration, but Harriet was my rock. I feel kinda lost and unmoored without her. There's a moment in each day when I start to reach for the phone to call her before I realize she's not there. It hurts." He put his arm around her.

The bike ride back was hard, their shirts soaked with sweat. They high-fived each other, placed their bikes in the rack and lowered themselves into the car. She handed him a bunch of red grapes she'd kept in a small cooler in the back, lowered the top of the convertible and played Keith Jarrett's "Koln Concert." They took back roads, enjoying the scenery, listening quietly to the music, circling through Napa Valley, before heading back across the Golden Gate Bridge under violet skies. Below them, the San Francisco Bay was filled with sailboats tilting like ballet dancers in syncopated pirouettes. "Someday I'm going to own a sailboat with a large bed and lots of brass and lacquered mahogany walls," she mused.

"I'm afraid I'd get seasick trying to sleep on one of those," he said.

It wasn't the response she wanted; but she was like a cat with a mouse, convinced that she would eventually break down his defenses.

37

Over the next two months he noticed his confidence returning, along with the passage to Spring. He was sitting on a bench across from the old carousel in Golden Gate Park, warmed by the sun, watching an African-American father lift his boy of about three onto a mighty dragon next to a little Asian girl atop a tall giraffe. In the background he heard the percussive rhythms of the Sunday morning drum circle as the merry-go-round started moving and the sounds of the Wurlitzer organ began. The mix of ethnicities and the infectious laughter of little children produced a feeling of general euphoria. Cary walked up holding two large steaming coffees. "Dude, what a gorgeous day. How are you?"

"Terrific." said Jacob. "Couldn't be better. How are you?"

"Same old, happy, horny and hungry."

"How's Deena?"

"She's good. Nothing ever changes for her. Very disciplined. Same routine every day."

Jacob pulled the lid off his coffee and sipped it. "Thanks for this," he said. "I love the scene here. I wish the whole world could be like this."

"You're an incurable romantic, Jake. Unfortunately, the world happens to be exactly like this. Everyone grows up and picks their fantasy horse to ride, hoping to beat everyone else. They go up and down through life thinking they're actually getting somewhere, and then they end up in the same place they started."

Cary took a sip and went on. "And these deluded parents, intoxicated on so much innocence, don't yet realize that all their cute little kids will soon grow into horrible, drug-abusing, acne-faced teenagers who will drive them to the point of hopeless despair."

"You're such an optimist," Jacob said.

"You should talk," said Cary. "Still carrying that key to your dark past?"

The key, in fact, never left him. "Honestly, I don't dwell on that anymore," Jacob remarked. "I decided to stop seeing any more doctors and therapists. If my memory comes back, it comes back. If not..." he shrugged. "I can't keep worrying about it. It's time I focused on the future, not the past."

But Jacob had to admit to himself that his optimism was not unbridled. He was conscious of a certain tentativeness in everything he did. He was no longer the recidivist risk taker he used to be. 'Even Cary, might not have noticed this,' he thought. 'He probably believes I'm simply maturing, shedding my inner rebel.'

"Glad to hear that," said Cary. "You've got it all, Jake. But if you're so smart, why aren't you getting any pussy?"

He didn't have a good answer, he realized. 'Cary's right,' he thought. 'Those lost years are holding me back.' He had to work at separating this black hole from his everyday life, like a well-trained athlete keeping his head in the game.

"Is that all you ever think about?" Jacob asked.

"Not all the time," Cary said. "Sometimes I worry about money." He paused, examining his friend. "What's up with you?"

Jacob prepared to give some glib, smartass answer, but then checked himself.

"This is going to sound really weird, Cary; but something strange's been happening to me the last couple days." He paused to take another sip of coffee. "I'm not sure how to explain it. But it's interesting. Sometimes I get an emotional reaction to a stranger I happen to be standing near. It's like I take on another person's feelings, kind of like a 'sympathetic reaction' you might have with someone you loved. It first happened to me in a supermarket." Cary eyed him warily.

"I suddenly felt an overwhelming sense of sadness and empathy for an old woman standing in line behind me... before I even saw her. I thought I was going to burst into tears. It took a surprising amount of effort not to. When I spoke with her I discovered she had just lost a daughter the day before."

'Cary's going to think I'm losing it again,' he thought. 'Maybe I shouldn't be telling him about this.' But he went on.

"Then, a week or so later, I had a similar experience with a vendor I met at work, who confided he had just received a diagnosis of pancreatic cancer." He stopped for a minute to let all this sink in. "I thought there was something morbid about this—I had perhaps a half dozen of these experiences in the last month—until I met a woman at the gym and, without thinking, congratulated her on being pregnant. She was astonished, hadn't told anyone yet, not even her husband."

Cary shook his head with a look of pure incomprehension. "It's usually not a good idea to tell a woman she looks pregnant," said Cary.

"I don't have a clue how these revelations come to me. I don't seem to have any control over them."

There was a silence between them. Then Cary spoke. "Sometimes I think you're like *The Man Who Fell To Earth*, Jake."

A sudden sense that he had heard these words before seized him, an intense déjà vu experience. He didn't say anything, waiting with a feeling of some anxiety for what might follow. But nothing did.

Cary said, "Honestly, I wouldn't worry about this. You're just a super sensitive dude. You should just put your worries aside and enjoy this fabulous life you've fashioned for yourself. How's the non-profit going, by the way?"

The change of subject was a relief. "Things are starting to take off," Jacob exclaimed. "The *Economist* ran a piece about us and ever since then we've been getting requests from all over the place. It's refreshing to work with young math geniuses who are more interested in the mission than in making the big bucks they could get in the private sector."

They finished their coffees in silence, then stood and walked through the park. Cary tried to interest Jacob in going to a horse show in Palo Alto, but he begged off. He did agree to join him on Saturday to hear Deena perform with the symphony and have dinner at their place afterwards.

"Why don't you ask Sara to join us? What's happening with you two, anyway?" Cary asked.

"I doubt she'd take time off from work," Jacob said. "I rarely see her. When we do meet, it's usually to go running together at dawn. She's totally into her job. I've never seen anyone more determined or competitive. She says her coworkers are put off by her, but she's in too much of a hurry to worry about that. 'I didn't go there to socialize,' she says. She obviously likes the challenges, loves tackling intractable problems."

"Well, you're a challenging intractable problem," Cary said. "You two should get along fine."

"We do. We laugh a lot and she helps me keep in shape. Three weeks ago she moved into her new apartment on Bernal Heights. It was hilarious. She didn't have a clue how to proceed. So, I picked out all her furniture and kitchen stuff for her. But it's all still in boxes on her beautiful hardwood floors. She's worse than I ever was," Jacob said, smiling.

Cary shook his head. "I don't get it. Are you two like fitness buddies or..." he stopped and rubbed his index fingers together in a sexual innuendo, "or what?"

Jacob smiled. "We totally enjoy hanging out together. I don't know where this might lead. Neither of us seems to be in any hurry. We're not searching for anyone else. For sure, the sexual energy is always present; but for now at least we're just happy being together. Maybe that will change someday. The risk of being rejected or changing our friendship probably prevents either of us from making a move."

Cary gave Jacob a ride home with the top down. "That was fun," he said, as Jacob jumped out.

"Yea, thanks. I'll see you and Deena on Saturday."

38

A few days later as Jacob was about to leave his office, Sara called. Usually they planned their outings in advance, but today she asked if he'd like to go for a sunset run and have dinner afterwards. "I'd love that," he told her. "Come get me."

She arrived fifteen minutes later. He was dressed in a pair of black running shorts he kept at the office and she in cut-offs and a company T Shirt with the big Apple logo. They took off through the Presidio towards Fort Mason and then west along Lincoln Boulevard, Sara setting a fierce pace. "Time to burn off a week's worth of stress," she said. When they passed 32nd Avenue, she threw down the gauntlet. "Let's race to the Legion of Honor." She sprinted ahead of him, but he kept up a few paces behind. As they approached the finish line he poured it on with everything he had. They ran alongside each other until the final twenty yards when he pulled ahead at last. Gasping for breath, they hi-fived each other and she playfully slapped him on his butt. "You cheated," she said.

"How?"

"You're wearing new shoes," she said.

"These aren't new. They're my old shoes." He knew how much she hated to lose, but he had been determined to beat her this time. "I'm sorry. I probably should have let you win," he paused, "like I usually do."

She cocked her head, unsure for a moment, if he were kidding or not. "OK, smartass, let's see who's first going back."

He threw up his hands. "No way. You win. I've got nothing left. Let's just jog."

The sun dipped below the Golden Gate bridge lighting up the sky with reds and oranges. They shifted to a walk when they crossed back into the Presidio and held hands. Neither of them said anything. 'Finally!' Sara thought. She'd been the pursuer, persistent but patient. Partly she'd been too busy to move any faster, but she also realized how gun shy he'd become. It'd been different with every other guy she'd been with. Jacob's reticence just made her want him more.

When they got back, Jacob put the bike he rode to the office on the rack of her car and got in the passenger seat. "How about Thai food?"

"Great," Sara said, and then suddenly exclaimed, "Shit! I forgot they turned off the water in my flat today, some major plumbing problem. I smell like crap. I've gotta get a shower first."

"You can take one at my apartment, if you'd like," Jacob offered, "then we can walk over. There's a new place I've wanted to try just two blocks away." She placed her hand on his. He did not remove it, but turned it palm up to hold hers. He watched himself with some trepidation. 'Am I ready for this?' he wondered, but the connection felt so right. She pulled her hand out to shift gears and placed it back on his again. They were silent.

Jacob's apartment was neat and clean, unlike the chaos of boxes and piles of clothes on the floor at her place. It was the first time she'd been there. He showed her around and handed her a glass of Pelligrini with a slice of lemon. They stood in the kitchen and snacked on pistachios, then he showed her the bathroom and the large steam shower and handed her a fluffy white towel and a rich red bathrobe. "I'll look for some clean sweats you can put on," he said.

Above the sound of the steam hissing, he could hear her singing softly.

After a while she shut the shower off and peaked her head out of the bathroom. "Do you have a hairbrush I can borrow?"

He returned a moment later with a wood-backed brush. She was standing, hair still wet and wild, holding her bathrobe closed with one hand, the other outstretched to him. He handed her the brush. She didn't break his gaze. Slowly she put the arm holding the brush on his shoulder and, rising on her tip toes, stepped forward. She placed her mouth against his. He kissed her without hesitation, pulling her closer.

Then he pulled back, held her off with stiff arms. "Are you sure you want this, Sara?" He was shaking inside, heart beating fast. He didn't know what to think. He opened his mouth to speak, but nothing came out. She moved close to him, let the bathrobe slip from her shoulders and, lips inches from his, whispered, "Checkmate."

39

"Wake up Jacob, wake up!" Sara shook him by his shoulders. "You're dreaming. Wake up." His eyes fluttered, trying to open. His hair was matted with sweat. He was breathing hard, chest rising and falling, heart pounding. "Jacob, it's Sara. You're in your bed at home, safe. You've been dreaming. Everything's OK. Wake up."

He sat up quickly, opened his eyes, staring ahead of him blankly. His breathing was still hard. He tried to say something, waited, letting his heart slow. He turned his head and looked at her, his expression full of terror and wonder. His face was ashen. "I, I," he couldn't get the words out, he realized, because it was just too big to describe. He saw the fright in Sara's face and managed, "I'm sorry." He was still breathing too fast to speak easily. "Had a dream. About to go off. Had to stop it before…"

She took him in her arms, cradled him like a child, rocking slowly back and forth. "It's OK. It's only a dream. You're fine."

He let out a loud breath, rubbed his hands through his hair and turned to face her again. "Oh, Sara. I'm really sorry. I've never experienced anything like this before."

"It's OK," she said. "Just a nightmare."

His eyes widened. "No, no, it was more than that. I can't explain. It was frightening, but it was also, how can I explain; it was also the most wonderful, most beautiful feeling I ever had." Part of him wanted to go back there, wanted desperately to hold onto it. "I was," he paused for a moment, hesitant to tell her, afraid his telling would turn the experience from something real to just a story. "I was like some kind of Messiah. I could understand everything, feel everything. Everyone's thoughts, all their feelings were my own. I was their body, their heart. I had come to redeem them."

He knew how crazy this sounded, how preposterous; but it needed to be said out loud, once, at least. The dream needed to be weighed in the light of day. "I walked among them and could read each of their minds, know what they were thinking. I was in the city where I got hit by the truck. I was dressed in white. The world was coming to an end, the end of days; but I was there to stop it."

He paused again. His breath was steadier. His eyes remained wide with wonder. He connected with her now. "I knew, somehow, that if I could just open my heart wide enough, encompass all this pain and suffering, I could stop the Armageddon that was coming. But there were these men, dark and evil men that wanted to obliterate everything. I ran to stop them and I heard my voice screaming, louder than thunder.

The whole of heaven shook and I knew there were only seconds before I would be too late, and then, and then," his eyes blinked, "and then I woke up. I don't know what happened, how it ended."

She was frightened to see him this way, confused, not knowing what to say. "Have you had dreams like this before?" she asked.

"Never," he said and reached over to hold her. He whispered, "It felt like I saw God or the end of time. It was terrifying, but it was also an epiphany. I had a very real experience of total love. It was the most glorious experience I could ever have. I feel so lucky to have had it." He looked at her carefully, saw her confusion. "I'm only sorry to have scared you like that. Please don't be alarmed. It's not something I do each night. I promise. I think our love making may have provoked something deep within me."

She shook her head, totally unable to know what to say or even to think. There was something about Jacob Alejo she could not comprehend. She might win his affection, but would she ever be able to have all of him, she wondered?

40

"How's Goldilocks?" Cary asked, as they traded volleys in the handball court. It had been six months since Jacob and Sara had begun seeing each other. "Has she eaten all your porridge?"

Jacob smashed his return shot with a vengeance. "I thought you approved."

"Oh, I do. I'd give my right testicle to be you for a night," Cary answered, lobbing a shot that landed deftly just outside Jacob's reach.

Jacob wiped the sweat from his eyes with the sleeve of his T-shirt. Both men were drenched. "It's going really well, in fact. She makes me laugh and she makes me come. The sex is phenomenal. Neither one of us likes to cook; but we both love eating out. Of course, I'm ten years older than her, so we have some differences in terms of what we want out of life. She's still feels the need to prove herself.

"I worried that she wasn't going to be user friendly," quipped Cary, "but it seems she is." The sounds of their voices and the squeaking of their shoes reverberated off the walls, as if they were inside a drum. They lunged forward and back, darted sideways, and cursed when they missed a point. "Cary, you asshole," he yelled at himself after missing an easy score. He bent over, hands on knees, panting.

"And what about you, Care? How are you doing?" Jacob asked.

"Pretty well, I guess. You know what a hypochondriac I am. I was convinced I was dying from prostate cancer because my PSA jumped half a point in just a few months," Cary answered. "I get it checked every quarter given my Dad's history. My doctor thinks I'm nuts, but I like the reassurance it gives me, except when it doesn't. I got it checked again and it had gone back down. I'm drinking a quart of pomegranate juice every day now just to be sure, though. Apparently, the PSA test results can be off if you've ridden a bicycle or fucked in the past 24 hours and I had done both."

"With Deena?" Jacob asked.

Cary laughed. "No, with one of those Asian girls at my Happy Endings spa."

"I didn't know they rode bikes," said Jacob.

"Very funny. I think Deena suspects I'm getting some on the side because I've stopped begging her; but she never lets on, if she does. We're getting along fine. And, what about you, Jake? Are you and Sara going to succumb to marital bliss and make babies?"

"Babies are out of the question," he responded quickly, driving his shot with a forward swing down the sidewall. "We're not masochists. Neither one of us want them. The planet certainly doesn't need them. I think they're God's punishment for our vanity. Sara definitely wants to get married, though, wants a big wedding. She's obsessed with *Sex and the City*. She's always pointing out houses she'd like to buy and I suspect she's already picked out her dress, but I'm not going there."

It was match point and Cary smashed the ball down the right wall. Jacob returned it with a soft lob to the left, catching Cary going the wrong way. Advantage Alejo. "Fuck you, Cary!" Cary yelled at himself again, shaking his fists in the air.

Turning suddenly to face Jacob, panting hard, he said, "You know, you're a pussy, Jake. You're afraid to make a commitment. You think freedom is all about not being beholden to anyone or anything, but you're missing out on the real fun. You're just skating on the surface. If you want to know true love, you're going to have to take some chances, put down some roots, invest yourself."

"Like you?" said Jacob. They volleyed ferociously, pushing themselves to their limits, Jacob's winning shot catching Cary in a corner with no room to maneuver. They both collapsed on their backs wiped out.

When his heart rate finally slowed a bit, Jacob sat up, arms hugging his knees, and said, "I'd love to be able to commit to her, throw all my marbles in her basket; but if I'm really honest with myself, I have to admit something's holding me back. There's still this hole in my past."

Cary struggled to sit up. "That's bullshit. You had trouble committing before you ever even left here. You want to blame everything on your amnesia. But someday you're going to have to stop being so cautious with women and just take the plunge and don't look back."

"But that's the problem. I can't look back," Jacob responded. "There's just too much I don't know. It wouldn't be fair to Sara. I've left some part of me back there. I'd like to give her all of me, but I honestly can't. No matter how close we get, something's missing."

"You're an asshole, Jake," Cary said, shaking his head as he stood. "You've got a sensational woman who's madly in love with you. Yea, she might be a little on the control freak side, a little too ambitious, but no one's perfect. You're never going to find anyone smarter, or more beautiful or more adoring of you. God knows what she sees in you. You'd be a jerk not to grab her." He reached down, grabbed Jacob's hand and helped him to his feet. "Throw away that fucking key you carry and get a life."

41

"Boomer!" exclaimed Jacob, throwing his arms around his old friend as he stepped into Jacob's office.

"Bean," replied Boomer. "It's great to see you."

A former All-State linebacker and a defenseman on Jacob's Georgia Tech lacrosse team, Boomer's real name was Henry Brickman. Balding and forty pounds heavier, his profile was more square now, someone it would be hard to knock over. He was dressed in beige chinos and a blue blazer that he had somehow managed to button in the middle.

"You look terrific, Bean, skinny as always," said Boomer, surveying his old friend.

"What are you up to, Boomer?" said Jacob, patting him on his stomach. "They must be paying you well."

"Managing some construction projects in Atlanta. They don't pay me nearly enough," he said. "But I love the work."

"You and Cheryl still a team?" asked Jacob.

"Twelve years. Just celebrated with a cruise to Aruba. Got two kids, twin boys. What about you, Bean? I'm surprised you aren't hooked up yet, or are you?"

"Not yet. I've been dating Larry Cornish's daughter, Sara," said Jacob.

Boomer smiled. They walked through the office into the back room and sank next to each other on the purple couch.

"Sorry I've been so out of touch the last few years," said Jacob. "Catch me up. What's been happening with Jerry and Eddie and Kroger and the others?"

"Yea, I heard from Cary about the accident and your amnesia," Boomer started. "Too bad. Sounded like another of your lame excuses to get out of trouble though, if you ask me. Cheryl would never believe it, if I tried to pull that on her." He punched Jacob playfully on his arm.

"Jerry and Eddie I see all the time. Our wives are close too. Eddie married a big deal Atlanta city councilwoman. He's doing very well with his architecture business. Stay at home dad, works from there. Kroger is still Kroger, hasn't changed a bit, stoned all the time. He was married for a while; but the story is he came home one afternoon and found his wife fucking his next-door neighbor. As he tells it, he handed the guy the keys to his house and car and said, 'You can have my wife, my house and my car, but give me your motorcycle.' They traded keys and he took off for California. Showed up here two years later with another girl, but that didn't last either. I'm not sure what he's doing now. Haven't seen him for a few months."

"And you probably heard about Franklin getting killed in some freak accident in Iraq—electrocuted himself in the shower is what I heard. Fucker was the best goalie I ever saw.

Should have been All-American. Probably was jerking off when it happened." He shook his head. "What a waste."

They sat silently for a minute reminiscing. Boomer started to ask, "What ever happened to," but before he could finish Jacob interrupted.

"Carly Reynolds?" he asked.

"How'd you know I was thinking about her?" Boomer asked.

"I don't know," answered Jacob. "I just did." He thought about that for a second. "I lost touch with her after graduation."

"What was that story you used to tell about losing your virginity with her in my fraternity house?" Boomer asked.

"No, I didn't lose my virginity. I almost did. It was a total disaster. I came prepared. Bought the most expensive rubbers I could get, 4X condoms, lambskins. They came in these little blue plastic capsules. After I pulled her pants down, I tried to get the package open, only I couldn't figure out how to do it. I was frantic. Finally, I just broke it open with my teeth. But it cut my mouth and I was bleeding all over the place. By the time I turned back to her with my bloody mouth she had put her pants back on. Needless to say, it didn't happen that night."

Boomer laughed so hard his jacket button finally popped off, causing them to laugh even harder. Tears were rolling down Jacob's cheeks. "I haven't had this kind of fun in years," he said. "We've got to do this more often. Bring Cheryl and the kids with you next time and plan to stay longer."

"I will. Cheryl will want to pick your brains about travel. She's already planning a big trip when the twins turn thirteen in a year. Sounds like you've been all over. What's your favorite, Bean?"

"Hard to say. I've loved everyplace I've ever been," Jacob reflected for a moment. "Take the boys to see Ankor Wat in Cambodia. They'd love it. It's like Indiana Jones on steroids. Wait a moment. I've got a whole list of suggestions for Cambodia we put together for one of our staff who went out there to check on a project we were starting."

He turned back to his desk and pressed a button on his phone. "I've just hired a new assistant to keep track of everything going on here," Jacob told him. "She'll be able to find it."

"Yes?" an accented woman's voice answered.

"Hi. There's a file somewhere with information about travelling in Vietnam and Cambodia," he said. "It should be in a folder called 'Digital Trek, I think. Could you please make a copy, if you can find it, and bring it in?"

A moment later a striking young woman with olive skin and thick dark hair tied up in a bun entered. She walked erect on high heels, her long eyelashes and green eyes gave her an exotic look. She handed Jacob the folder.

"Leila, this is Henry. He's an old friend from college." They shook hands. "We played lacrosse together. Leila's from the city where I had my accident and lost my memory," he told Boomer. "She just started here a couple of weeks ago, but she's already become indispensable."

Leila smiled, exposing dimples on both cheeks. Henry asked her how she came to Alejo Designs. She told him that she had read the article about Jacob in the *Economist* and wrote to ask for a job. "I was desperate to leave my country and all its conflict," she told him. "Jacob's vision was inspiring, exactly the sort of thing that countries like mine need."

"I always wonder how people do that," asked Boomer. "I mean, how'd you go about getting a visa? Seems like it would be really difficult."

"It is. But I had a special hardship that allowed me to apply for political asylum. My husband was a hero who stopped a suicide bomber from setting off a bomb in a crowded market. He was chased by the terrorists and disappeared. I started getting death threats every day. And I was pregnant at the time, but I lost my baby. He was born prematurely and died a week later."

"I'm really sorry," said Boomer. "Did they ever find your husband?" he asked.

"Not yet," she said.

"She's impressive," Boomer remarked.

Watching her walk down the hallway, Jacob felt pride in his new employee. 'She's graceful, a real beauty, such penetrating eyes and the poise of someone who's experienced life,' he thought.

He looked back to Boomer. "It was uncanny," he told him. "When I saw the return address on her letter with the city that holds such mystery for me, I didn't know what to expect; but I had a premonition it was something important.

The story she just described about her husband and her child deeply affected me. Apparently, she was a pretty well known photojournalist. Worked for several Western news organizations. It wasn't a letter I could ignore. But what really got me was how precisely she seemed to know me. She wanted exactly the same things I do—more about changing the world than making a profit. It was a blink decision to hire her. I never doubted it for a moment."

42

Leila ran out the back door, closed it behind her, tears running down her cheeks. She imagined talking to Muna. 'I'm not sure I can do this, Muna. I want so desperately to throw my arms around him, to scream his name, to shake him. I look in his eyes and he doesn't know who I am. How could he not recognize me?' She collapsed on a bench by a trail along a row of eucalyptus trees quietly crying.

She had not called Muna since she arrived, had not even written to her except for an email to say she was all right. She had prepared herself as best she could. Dr. Solomon had warned her not to expect anything, but she still harbored the hope, however slim, that seeing her would provoke repressed memories. When they met for the first time in Jacob's office, it was the hardest thing she had ever done, to keep her composure, to not blurt out the truth. He was kind, just like the old Jonathan, but there wasn't the slightest spark of recognition.

She knew, however, that if she told him, he might act out of a sense of obligation, but not of love. That would be like him. No, she would need to win his love again; and if she could not have that, she would at least be close to him. But on her third day in the office, when she saw him with Sara, it had torn her insides to shreds.

With each day she began to think she had made a mistake. The pain was too much to bear. She could not grieve for him while he was so alive in front of her, but she could not have him either. If she stayed, she would be torturing herself every day. Her despair came in waves, 'Oh Jonathan, Jonathan!'

43

"They're beautiful," said Deena, taking the flowers from Sara while Jacob handed a bottle of wine to Cary. "Please come in."

They entered. The apartment, with its floor to ceiling windows, seemed to float above the city. Sara followed Deena into the kitchen. "I love your hair," Sara said. "I've been thinking of cutting mine. Long hair takes so much work. I don't want to waste my time taking care of it anymore."

"Oh, please don't," Deena pleaded. "Your hair is gorgeous. I'd give anything to have hair like yours. I just cut mine a week ago. But mine was so mousy."

Sara smiled. She liked this woman, appreciated how uncluttered her apartment was, how well she'd dressed in a simple skirt and blouse and how expertly she'd done her makeup. She looked around the kitchen admiringly, making a note to herself that she should get a set of copper pans and a pot rack like hers.

"What can I get you?" asked Deena. "The boys'll be opening the wine out there. But I was going to make myself a gin and tonic."

"That sounds divine," said Sara. "Jacob tells me you play violin for the symphony. I can't imagine anything more exciting. Do you love it?"

"I do, very much. There are aspects that can be very frustrating—the politics for example—and you have to practice for hours each day. But it's worth it when the conductor tips his baton and you start playing. When it's over, I feel like time has disappeared. It's like nothing else I've ever experienced." She pours gin into a tall thin glass with ice, adds tonic and hands it to Sara. "Tell me about yourself," Deena asked. "Cary says you landed a great job at Apple."

"I was lucky," Sara answered. "They were looking to hire more female programmers and my father's something of a legend, so they made me an offer I couldn't refuse."

"How do you like it?"

"It's kind of what you just described about music. I start writing code and all of a sudden the day's gone. Time doesn't exist. I love it. It's something I'm good at, that comes naturally; but I haven't learned how to control it yet. It's like a runaway horse. I can't seem to get off of it to do anything else with my life."

Deena nodded sympathetically. 'Sara's so young and beautiful, very poised, too. I can see why Jacob fell for her' she thought. 'What man wouldn't? She's obviously smart, at least with numbers, but is that all there is? I love her shoes.' "Let's join the men," she said, taking Sara's arm and leading her into the living room.

Jacob and Cary were spread out on the ends of a large white L-shaped couch with their feet up on a square leather ottoman, their shoes off. They each had a glass of red wine. Cary held his up to the women as they entered and said, "Please join us. We were just discussing fashion and nail polish and the sale they're having on accessories at Gumps."

"Yeah, right!" said Deena. "More likely the stock market or the new model Tesla."

"You're a mind-reader," said Cary.

"Just married to you for thirteen years," said Deena.

"That's something to celebrate, I would think," added Sara. "You must know each other inside out."

"Literally," quipped Cary.

"You two seem so happy together," said Sara. "With some couples, when you meet them, you can feel the tension. What's your secret?"

Deena and Cary looked at each other and Deena said, "I let Cary be Cary. He lets me be me. I get to play music and study cooking and he gets to remain a boy with his cars and…" she hesitates and stops, raising her eyebrows as she looked at him.

Cary placed his wine down on the ottoman, "It's a fair trade, but the cooking is starting to take its toll," he said patting his stomach.

Deena stood. "That reminds me, I'd better get the roast out of the oven."

Deena came in with the dinner and they moved to the dining room with its view of Coit Tower and the Pyramid.

They chatted about their lives—Sara about the intense secrecy at Apple, Jacob about his latest project and the woman he hired from the city where he lost his memory, Deena about the new conductor for the symphony and Cary about his latest investments in emerging markets.

The food was pure haute cuisine decorated with a bouquet of edible flowers. Sara couldn't help comparing herself to Deena. 'Will I ever have the time to learn to cook like this?' she asked herself. 'Deena seems to do everything without effort. I'm just a klutz around a kitchen.' "This is amazing, Deena," she said. "I've never eaten a better meal. You are an artist. I can't imagine doing what you do."

"Well, I certainly can't imagine writing code," responded Deena. "Young programmers like you amaze me. You're so fluent in a world I don't even know. For me it's like a foreign country where I don't speak the language."

"Yes, and to think it is mostly written by young white males with Asperger's syndrome," interjected Cary. "Kinda frightening."

"I'm worried about what it's doing to American culture," says Deena. "It's pushing us further and further apart from each other. We've created electronic ghettos that confine us to our 'friends' and 'followers.' We only read books recommended by people who liked the book we just read. I wish there were a Facebook for people who weren't my 'friends,' who didn't 'like' me."

"You'd be very popular," joked Cary.

Deena got up from her chair. "Well, it must be time for dessert," she said, clearing the dishes. Sara stood and helped carry them into the kitchen. A moment later Deena emerged with a flourless chocolate cake doused with crème fraiche. Am I popular now?" she asked.

"You're the best," said Cary.

"Jake, tell me about the new girl you hired," asked Deena.

"She's gorgeous!" interrupted Carey.

"She's a photojournalist," said Jacob. "I think she's been badly traumatized by the war. Her husband disappeared and is presumed dead. She doesn't talk about it much, so there's not much I can tell you. There's something intriguing about her, though. I suspect she's way too qualified for this job." He looked over at Sara and tried to read what she was feeling, but she changed the subject.

"I love the painting over the mantle," she said, pointing to it.

"It's by Connie Tzu," says Deena. "She's Taiwanese but lives half the time here in the city. I love her work. Cary just bought me another one for our anniversary. I haven't framed it yet, though."

"Where is it?" asked Cary. "I'd like to show it to them."

"It's in the closet in the guest room," Jacob answered without thinking.

Cary and Deena looked at each other.

"How'd you know that?" she asked. "I just moved it in there this morning."

"I don't know," Jacob responded, shrugging his shoulders. "I just did."

Cary shook his head. "Sometimes you just scare the hell out of me, bro."

44

Sara walked into Jacob's office the following day and closed the door behind her. He stood to greet her. "Hi, darling," she said, kissing him lightly. "I was in the neighborhood, wondered if you wanted a ride home. I'm off to have dinner with Alison, my old roommate and Jacques Renaut, the French guy I told you about who climbed Everest; so you're a bachelor tonight, my dear."

"No, thanks," he said. "I've got to finish this proposal and I'm almost done."

"Don't forget we're going sailing with Cris and Henry tomorrow," she told him. "It's a three-day weekend and everyone it seems, including us, has plans. I'll come find you in the morning."

He smiled, put his arm around her waist and pulled her closer to kiss her more seriously. She gave his butt a playful squeeze, then turned and walked out, leaving his door open.

Jacob ran his hands through his hair and stretched. After a half hour, he walked upstairs, stopped at Leila's office and tapped on her door. She was wearing light blue leggings and a crisp white collared cotton blouse, her hair down, the first time he'd seen it that way. "Everyone's left for the long weekend except you and me," he said. "Would you like to share a glass of wine?" His face dropped slightly, fearing he may have made a faux pas. "I'm sorry. I should have asked. Do you drink?"

Leila smiled, a beautiful smile, he noticed. "I'm not devout, if that's what you mean," she said. "I'm not really a practicing Muslim at all. Drinks sound great. But I think I'd like my own, thank you."

"I guess I don't know that much about you. This will be a good opportunity to fill in the blanks." He suggested they go to a restaurant near her home in the Petrero Hill neighborhood, not too far from his own house, and called for an Uber.

They turned out the lights, turned on the alarm and rode to Chez Papa's on 18th Street. It was still warm enough to sit outside. There was a table open and they grabbed it. Next to them an eccentric old woman fed pieces of steak to her Bernese Mountain dog. "O, Sammy," they overheard her say, "I hope this isn't too well done for you." Leila and Jacob laughed discretely.

He ordered a glass of Pinot Noir, she a Kir. The waiter left menus. "We can also eat here, if you'd like," he told her. "I'm free all evening."

She smiled and said, "I'd love that."

He pushed back his chair and exhaled. "It's been a long week," he said. "But, tell me, how's it been for you so far? San

Francisco's a great town, but I can imagine it might take awhile to learn it. Have you had a chance to explore?"

She put down the menu. "I'm loving it already," she said. "Last weekend I took a bus to the Palace of the Legion of Honor. I usually get overwhelmed in art museums, but this one was small enough that I could take it all in in a couple hours. Then I walked for miles at Land's End and along the cliffs near there. Those houses are beautiful. It's so peaceful here. You can't imagine what a change that is for me, what a huge relief to get away from the bombings and the constant fear of living in the middle of a battle zone." She paused for a moment, studying his face. "The first day I arrived I heard a car backfire and I dove to the sidewalk. A very nice gentleman helped me up and reassured me, but I was so embarrassed. I think I'm finally relaxing now, though. It seems almost too good to be true to be back in a normal country. I had almost forgotten what it was like."

"Did you see much of the war and the violence?" he asked.

"Way too much," she answered. "As a photojournalist, I was often the first one on the scene after an attack. I wanted to show the world the reality of what was happening, to shock it into stopping the war somehow; but one day I noticed I wasn't as traumatized as I used to be and I realized it was destroying whatever sense of humanity I had left."

He saw the pain and the dark memories in her eyes. He did not look away. "I think the whole world has grown too accustomed to seeing the violence on television," he said. "After Syria, we've become numb. I guess that's the ultimate tragedy."

They were silent. She looked away from him, watched the old woman patting her dog. Her mind and her heart raced ahead, but she maintained her outward composure. The waiter brought their drinks and asked if they were ready to order. They quickly scanned the menu together and decided.

"Was it hard to leave without knowing what happened to your husband?" he asked.

The irony of her situation threatened to overwhelm her. If she were to have him, they would need to fall in love all over again. That possibility, unfortunately, seemed remote, given his deepening relationship with Sara. Being alone with Jacob now, though, was a dream come true. For months she was sure he had been killed.

"We were very much in love, recently married. This was going to be our first child. He did something very brave, stopped a suicide bomber before the guy set off his explosives in a crowded market. It was the big story on the news for days. They had video of the whole thing and he became a kind of national hero, but he was never seen again. But for a couple of months afterwards I got death threats every day, sometimes phone calls, often letters left at my apartment with gruesome photos of previous victims. Between not knowing what had happened to my husband, the incessant media coverage and the threats from the Jihadists, I could barely keep it together. After I lost our son, I had to escape. Luckily, I was granted political asylum. This job is a lifesaver for me, J…"—she started to say "Jonathan," but stopped herself—"Jacob."

His attention was riveted on her. That overwhelming empathy she had known so well before, like a force of Nature, enveloped her. She remembered the first time they met when he told her grandmother and her about the torture he had witnessed, how his eyes relived the experience as if had been him. Now those same eyes, those same infinitely deep blue eyes, reflected her own pain.

"I'm glad you are here now, Leila," he said.

Tears ran down her cheeks. He moved over to her, crouched by her, and held her in his arms. She felt herself on the verge of letting go, of total hysteria, but managed to keep some semblance of self-control. The smell of him went right to her heart. She was cleaved between love and grief. He handed her his handkerchief.

She wiped away her tears and pulled her head back. "I'm sorry," she said. "I haven't talked about this with anyone since I left. It seems a million miles away and yet so close. Thank you for listening."

He sat back in his chair again. She handed him his handkerchief and asked, "Do you remember anything at all about your time there?"

He told her what it was like waking up in the ambulance and not having a clue how he got there. "I think one of the reasons I made the decision to hire you was that I wanted somehow to keep a connection to this place that holds so much power over me. You are the only living link I have to it."

She looked at his hand and saw that he was holding something. Feeling like her whole stomach had dropped to the floor, she recognized what it was.

He looked down at the big iron key. "This is all I had when I left. I don't know what it means," he told her. "I carry it with me all the time. I keep praying that it will someday unlock the past. Until that happens I feel lost. I can't shake the feeling that an important part of me was left there." He handed her the key.

Her hands trembled. She felt like she was suffocating. The key held the unbearable weight of reality. She fought desperately to keep from telling him all. "Why don't you go back there?" she asked.

He took the key from her and put it back in his pocket. "I will someday. I'm just not ready, I suppose. I don't know yet what I'd be looking for."

The waitress brought their food. They picked at it silently for a few minutes. 'This must be what it's like to see a loved one with Alzheimer's,' she thought. 'He doesn't recognize me or even know who he is. But I do.'

"I feel like I have to find my place here, first, " he said. "I'm a little unmoored. I need to discover who I am in the present before I can rediscover my past," he reflected. "My life is perfect. I have everything a person could want and yet," he paused, "and yet I feel like I'm not fully here, not wholly alive."

She wanted so desperately to kiss him, to take away his pain. It took every ounce of her strength not to. "And what about Sara?" she asked.

45

Cris and Henry Reynolds were college friends of Sara's who was the Maid of Honor at their wedding. Henry was two years ahead of them at Stanford and had been struggling with a Silicon Valley start-up he and his brother created, which had failed to attract investors. Cris was the assistant marketing director for a San Francisco-based organic cosmetics company. They were in the process of selling the sailboat, which had been a graduation present from her father, she told them, almost apologetically, as they glided towards their berth in the Sausalito dock.

Henry was tall and thin, adept at sailing and mostly quiet. Cris, Cristiana, was a honey colored Chilean with raven black hair and an athletic body. She and Sara, inseparable around campus, were known as the "Gobstruck twins" for the effect they had on men. Both were sporting the same Victoria Secrets bikinis, white for Cris and black for Sara.

It had been a fun day of sun and wind and old stories, a carefree few hours in the dazzling beauty of the San Francisco Bay away from any thoughts of work. The conversation shifted to places they loved. "Everyone thinks Brazil is the best," said Cris. "The people are all gorgeous and the music is everywhere. Women samba instead of walk. But, of course, I prefer Chileans. The people are more real. Have you ever been?"

"Not to Chile, but I was once in Brazil," Jacob replied. "It was one of the most humiliating experiences of my life." He noticed Sara roll her eyes, as if she'd heard the story too many times before. He could tell that something was upsetting her today.

He continued. "I was invited to give a keynote speech to a conference in Sao Paulo on Gregory Bateson and cybernetics. Frankly, I was a little over my head. Throughout the day—my speech didn't begin until 10pm—I kept making eye contact with an adorable blond usher who blushed whenever we looked at each other. You're right about Brazilian women. They are beautiful; but this one stood out even in that crowd. I was returning from the bathroom, dressed in my new white linen Panama suit, feeling pretty good about myself, when the girl I was crushed out on walked directly towards me. I was so excited. My heart was pounding. 'Senor Alejo,' she said, looking up at me with those beautiful blue eyes, slightly embarrassed, 'you have some toilet paper stuck to the back of your pants.' And sure enough, there was a long line of toilet paper that trailed behind me like a tail from the back of my suit."

Cris spilled champagne on herself, laughing. But Sara, Jacob noticed, had only managed a slight smile. 'What's up with her?' he wondered. They leapt onto the pier and tied down the boat and said their good-byes. "We'll have to do this again before we lose this boat," Henry said.

"We'd love to," replied Sara. They hugged and went their separate ways. Sara and Jacob walked silently to her Miata.

"What's wrong?" he asked her.

"What do you mean?"

"You're upset. I can tell."

"What are you, a mind reader?" she said.

"Come on, tell me what's bothering you."

She looked at him severely. "I don't like it when you show off like a peacock around women. You were like fawning over Cris. It was embarrassing for me."

"You've got to be kidding," he said.

"Be real, Jake. I'm sure Henry saw it, too. You had to make a show out of lathering sunscreen on her and turning it into a little massage. You're so obvious."

"That's ridiculous," he retorted. "I put sunscreen on Henry's back, too."

"Not like you did with Cris. It was embarrassing. I was worried you were going to reach around and massage her tits. She's my girlfriend. I don't appreciate you trying to seduce her right in front of me."

He shut his eyes for a moment. "I wasn't trying to seduce her. You're overreacting."

Sara suddenly pulled off onto the exit to Fort Cronkite and found a place to park on the side of the road. "And what about your inviting her to go with us to Yelapa? You don't think that's something we might want to discuss first? You think I want to spend my time on the beach watching you go gaga over my best friend?"

Jacob looked away from her, but turned and said, "You're right about that. I shouldn't have invited them without talking with you to begin with. I apologize."

"Our first vacation alone together and you're inviting a girl you've got the hots for," she shook her head. "Maybe you ought to join a swingers club. There'd be a lot of girls who'd love to have you massage them and take them to Mexico."

"Look, I'm sorry. I shouldn't have invited them like that and I'm not at all interested in having sex with your girl-friend."

Sara took off her sunglasses and looked carefully at Jacob. "You know, I didn't say anything this morning, but Jacques came on to me pretty strong last night. I made it clear I wasn't interested at all. Handsome man, though, great body!" she said, provoking him. "How would you have liked it if I had flirted with him the way you did with Cris just now?"

"Sara, stop this. I'm glad you had such a good time last night. Your friend obviously has good taste. But I trust you not to do anything inappropriate. I don't know what's gotten into you, but I wasn't flirting with Cris. I swear. I'm totally committed to you."

"Jake, I think that's the real problem. You're afraid of commitment. Part of the reason I'm so upset is that I look at Chris and Henry and see how devoted they are to each other. You and I are still dating like we're back in high school. We even split the check when we go out. I want it to go deeper, but I think you're afraid to. I need to know whether this is going somewhere or if one day you'll decide you're bored and end it. It takes a real commitment to hold a relationship together through all the ups and downs. Sometimes I think you're in it only for the good times. Neither of us wants to have a baby; but are we just going to remain two single people going steady or are we going to build our lives together as a committed couple?"

There was a very long silence between them. Jacob wanted to reach over and hug her, but something held him back. Finally he said, "I'm committed to you. I love you with all my heart and I'm in this for the long run. I want this to work. I like that we have our separate spaces. But maybe we should consider moving in together."

Immediately, without forethought, Sara responded, "Maybe we should get married," surprising them both. There was a stunned silence.

"Was that a proposal?" he asked.

The absurdity of the situation in the middle of an argument finally broke the tension. Laughing, he reached over and hugged her.

"Sara, I want us to go further, to get married eventually; but I'm not quite ready. It's a big decision. I know you think it's crazy, but those two years that were erased from my life keep me a little unsure of myself. I feel like I left some part of myself there. I want to come to you with 100% of my being, but something's missing inside me. It doesn't have anything to do with you or my feelings for you. I know I'll get over it, but it's going to take a little more time." He kissed her. "Please have patience with me."

Sara stared out the side window for a minute, then turned back to face him. "I do. But you've got to look to the future and not just stay stuck in the past. It's the same thing with your work. You want to just play at it, like it's a hobby. You struggle to keep it small, afraid to let it grow, to take it to scale. Just like us. There comes a moment when you have to choose, to make a stand. I would love to marry you, but I need for you to ask me when you're ready.

"OK," he says. "When I'm ready."

46

A face emerged on the screen like a revelation.

"Dr. Solomon, can you see me?" Leila asked.

"Yes, perfectly. What time is it there?"

She looked off to the side. "It's 4am here. I thought this might be a good time to catch you. Thanks for answering my text."

"It's a delight to see you, Leila. I can't quite get used to this technology. The world has shrunk so much. How are you?" he asked.

"I'm good, really. It's been quite an adjustment living here, though. The sense of peace and security was unsettling at first. It made me even more nervous than I was at home. I didn't know what to expect. But I've gotten used to it now. It's like la la land here. People are actually happy."

"What do they know?" scoffed Dr. Solomon.

"And how are you?" she asked.

"I'm good. Just got over a wicked cold, but now I'm better. The weather here has been miserably hot," he said. "I'm almost finished writing my article about Jonathan's amnesia and clairvoyance. It's for my own sake, a way to stay connected to him, and for posterity, I suppose. I won't publish it, of course, as we agreed. Too many bad guys would want to get their hands on him. But it needs to be documented, for science's sake." He paused and then continued.

"Otherwise, life is more or less the same. There are still suicide bombings in the city, but significantly less than when you left. You'll be pleased to know there's been no mention in the news about the 'Market Place Angel' for several months now." She smiled and he continued.

"Muna and Khaled stopped by to visit on Friday after work. We've become quite good friends. It turns out the three of us share a love of 1930's jazz, so we've been trading old records. I think we're the only people left who still have turntables. They took me last weekend on a visit to your village to see the cottage. It's so romantic. They are keeping it up for you, expecting you'll return here someday. They seem really happy. Muna has started showing some. It's hard to imagine how they're going to balance their workloads with a baby. It's a real leap of faith to have children in the middle of this violence. But their courage about everything never ceases to amaze me."

He gestured with his hands towards her and asked, "And how is Jonathan doing and how is it for you being around him so much?"

The screen flickered for a moment. "Hugely difficult at first, as I wrote you. It was the greatest disappointment of my life when he didn't recognize me. I knew in my head to expect that—you warned me—but my heart kept hoping, and still does. It's been an emotional rollercoaster. Being so close to him fills a huge hole inside me; but his not knowing me, not knowing himself, is very confusing. It's hard to even remember what name to call him. At least he's alive and healthy."

Dr. Solomon moved his head back and forth. "I can't even imagine how painful this must be for you," he said.

"It is. I love him so passionately, but I can't even touch him. It's so strange. I'm playing a role I don't want to play. I can't be myself at all."

Dr. Solomon responded wryly, "So ironic. He doesn't know who he is and you are pretending to not know who you are."

Sara bit her thumbnail. "I don't know how much longer I can keep up this act," she said. "Watching Jonathan with his girlfriend tears me apart. She's nice and I want him to be happy, but I can see that they're not as in love with each other as we were. Almost every day I struggle whether to stay here. It's so hurtful. I cry myself to sleep most nights. I need to stop hoping. It just makes the pain so much worse."

Dr. Solomon paused, scrutinizing her. "How does he seem to you?"

"Actually, he seems more and more like his old self," she said. "Not mind-reading or anything like that: there's no hint of that. But he's lighter. He smiles a lot more. We've become close as colleagues and also as friends. It gets very awkward when he confides in me about Sara, his girlfriend. She keeps wanting more of a commitment, he says. Who wouldn't?" She paused, considering her words. "She's very attractive, a very up personality. But I think she's spoiled and too ambitious for Jonathan. He believes she'll outgrow all that, but I keep hoping that he'll see that their values are not the same. Part of me knows this is wishful thinking. They're obviously smitten with each other and it's inevitable that they'll tie the knot. I'm torn. I love working here and I love being around him, but I don't think I could make it, if they were to marry. I know I couldn't. Sometimes I think I should just return home and pretend that my husband is dead."

He remained quiet for a moment, and then said, "You've put yourself in an impossible situation, Leila. I hate to see you get hurt. I know you were hoping he'd suddenly get back his memory when he saw you, but sadly that didn't happen. If seeing you didn't jolt him, it's probably unlikely he'll get it back anytime soon. At some point you may just have to let him go."

Her eyes welled up. "I grieved for him so hard when he disappeared. Then, when Khaled showed me the *Economist* article, I thought I'd gone to heaven. I was certain he'd recognize me when he saw me. I don't know whether I have the courage to grieve him again." Her face was contorted with pain. She covered her mouth with her hands to stifle a cry. "I'm sorry," she said.

"Not at all. It's all such a tragedy. I'm not sure what you should do." He paused. "Maybe you should tell him the truth. At the very least it will make him whole again."

"I can't. Don't you realize what that would do to him? I think about it constantly. It takes all my strength each day not to reveal everything. But what could he do? He doesn't love me now. I'd be a nuisance for him. Even if he knew the facts, he wouldn't remember the feelings that went with them. I could tell him we were married, that we had a child; but he wouldn't remember what he felt for me. I'm a stranger to him, an employee. That's all. If he didn't recognize me when he saw me, he's not going to suddenly get his memories back just because I show him a marriage certificate. What he would know would be so much less than what he had felt."

Dr. Solomon raised his eyebrows and whispered, as if to himself, "And to that precise extent, we are so much less than what we are."

She tilted her head, looking confused. "What?"

"That's a quote from a psychiatrist, R.D. Laing," said Dr. Solomon. "'What we think is less than what we know: what we know is less than what we love: what we love is so much less than what there is. And to that precise extent we are so much less than what we are.'"

She closed her eyes. "What should I do?"

"I don't know, probably give it a little more time and see if anything changes. But at some point it may be best to tell him the truth. You need to be true to yourself, too," he suggested.

She pictured herself telling Jacob and feared what his face would reveal: the look of shock, of remorse maybe, even worse, pity. 'If only he would show some attraction for me,' she thought. 'I would hold nothing back.' She tried to imagine

him alight with recognition, in the fullness of his unconditional love, as she knew him before; but this was pure fantasy,
she realized.

47

It was a cloudy, windy day; a portentous afternoon with leaves blowing and the sky darkening, threatening rain. He ended his run in front of the Palace of the Legion of Honor and sat on a bench with his hands on his knees catching his breath. A young Hispanic man walked by tethered to six dogs on leashes, three small ones and three large. They excitedly sniffed the ground, tails wagging, and moved in stuttering steps, following whichever dog lead forward. A woman in a red coat pushed a baby carriage. Two children threw breadcrumbs to the seagulls that fluttered around them noisily. An older gentleman dressed in a black raincoat approached with a cane. "Mind if I sit here?" he asked.

"Not at all," Jacob responded, gesturing for him to sit next to him on the other end. They were quiet, lost in their own thoughts. Jacob was thinking about Sara, wondering why he held back from proposing to her. They had so much fun when they are together, yet he also loved his solitude. The puzzle of his lost years were an enigma; but if truth be told, he thought about it less and less. 'Perhaps I'm using it as a convenient excuse for not making tough decisions,' he admitted to him-self. 'Maybe Sara and Cary are right. Am I afraid to commit? Or am I just being true to myself?'

He noticed the man next to him staring at the threatening sky and saw him wipe a tear from his face. Suddenly, he heard or imagined he heard the man's voice talking to his wife. He could picture her in a hospital bed with tubes running from her arm and mouth and monitors scrolling orange graphs and numbers to a metronome of beeps. The man was telling her he would be all right. The kids would look after him. It would be empty without her, but he would keep busy.

Jacob's heart was filled with sympathy, but his mind was reeling. 'What's going on?' he asked himself. He saw that the man's lips were not moving and yet he clearly heard his voice in his head. The images of the man's wife—Katherine she was called, he somehow knew—must be in the man's mind. Or was he making this all up? He looked around furtively to see if anyone were watching. The man seemed oblivious to him, lost in his thoughts. 'Surely I'm imaging all this,' Jacob thought. Yet he knew it was more real than that. He remained perfectly still.

The man was terrified, afraid of the future, of the loneli-ness he would feel. He thought back to happier times, to vaca-tions together by the sea, to walks in Paris and her seventy-fifth birthday in Prague. And he pictured her in pain at the birth of their first-born and sitting Shiva for the boy when he died at 14 and how he could not console her; how she cried for days and weeks and was never really the same after that. All this passed through the man's mind and with excruciating clarity through Jacob's as well.

He wanted to do something, to acknowledge the man's suffering, but he was frozen in the grip of a vortex of memories not his own. Confused and transfixed by these thoughts and images, he could do nothing to stop them. He wanted to escape, but whatever he was experiencing was too close to run from. His own pain was no less than the man grieving next to him. It was the same pain. Finally, he turned to face the man. Their eyes met and in a moment, in an instant of recognition, the pain lifted and he saw in the man's eyes a look of redemption, and, a moment later, a look of awe.

48

A burst of hot air greeted them as they stepped off the plane in Puerto Vallarta, plunging them into pure vacation mode. Instantly, their moods went from mildly happy to ecstatic. As they waited in the terminal for their bags a motley band of Mariachi players transported them into the laid-back ambience of Mexico. Leaving behind the busy freneticism of work and city, they set out on a molasses-paced five-day siesta with nothing to do. Jacob exhaled a long slow breath. Sara put down her floral beach bag, threw her arms around him and kissed him, wide mouthed and hungry.

They grabbed the duffel bags, mostly filled with snorkel equipment purchased in San Francisco that very morning, and walked out into the blinding mid-day sun. A yellow taxi with green-checkered trim and Christmas decorations inside was waiting by the curb. Jacob chatted with the driver in the little Spanish he knew and they set out to the port to catch the ferry to Yelapa, an Indian preserve on a nearby peninsula that Sara had once visited as a ten-year old, a low-key vacation destination that had neither cars nor roads.

They drove on a paved two-lane highway with little traffic. Thatched-roof huts advertising cold Fanta and Pepsi punctuated a flat tableau of scrub brush and Pacific Ocean blue. Sara couldn't wait to get out of her clothes and into her new bikini. Jacob continued his small talk with the driver.

In the other lane coming at them a truck pulled out to pass a slow moving tanker and appeared not to have the speed to overtake it in time to avoid a head on collision. The road was elevated and there was no shoulder to swerve onto. The angry blast of the truck's horn filled the air with fear. Their driver jammed on his brakes and the truck managed to pass miraculously just before impact.

Sara's left arm was raised in front of her face and her right squeezed Jacob's hand on the seat next to her, her mouth still open for a scream that had not been needed. She turned to look at him, wanting him to hold her; but he was absolutely frozen, sitting straight and rigid like a stone figure. "Jacob," she cried anxiously, but he did not seem to hear her, as if his mind were miles away. "Are you all right?"

He still didn't move. She shook him and, slowly, as if waking from a dream, he turned to face her. "I remember," he said, eyes startled but without fear. His unnatural passivity alarmed her until his ocean blue eyes came to life with a vividness and excitement she had not seen before. He blanketed her in kisses all over her face, held her shoulders in his hands, peered into her eyes and bursting with elation said, "I remember this, something just like this, that happened to me over there. It's the first memory I've had." He was practically jumping up and down. "Sara, do you realize how important this is? This might open the gates to the mental prison I've been in."

She looked at him with a combination of joy and concern. The adrenaline was still racing inside her, but a higher drama seemed to be playing out in front of her. She soon grasped the magnitude of his revelation and moved to meet his excitement with her own. "Oh my God, Jake, what is it? Had you been in an accident before? Maybe that's what happened to you. Maybe you spent two years in a coma or something. It would explain everything."

His mind was racing, searching for more data, more fragments of memory, but none came. "Yes, that makes a lot of sense, doesn't it? It's a clue for sure, a big one. But whatever happened to me, I know I can return there in my mind now. I've lifted some veil. This is only the start." He kissed her on her mouth in celebration.

"Are you sure you had an actual memory of a real experience?" she asked, not wanting to dampen his enthusiasm, but hoping to avoid a dead end. "Could it be a sense of déjà vu or something? What exactly do you remember?"

"No, it was a real experience, I'm certain. I was in a van riding with three other people. I can't actually see their faces now, but I know how they were seated. There were two trucks just like the ones we just missed, but green or brown, not silver like these. And there was singing. I remember that. In Arabic I think. I know it happened. I'm absolutely sure of it."

They stopped by the port and the driver directed them to a small shack where they could buy tickets for the ferry. Sara had never seen Jacob so carefree and alive, like a six-year old. They sat under an awning at one of the endless beachfront restaurants and ordered marguerites, chips and guacamole to pass the time until the ferry returned from Yelapa.

An hour and a pitcher of marguerites later, the Princess Yelapa Bay Cruise boat finally lumbered in to dock. The ride to Yelapa took 45 minutes. When they arrived a small flotilla of rowboats took the hundred or so happy tourists dressed in brightly colored shirts and straw hats from the big boat to the pier. They would all return in a couple hours for the last sailing back to Puerto Vallarta, except for Sara and Jacob and one other couple who planned to stay overnight. At the pier an old Mexican man greeted them by name, as if he knew them and carried their two bags, one over each shoulder, up the winding path, crowded with bougainvillea, alive with the exotic squeals of macaw, to ever-greater views of the golden sand beach below. "This is paradise," exclaimed Jacob.

The palapa they rented was a single story thatched-roof villa without walls completely surrounded by flowering plants and vegetation. There were views of the ocean from every room and no other dwellings within sight or sound. The master bedroom had a large bed suspended from the ceiling two feet off the ground by chains that held up each corner, "to keep away from the tarantulas," the old Mexican told Jacob ominously. There was, in fact, a gigantic black and yellow spider of some kind the size of a grapefruit attached to the shower wall in back that Jacob managed to scrape into a large soup pot and throw into the jungle.

The air was thick with smells. Sara quickly changed into her hot pink bikini and lay on the swinging bed. Jacob, still feeling a little tipsy from the marguerites, carefully climbed in next to her, spooning her as they stared off at the endless expanse of blue ocean. When she turned to face him, he reached behind her and unfastened her top. Their mouths met and they struggled to undress on a bed that rocked back and forth like a rowboat. With balance and restraint they came to each other, eyes wide-opened, bodies wet with sweat, and he entered her deeply and slowly. Miraculously, the bed did not collapse and they fell into a delicious post-coital sleep.

When they woke it was already dark. They took flashlights and walked down the path towards some twinkling lights in the distance. Sara explained that when she was last here as a ten-year old there was no electricity. Now there was some and it had inevitably changed the place, less charming for visitors like them, but probably a God-send for the native villagers. "Progress always comes with a price," Jacob commented.

But charm there still was. The lights that drew them came from one of several makeshift restaurants scattered on the hillside, each with a few mismatched wooden tables and chairs, Christmas lights strung through the canopy, and votive candles in glass jars on the dirt floor. Below were lights from the few sailboats that were resting in the harbor. There was fresh fish on the menu.

Sara picked up her pina colada and toasted his break-through in the cab, "If your memory returns, I don't think there'd be anything holding us back anymore," she said. "That was a really big deal, a turning point, I believe."

"For sure," he said. "If it all comes back, I'll be the happiest guy in the world. I really do want to marry you. But I'd want you to know that I was committing with 100% of me."

She nodded. "I'm excited for you. I don't want you to have any doubts. I want all of you, every last morsel of you. I love you, but it should be all or nothing," Sara said, reaching over to hold his hand.

The next morning they walked down to the beach, which had a line of small bungalows along with a snack bar and restaurant. They rented beach chairs and settled in. Soon, one of Yelapa's renowned "pie ladies" meandered towards them carrying a basket of fresh baked pies on her head. "Pies? Limon, coconut, chocolate," she sang. They took one of each.

"What are you reading now?" Sara asked.

"I'm actually rereading one of my favorite novels, "The Time Traveller's Wife," Audrey Niffenegger. It's a real mindbender, but ultimately the most romantic story I've ever read. They get to know each other at different ages in their lives. At least I had the advantage of knowing you as a teenager, but I wish I knew you when you were really little. Wouldn't you have liked knowing me as a child, as an adolescent?"

She laughed, picturing him so young. There was something so innocent about him, she realized, and yet he had a certain reserve of someone much older.

A young man settled himself down with some difficulty on a beach towel about thirty yards from them. He was wearing a purple Hawaiian bathing suit, a white T-shirt and a red base-ball cap with a yellow star on it. He struggled to lower himself and Sara noticed that he was wearing prostheses for one of his arms and another for a leg. Jacob glanced over to see what she was looking at. "I'm always blown away by guys like that," Sara said.

"I used to have a friend who had only an arm and a leg," said Jacob. "A young soldier named Sami, a really funny guy."

"Where'd you know him from?" asked Sara.

Jacob's smile suddenly turned into a frown. His expression tightened like a knot. He stared straight-ahead, out towards the surf lapping at the beach, concentrating, intensely focused. He put his hands on his head. He turned to face her. "Sara, it was there, in a hospital ward of some kind. It's another frag-ment."

49

Leila walked down the hall to Jacob's office lost in thought. The blinds were drawn, which meant Jacob hadn't arrived yet. She opened the door without knocking. Standing there were Jacob and Sara in a passionate embrace, both tanned and radiant. "I'm so sorry," cried Leila who tried to say something about the blinds, but couldn't get it out.

Jacob disentangled himself. "It's OK. Please come in. We're trying to decide whether to elope or have a real wedding. You're the first to know."

Shock and despair sliced through her. She felt shattered like broken glass. She couldn't move, couldn't speak. Jacob was talking, but it was like the sound of an airplane flying over and she could not make out what he was saying.

Sara looked at her strangely. "Are you alright?" she asked.

She tried to answer, but the muscles in her face wouldn't move. She willed herself to smile, but felt her face cracking instead. The air seemed to have been sucked out of the room and she began to faint. Catching herself on the door handle, she managed to stay standing. She heard her voice say something. "I'm so sorry. I shouldn't have come in today. I'm not feeling well." She held a hand over her mouth and the other over her stomach as if she were going to throw up, turned and ran from the office.

Jacob started to run after her, but Sara grabbed his arm. "Let her be," she said. "She's obviously in love with you, Jacob."

He turned to face her. "No, it isn't like that between us. We're friends. She's never shown a hint of wanting anything more. I'm sure of it."

Sara rolled her eyes. "Men are so naïve. I always knew she wanted you. She tried to hide it with her professional bearing, but I've seen the way she looked at you. She's been hoping all along we'd break up and she'd get you by default. Why do you think she's never dated? You're so innocent."

"Don't be jealous, Sara," Jacob responded. "It's not very becoming. I think she's just sick. You don't have anything to worry about. We're friends. That's all. Anyway, I'm yours and that's all that counts." He moved close to her, took her hands and wrapped them again around his back. "Now, where were we?" They kissed and then sat on the couch.

"I want to get married as soon as we can," Sara began, "but I don't think we can elope, though that is very romantic. I couldn't do that to my father. He'd be so hurt. And my brothers and some of my close friends, I'd have to invite them. But let's plan something very small and very soon."

"How soon?" he asked.

"Just a month or so, as soon as we can make arrangements. I know a wonderful place, the perfect spot. A friend of my Dad's owns it. I've wanted to take you there for some time. It's called Lake Leonard. It's the largest natural lake in Mendocino County, just outside Ukiah. The lake's about a half mile across, surrounded by a thousand acres of virgin redwoods. There's never been a motor in it. John Philip Sousa once played there. An old 1930's homestead house overlooks the lake. I think it can sleep 30 people or so. It's beautiful. We could house everyone and make a two-day event of it," she said with the pleading look of a little girl.

Jacob smiled. "Sounds ideal. Why don't you see when it might be available."

50

Leila shut the door to her office and crumbled to the floor sobbing, holding a hand over her mouth so no one could hear her. Then, terrified that Jacob would see her like this, she forced herself to stand and composed herself as best she could. Her head was throbbing. She felt like it would actually explode. Nausea rose to her throat. Panic seized her. 'I've got to get out of here,' she thought and went to grab her laptop, but then sat abruptly at her desk instead.

She took out a legal pad and, hand shaking, began to write.

Dear Jacob,

Please excuse my behavior just now. I received some very bad news this morning and it's made me quite sick. I wanted to congratulate you and Sara, but when I opened my mouth, I thought I was about to throw up. Of course, I can only wish you two the best of luck. You are a beautiful couple and you will be very happy together.

You remember I told you about my husband who's been missing since he interrupted a suicide bomber? Well, there's been some news about him and I'm afraid it's very bad. I need to return home at once. Please forgive me. I do not have a choice. I don't know how long I will have to remain there.

Please excuse this letter. I know I should tell you this in person; but after this last scene in your office, I don't think I could face you two just now. You looked so very happy. I don't want to rain on your happiness. Please don't be angry with me. I know that the organization can run fine without me. I will miss you horribly, more than these words can convey. Please promise me that you won't try to contact me. I will write you as soon as I'm able.

I have to pick up the pieces of my life, which have just been shattered. I wish I could share more with you now, but please trust that I'm doing what's right. You have been the kindest person I've ever met and I value your friendship more than you will ever know. Give my love to Cary and everyone on the staff. And be good to yourself.

Leila

Tears had smudged some of the words, but she didn't have the heart to rewrite the letter. She gathered her things and left the note under a small vase that held a single red rose on her desk. She opened the back door. Wind wrapped her hair around her throat. The joggers and bicyclists outside appeared alien to her. She walked hurriedly away from the building, her heart an open wound, more painful, she realized, than the birth of Jonathan's son. The two tragedies merged into one. "I have lost him. It's over," she said out loud to herself. It was the final act in the play.

She Facetimed Muna. It rang incessantly. She clenched her free hand in a fist and pleaded for her to answer. 'It's only 9pm. Muna should still be up.' Finally, the screen flashed tentatively several times and the grainy pixels coalesced into a shape, Muna.

"Leila, what's wrong?" Muna exclaimed, seeing the tears and distress on her face.

"Muna, O! Muna," Leila cried, tears flowing uninterrupted. She stood on a street corner breathing heavily, unable at first to speak. "I'm coming home. It's all over here." She gasped. "They're getting married. I can't bear it."

There was a long silence as if it took several moments for these words to cross the distances between them. "Yes, please come home," Muna said. "Let us take care of you. I knew this would happen. I'm so sorry. What did Jonathan say when you told him?"

"I just left him a note—my husband died or something. I guess he is dead to me, isn't he? It's obvious how in love he is with Sara." She stopped to catch her breath. "You were right, just as you predicted. I should have listened to you. I don't know if I can survive this. I just know I have to leave on the next plane."

"Leila, it's Khaled. Can you see me?" He had moved next to Muna. "Be careful how you do this. Don't fly directly here. It might screw up your application for political asylum. Fly somewhere close by and take a bus. I know you don't care about that now, but someday you might. It's still dangerous here. We may all have to leave."

Leila just shook her head. "OK, I'll do what you say. I'm going to stop by my apartment and get a few things and head to the airport. I'll text you when I know something."

"Leila, don't hurt yourself," Muna added. "You have a whole life ahead of you."

Leila considered what Muna said and shook her head. "I promise not to do anything stupid; but, Muna, when little Jonathan died, I thought I couldn't go on. The only thing keeping me alive was the hope that I might one day be with Jonathan again." She tried to compose herself, but could not. She sobbed uncontrollably. "I guess I'm glad I had this chance, to see him alive." Unable to continue, she ended the call.

51

Cary arrived for a tour around the private, pristine lake and the groves of redwoods where Jacob and Sara were to wed. Jacob's tan had begun to fade. He looked tired and seemed uncharacteristically distracted. "Are you OK?" Cary asked, as they ambled down the grassy slope to the little dock. "You seem down. Getting cold feet?"

Jacob managed a smile. "No, not exactly. I'm fine. I just didn't sleep well last night. I guess I was worried about Leila. It seems strange that she would leave so abruptly like that. But everything else is going well. Sara's up at the barn looking at the horses. We settled on the site for the ceremony. I'll take you there in a bit, but I thought it might be fun to go out on the lake first."

They walked onto the floating dock and Jacob untied the rope holding one of the canoes and pulled it around so it lined up snug against the side, then held the boat steady as Cary climbed in. "I was shocked when you told me about Leila. I had never heard the full story of her husband before. It sounds pretty awful," Cary said, holding onto the dock with one hand while Jacob got in behind him.

"She never talked about him," Jacob said. "I think there's a lot about the story that's murky."

"What's happening with you? On the phone you said you were starting to get back your memory and you'd tell me all about it when we saw each other. What's going on?" Cary asked.

Jacob used his paddle to push away from the dock and guided them in a wide arc towards the middle of the lake. A flock of startled geese took off sputtering noisily into the air before them. "It's a big deal, Cary," Jacob began. "It happened when we were driving into Puerto Vallarta from the airport. A couple of trucks came close to crashing into us and I suddenly remembered a similar close call. Later I had a clear memory of talking with a young soldier whose leg and arm had been amputated and there have been other, smaller, fragments. None of them fit together yet, but the door has been opened."

"Like what?" Cary asks. "What else?"

"Just some vague flashes or impressions—someone chasing me or looking at the stars on a rooftop on a hot summer night. Things like that."

"This is amazing," Cary said. "You must be ecstatic. You've been so hung up about this."

Jacob didn't answer for a few moments. "I guess so," he said. "Part of me is thrilled. I've wanted this so badly. I needed it. Not knowing has been a big dark hole in my life holding me back. But it's also a little disconcerting. I can't stop thinking about it now. I should be concentrating on this wedding, but I feel myself being pulled back there."

"Maybe you just need to let it all play out, get all the memories out and put the puzzle back together," Cary suggested. "Once everything comes into focus, you won't have to be thinking about it anymore."

"Maybe," Jacob sighed. They glided silently across the water, surrendering to the inertia and the utter stillness, savoring this magical interlude between time and space.

They remained quiet this way until they returned to shore, not wanting to disturb the sublime perfection of floating in the moment.

"That was divine," Cary said.

They tied the canoe, walked up the lawn towards the big house with its decks spread out like large skirts and turned up the steep path to the woods to see the "angel ring," nine cathedral-like old growth redwoods in a circle, where the wedding would take place. Off to their right someone was working with a small generator and a bank of batteries by a converted barn. As the workman attached a set of cables to the generator, Jacob suddenly gasped and fell to his knees, his head in his hands. "Oh my God!" he cried out in a voice of unspeakable anguish and despair.

"Jesus, Jacob, what's wrong with you?" Cary yelled, putting his arm around Jacob's shoulders.

Jacob's body shuddered with the memory. When he looked up at Cary his eyes showed terror, his sight obliterated by some hellish inner vision. His body convulsed in a paroxysm of grief. "Oh God, Cary. Oh God."

"What is it? What's happening," Cary implored him.

"I just saw someone being tortured, electrocuted, hanging from a chain in a dungeon. Then a door slammed in my face. It was real, Cary. I remember it. I felt it. I saw it. I was there. But I must have been tortured, too. I remember the pain, the electricity in my teeth, the smell of burnt flesh. Oh God, help me." He was shaking.

Cary held him in his arms until the shaking slowly subsided. He had never seen such a look of terror in anyone's eyes. They stood unsteadily and walked up the path in silence. Cary was frightened to his core. They walked into the middle of the angel ring, which was like a sanctuary, and sat on the soft, decomposed earth.

Several minutes passed before Jacob was able to speak. "I can see now why I wanted to block those memories," Jacob started. "I witnessed something horrible, some unimaginable depravity. I felt it also. Maybe I was tortured, too, or maybe I just imagined the man's pain. But I didn't imagine what I saw. It was real, all too real."

Cary wanted to respond, to say something soothing, to offer some advice, but he couldn't think what was right.

After a moment, Jacob continued talking. "I have to get to the bottom of this. I need to know everything I experienced there. Having these pieces come back but being unable to see the whole story is worse than when I couldn't remember a thing." He paused for a moment, considering his options. "I need to go back there."

"Are you crazy?" Cary said. "It's dangerous as hell. Whatever you just saw could happen again. I think you need to wait until you can remember everything before you jump back in. Besides, you're getting married in two weeks."

With this, Jacob looked up and stared wildly at Cary, like a man about to jump from a cliff. "There's something else. It's not just the terror. I realized something just before you got here. I've been afraid to put voice to it, but the truth is I feel a stronger pull to return there than I do to go on here. The things I'm starting to remember are mostly provoked by deep-seated fears. But there are also other feelings, good feelings, which are drawing me back. I've only caught glimpses of places and images; but the feelings and emotions are vivid and real. I can't get them out of my mind. Maybe they're siren calls luring me back into danger, but it feels more like…" He can't say the word.

Cary looked at him gloomily. "Have you shared any of this with Sara?"

Jacob shook his head.

Outside the ring the sound of someone approaching interrupted them. It was Sara, dressed in bright purple floral shorts, a white, wife-beater shirt, and sunglasses and wearing a large-brimmed straw hat. Cary jumped up and walked towards her. Her movie star smile disappeared when she saw the look on his face. He passed by her in silence. She watched him walk down the path, then turned back to Jacob in the ring of redwoods.

Jacob stood, unsteadily.

She removed her hat and sunglasses and walked up to him. She noticed the key in his hand. In an instant she saw everything in his tortured eyes, saw the parts of him he couldn't share, the disappointment, the grief, the fear of hurting her; but more importantly, she saw the thing that was taking him from her, that was pulling him away. Fear flooded through her. The bottom fell out of her stomach. She wanted to reach out, to beg him, to prevent him from leaving. But she was also aware of an unspoken truth she couldn't deny. She realized in an instant that it was her determination that had bound them, not his desire. She understood that she must let him go, however much it would rip her apart. And, strangely, accepting this truth ennobled her. He was her teenage crush, but she knew fully now that he did not love her as she loved him. A single tear fell. Her heart held its breath as she whispered, "Do what you have to, my darling," and kissed him good-bye.

52

"You got everything? Passport, visa, credit cards, cell phone, cash?" Cary asked, as they drove in the Lexus towards the International Terminal at the San Francisco airport. Jacob nodded. "What about Leila? Any luck figuring out how to contact her? She would be invaluable."

Jacob shook his head. "I've tried everything, but it's all been a dead end."

"How do you plan to get around? Are you going to hire a translator? What about a private investigator?" Cary had given up trying to talk him out of leaving.

"I'll figure it out when I get there somehow."

"Where will you even start?" Cary asked.

"I'm not sure. The only clues I have are memories of a near collision with two semi trucks, a double amputee named Sami—I don't know his last name—and being chased, but I don't know where. It was a downtown, I think, busy streets, maybe by a department store. That's probably how I ended up getting hit by a truck. There's also the rooftop, but that could be anywhere and, of course, the dungeon, or whatever it was, where I saw a man being tortured."

Cary let out a deep sigh. "I wish you'd reconsider, let someone else who speaks the language try to figure things out for you."

"One thing more," Jacob said, interrupting him. "I had a dream last night. I don't know what it means, but I know it's important. You'll think I'm crazy, but it's why I have to go back there. I've got to figure out how it ends. I had the dream before, the first night I slept with Sara, but this time it was different."

He noted a look of incredulity on Cary's face, but continued. "I was back in the city where I got hit by the truck. I was running in a big crowd of people. In the dream I could read everyone's minds, feel all their feelings. The world was about to end in a kind of Armageddon and I was the only one who could save them. It was the end of time."

Cary's expression turned from incredulity to real concern. But Jacob couldn't stop. "I had to do something, but then suddenly the scene changed and I was walking up a path in the mountains behind a woman with long black hair. She stopped, and in front of us, grazing on some grass, was a white deer, a young buck with antlers."

Jacob turned his head and looked at Cary. "In the dream I knew I was in love with this woman with a certainty I've never felt before. It was an overwhelming experience of total joy, of rapture really. But I had to make a choice, save the world or follow her. When I woke up and realized I was only dreaming,

I was angrier than I have ever been before. It was like God had cheated me of infinite happiness. I actually took the clock by my bed and smashed it against the wall. That's when I knew I had to go back there and find her."

"Jake," Cary said, "You need to see your old psychiatrist. I'm serious. You're saying things like you did when you were in the hospital. I think you may be going psychotic again."

"I'm not," Jacob responded. "I've never been more lucid in my life. I felt these things. The mind reading, the memories, they're all real. I've experienced them."

Cary glared at him. "For God's sake, Jake, did you ever consider that your brain is playing tricks on you because you feel guilty breaking up with Sara? This all started, all these so-called memories and dreams, when you went to Mexico to propose to her."

Jacob turned to face him. "I didn't plan to propose to her. In fact, I didn't. She did." He paused. "I never felt for Sara the kind of love I experienced in that dream. I don't feel guilty at all that we didn't go through with the wedding. It wouldn't have worked out well for either of us." He took the key from his pocket and held it up to Cary like a religious relic. "This key is real and it's connected somehow to the woman in my dream. I know it. I have to find her."

Cary shook his head. "I still think it's crazy and insanely dangerous. I wish you'd just give it a couple days before you do something this rash."

They arrived in front of the International Terminal. Cary was visibly distraught, but Jacob was serene. His eyes shone with optimism. He reached over and squeezed Cary's arm, tapped the key against the St. Christopher medallion that hung from the rearview mirror, and said, "Don't worry about me. I'll text you when I get there. Thanks for all your concerns. I mean it."

53

He arrived in the early morning before dawn. Security guards were everywhere toting AK47's. Outside the air-conditioned terminal, the air was hot and dry. There were few civilians. A taxi disgorged a family of six loaded with heavy bundles and suitcases. He waited patiently as the father paid the driver before he approached. "Embajada de España?" he asked. The driver looked at him suspiciously, not understanding. "Spanish Embassy?"

The driver reached into his cab, pulled out a pad and wrote "200 Dinars."

Jacob looked at him and smiled. "OK," he said, and got in the back.

"Yalla," said the driver. "Let's go."

They passed through three separate checkpoints to exit the airport. Jacob checked his phone for connectivity and looked for messages. There was nothing except a smiley face from Cary and "good luck bro."

He texted back. "Arrived safely, too excited to sleep on the plane. Heading to the Spanish Embassy, the one place I know I've been for sure."

The light of another day began to crest on the horizon, rose-colored against a gun barrel grey sky. There were intermittent stops along the way where sleepy soldiers checked their papers and searched the trunk and the underside of the cab. After about 20 minutes Jacob suddenly yelled for the driver to stop. "What's that?" he asked, pointing to a tall, red brick building, its front entrance manned by guards carrying assault rifles.

"Moustashfa," answered the driver and then repeated it louder this time, holding the back of his hand to his head in pantomime. "Hopital" he tried. Jacob's heart raced. He recognized the place. He thrust two hundred Dinar notes into the driver's hand and jumped out of the cab. The driver waved a friendly good-bye and took off.

Jacob walked up to the front gate and showed his passport to an approaching guard, who was shaking his head no. A sign next to the guard post identified it as a military hospital. Undeterred, Jacob took out his wallet and offered the guard 100 Dinars, then 200, but the guard refused to budge. At 500 Dinars the guard looked over to another who angrily dismissed Jacob with a wave of his hand.

Jacob turned and walked away, snapping a picture of the hospital and jotting down its name in his iPhone. He walked through the still sleeping streets, lost in a jumble of thoughts. The sun had now risen above the one-story shops that lined the road leading towards the center of the city. The odors of rotting garbage, donkey shit and kerosene began to give way to the smells of a city coming alive around him. Everything looked familiar to him, but nothing specifically.

He walked for two hours carrying a small backpack, all he brought with him, as the temperature rose and the heat radiated from the asphalt road. He forgot even to bring a hat. There were no taxis here. His legs were wobbly. Up ahead of him was a truck stop of some kind and a run-down hotel. He decided to take a room and sleep for a few hours through the hottest part of the day.

He texted Cary again. "I stumbled across the hospital where I think I met the boy, Sami, but they wouldn't let me in. Gonna take a nap now in a flea bag hotel. Hot and tired, but excited. Much is familiar." The room was bare concrete-block with a single light bulb dangling on a wire from the ceiling and an old army cot with a thin, worn mattress. Jacob swallowed an Ambien and a Xanax and fell into a deep sleep. When he woke it was pitch dark, 5am. He had slept for most of a day. It was cooler now and he decided to trudge back up the road to the army hospital, but was again turned away.

Despairing, he waited in front of the hospital for more than an hour until a taxi finally came along and had it drop him off at the Spanish Embassy. After waiting a few more hours on the sidewalk outside for the Embassy to finally open, he presented his passport and asked to see the young man who helped him after the accident, but the man was no longer there. After a very long wait, another consular officer informed him that they didn't have records going back that far and Jacob left the Embassy empty-handed.

He took a cab back to the military hospital, but was turned away for the third time. He had no idea how to proceed. He decided to hire a private investigator as Cary had suggested, but in the meantime he flagged another taxi and had it take him back to the hotel where he stayed the night before. At least the neighborhood and the shops were familiar. He got out and continued his walk towards the center of town. Stopping at the sight of propane canisters stacked along the side of the road, something clicked in his mind. He closed his eyes, remembering the sensation of being pressed close to a woman in a tiny kitchen with a propane stove and himself dressed in a ridiculous apron. He even recalled the scent of her hair, though he could not see her face. He opened his eyes and continued walking down the street, buoyed by this new memory.

He walked for more than an hour. It seemed that the further he walked, the more familiar things became. A merchant swept the pavement in front of his shop. A man pushed a cart loaded with watermelons. A rooster crowed indignantly. 'If I have to walk every block of this city, I'll do it,' he thought. Maybe I'll just run across her somewhere. If I lived here for two years, there have to be places I will recognize.'

Across from him a woman was unloading flowers from her car and carrying them into her store. He froze. He felt his heart race and his head fill with memories, too many to sort out. He'd been here before, in this spot. But something else demanded his attention. The flowers. He closed his eyes in concentration and he remembered. Flowers. Something terrible about to happen. He ran down the street desperate to find a taxi. 'Why didn't I keep the taxi with me?' he chided himself. Up ahead at a large intersection he found a taxi stand, but it was empty. Finally, he saw a taxi letting off a passenger a block away and ran to catch it.

54

The driver greeted him with a wide grin, looking him up and down. "Salam alaykum," he said and Jacob responded, "Alaykum Salam."

"Do you speak English?" Jacob asked.

The man laughed, "A little."

"Is there a big flower market somewhere?"

"Yes, in the center. But it won't be open yet."

Jacob's eyes brightened. "That's alright. Can you take me there?"

He felt like a dam had broken. Pictures on a billboard, smells from restaurants, the sounds of traffic provoked fragments of memories that flowed like a torrent. Now it was a matter of making sense of all this, 'the old noise to signal ratio,' he realized.

When they arrived, vendors were just unloading their trucks and filling their stalls with yellow chrysanthemums and pink orchids, orange ranunculus and long-stemmed white and yellow daisies, purple iris and red and white roses, a cacophony of colors. He paid the fare and leapt out of the car. Every detail was familiar, but he could not recall what happened here, only the sense of panic he felt, the razor-edged urgency of action. He walked through the empty market, drawn to a café on one corner where waiters were busy wheeling their umbrellas out to the curb.

'I've been here!' he thought. 'With her!' He ordered a cappuccino and sat at one of the small tables, hoping upon hope to catch sight of her. 'She brought me here,' he remembered. 'This is probably a café she frequents. If I come here everyday I may well see her.' He worried, though, whether he would recognize her. He had not yet conjured up her face.

Images of places and things continued to flood his mind, but their meanings still eluded him. He was on a carpet, sitting cross-legged, eating in front of an older woman, in a hallway looking at old photographs on a wall, dashing men with oversize moustaches wearing fezzes, one mounted on a white horse holding a long barreled rifle. He pictured himself at another café seated with the same older woman warning him of danger. And her. She was there, too, but he couldn't make out her face; only her voice was familiar, strong-willed, confident but kind.

He opened his eyes and watched the merchants quietly arranging their flowers with care. Across the square a policeman blew a shrill whistle. Suddenly he felt a rush of adrenaline and remembered people yelling and running. He closed his eyes again and saw a line of school children each holding a knot on a rope and experienced a bitter taste of fear in his mouth. He gulped down his coffee, dropped a 5 Dinar note on the table and headed through a side street, retracing the steps he took when he was chased. 'But by whom? Why?' He turned onto Suleiman Street. In his mind he heard car horns blaring, the wail of sirens that converged on the Flower Market behind him, the screech of brakes and the cries of onlookers as a truck slammed into him.

'It was here where I was knocked unconscious,' he realized. There were no sirens now, no real panic, few shoppers yet on the street. A truck screeched to a halt at the light and, again he flashed on the two semi-trucks that came barreling towards him, the very first memory he had. 'She was in the car next to me then,' he was sure. 'Where were we going?' he wondered, holding his head in his hands. 'Somewhere in the mountains,' he thought.

The taxi driver who had dropped him at the Flower Mart ten minutes earlier pulled up next to him and rolled down the window. "Hello, my friend, do you need another ride somewhere?"

Jacob opened the front door and got in next to him. "Salama alaykum," Jacob said in greeting.

"Alaykum Salam," responded the driver with his big grin.

His mind racing ahead, Jacob said, "I need to find a village. I don't know its name, but it's somewhere in the mountains, in the foothills."

The driver laughed heartily. "There are many villages, my friend."

"It's only about 50 kilometers or so from here. If you head towards the mountains, I think I might remember the way," Jacob said.

"By the meter?"

"Sure."

They drove in silence, Jacob straining to see any familiar landmarks ahead, the driver looking over at him every minute or so, hoping to discern what this tall Westerner was all about. As they reached the edge of the city, Jacob pointed to a highway sign and a two-lane road heading east. "I think that's the way," he said. "There was bunting on all the shops along here, some kind of festival."

The driver turned as instructed and they headed out of the city towards the ridge of mountains, which they could vaguely see in the shimmering light of the dessert. "Most people I take like this are running away from something," the driver said with an ironic smile. "But you, you seem to be looking for something." He examined Jacob, trying to discern his secret. He tilted his head. "It's not gold, I think. You have plenty. Why risk such a trip by yourself. It can only be love."

Jacob turned and laughed. "Is it so obvious?"

The driver sung a verse of a song in Arabic that amused him greatly. He turned and looked down at Jacob's hands. "My friend, you were in such hurry to go to flower market and you don't bring bouquets to your beloved?" he wagged his finger at him playfully. They both laughed, enjoying each other's company.

"It's not as simple as that," Jacob said.

"Love is never simple, my friend. Tell me about her."

Jacob considered explaining the strange circumstance of his quest, but decided not to. 'What do I know about her?' he asked himself.

"She is very beautiful, as you would expect," he began, "long thick black hair, a slim body, soft skin the color of cinnamon with a scent of lilacs." As he spoke, a deeper knowing of her surfaced to consciousness with a clarity that astonished him, revelations that brought back the feelings he had in his dream of falling in love with her. Instantly, his knowledge and his feelings about her broke through the veil of amnesia, stunning him. Yet, although he remembered what she was like, he still could not name her or see her face.

"She is very passionate, a little crazy perhaps, a risk taker like me. She works as a war correspondent, or something, though she somehow maintains a great sense of humor, an easy laugh. I think she's very brave, but also talented. She's intelligent, too, reads a lot, worldly. She was studying business on a scholarship at the University of Cardiff in Wales, but came back here after her father died to care for her grandmother who is old and deaf. I would say she's a true romantic, unusually loyal, very, very kind, strong and stubborn, someone you'd want on your side. Best of all, she loves me with all her heart and soul."

"Is that all?" the driver laughed his deep, belly laugh. "She sounds like a Goddess. She is your fiancée?"

"No, we are married," Jacob said without thinking. The truth of that stunned him. He held his hands to his head. His heart paused. He was unable to breathe. 'Oh my God, forgive me,' he thought.

"Are you alright, my friend?" the driver asked, seeing Jacob's face turn white. "Ah! I see. Now I understand. You and your wife had a fight and you are going to apologize. Yes, you must. But you should have brought flowers." He again wagged his finger at him.

Jacob was silent after that. In another twenty minutes he pointed to a narrow unmarked dirt road that led up to the foothills and the mountains beyond. A few yellow sunflowers and purple thistles provided the only color around. The land, dry as bones, turned more verdant as they climbed the mountain. The air smelled sweet. "Turn here," he said with excitement, his heart racing.

The road began a steep, bumpy climb. They turned right at a fork and climbed higher still, leaving the plains behind them. Sheep grazed along the side of the road signaling their approach to a village. The air was considerably cooler here. The sound of a mockingbird broke the stillness. They crossed a stream on a short wooden bridge. Ahead of them lay the first structures of the village. "We found it!" Jacob exclaimed.

He paid the driver twice what the meter read and let him go.

"Are you sure you don't want me to wait for you?" he asked. "I don't see any taxi stands around here," he laughed.

"No, I'll be fine. Thank you."

He walked through the village without seeing a soul. He felt himself being swept along, abandoned to his fate. Ahead of him was a familiar two-story cement and stone farmhouse and behind that a path, which he took, largely overgrown with honeysuckle and wildflowers.

His heart pounded in his chest, nerves on edge, his stomach churning as he walked. After ten minutes a cottage came into view at the end of the mile-long narrow lane, sitting by itself, separated from the village by fields of overgrown grass and occasional fig trees heavy with fruit. There was an old orchard, still bearing apples, pears and walnuts on one side, and a large garden. On the other side was a brook that ran down from the mountain, which rose steeply behind the cottage. The house itself was small, made of large stones and rough, hand-hewn wooden beams and a thatched roof.

Nothing in the world could stop him now.

He took out the heavy metal key from his pocket and walked up the three steps to the front porch and ever so slowly glided it into the lock. It felt as if his entire life had guided him to this spot, to this moment. The key turned easily, tumblers falling like grace, releasing the door that opened on its own before him. He recognized this was their home. In the center of the room was an antique cast iron pot-bellied wood stove with two rocking chairs by it. At the rear of the cottage was a large picture window that framed the mountain. He walked towards it and saw a woman bent over picking flowers by the brook.

He wanted to kneel in prayer. He felt this was the end and the beginning of the world. He was awed to watch her, to know that he was just a few moments, a few steps from all that he loved. The powers that he had when he was here before, powers that he remembered vividly in an instant, had no purpose for him now. He had made his choice. He could hardly breathe. He wanted to shout her name, but he could not. He saw her gather her flowers in her basket and start to rise.

He moved to the back door and opened it. She turned at the sound and saw him standing there, a look of surprise on her face that turned to quiet tears. She clasped her hands over her mouth. Slowly, he walked towards her, repentant, hopeful, transcendent. He, too, was crying. He imagined the sounds of angels singing. She did not move. Her feet were fixed to the ground. The basket of flowers fell from her hands. It was Leila, his beloved.

"Jonathan?" she said, her voice shaking.

He came to her cautiously, stood before her like a supplicant. He reached up and touched her hair. "Oh Leila, Leila, my love." She opened her mouth and he kissed her, surrendering himself, surrendering his very being to her completely. Eyes opened, past and future merged, he whispered to her, "I remember."

Acknowledgement

Editors are the unsung heroes of literature. If you read a work of fiction and can't stop turning the pages, you can bet that it was well edited by someone other than the author. I got my first taste of the editor's scalpel when my editor, Jane Rogers, cut out 10,000 words from my debut book, *Citizens Rising: Independent Journalism and the Spread of Democracy* (CUNY Journalism Press 2013), a non-fiction account of the role of media activists in recent history. I remember lying in a fetal position on the floor crying at the loss of what Stephen King calls the "little darlings." We writers get real attached to our progeny. In my most recent novel, Jane had me remove seven chapters. Ouch! But one gets used to it when we realize how much stronger the book becomes. It takes someone of great strength of character to speak truth to authors and an exquisite ear. Jane Rogers has both of these in surplus. But it is not only the art of excision. As my editor, she also contributed significantly to plot and character development. I feel the most profound debt of gratitude to Jane, who is in every sense of the word my partner. If my books have any value, a lot of the credit must go to her.